THE SEAL OF THOMERION

AN INTERACTIVE NOVEL

By Daniel J. Heck
Copyright © 2015

When you're finished with this book, please review it on Amazon. The author welcomes all feedback.

A sequel, entitled **The Gate to Thomerion**, is also now available in e-book or print format via Amazon.

Plus, check out Daniel J. Heck's author blog at:

http://www.theworldofthomerion.com

D0727794

Big thanks and acknowledgements!

I extend my deepest appreciation to the following people for their critically important roles in making The Seal of Thomerion happen:

Matthew Ridout, for critique and unwavering friendship

Cory Skerry of Chanticleer Reviews, for powerful developmental editing and critique

Peggy Elefson, for editing and fresh perspective

Michelle Herring, for motivation and undying love

Richard and Mary Heck, for raising me and instilling in me creativity and a burning desire to succeed

Big thanks to the test-reading crew!

Chris Acton
Kirsten Goddard
Peggy Golden
Kay Herring
Kristy Kozuki
Michael Rogers

Cover design by Andrei Bat, acquired via 99designs.com

Ambrosinian map generated by and downloaded from worldspinner.com

You may be wondering:

What is an 'interactive novel?'

There isn't just one story to this book. In The Seal of Thomerion, **you control the characters' actions** by making decisions every so often. When you come to a question, such as **What do you do next?**, don't just turn to the next page. Instead, turn to the page instructed, based on what you want to have happen next. When you reach an ending, simply start again. As you read, you'll find that a quest unfolds, and overall, the book contains **49 possible endings** that range in scope from utter defeat to glorious and complete victory!

That's not all. Some pages may instruct you to write down a **keyword,** for which you can use the space below. These words may help you down the road, as they have special meaning within the story. You can denote them in any order, but don't erase them, even if you start the book over. That's all I'll say about that for now! Thank you for reading.

KEYWORDS –

#1. - _____

#2. - _____

#3. - _____

#4. - _____

#5. - _____

#6. - _____

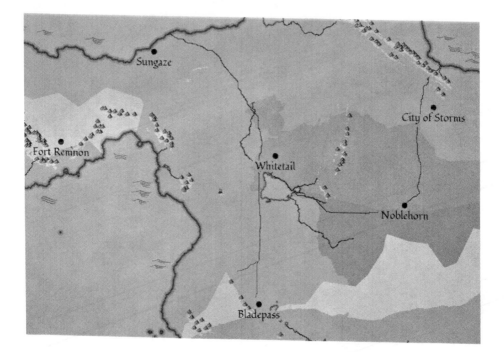

MAP OF AMBROSINIA

Deep within an endless expanse of beige Ambrosinian fields stands a hut of stone and brick, its chimney jutting out from the northern wall at an awkward angle. You selected this haven to be your own twelve years ago, to ensure the peace of your retirement from the royal infantry and for its proximity to the bustling capital city of Whitetail, just a quarter-day's travel to the west. Now, however, your heart is anything but at peace.

On a cot therein lies Fedwick, the flickers of a fire in the nearby hearth dancing across his brow. Arms crossed, head hung, you stare down at him. Autumn's breezes attempt to close a makeshift door several rooms away, banging it against its frame, and you suppress an instinctual annoyance. After all, nothing will wake this brother dwarf, for you have tried. In the heat of battle, he saved your hide on more occasions than you'd like to admit, but now appears more vulnerable than you'd ever imagined possible. Sweat pours from him, yet his leathery skin flashes pale, as his chest rises and falls in slow, belabored fashion. Heartsickness tugs at a part of you, but intrigue begins to grow from within as well.

Stroking your beard, you grunt, "Can you do nothing more, Bartleby?"

The bushy-haired, blue-eyed human leans into the wall at an opposite corner of the room, fiddling with a talisman representing the goddess of the sun. Although he subscribes to a different faith than you, the recent preoccupation of dwarven religious leaders with the construction of a new temple left you little other choice than to bring in an alternative healer. As a reputation for inclusivity preceded Bartleby, you'd gotten the impression that his peers think of him as something of a rebel. Now, however, his lack of confidence sets you aback.

"Fedwick's is no typical ailment," he says, "Nay, I would call it a curse. For only those of the magical persuasion, such as I, can even detect the sigil burned upon his forehead, a combination of skull and dagger. That is the seal of Thomerion, the god of destruction. The question becomes: who inflicted it, and why? What opportunity would they have been granted to do so?"

Your fists ball up. "You cannot remove it?"

5

Bartleby hangs his head. "My magic is not powerful enough. The disease may be treatable, but not by any spells I or my brethren can cast."

"How long does he have?"

"Unless something is done, perchance a fortnight."

You utter a guttural curse, and close your eyes. Sullenly muttering that you owe Fedwick whatever it may take to spare his life, you are tempted to cross your heart as you kneel by his side, but the oath has already been sealed.

Gripping the hilt of your axe, you stand.

"Where would you begin?"

He ponders for a moment. "There is an old warehouse near the limits of the city that I have been told serves as a temple for worshippers of Thomerion. The search for those responsible may be dangerous, but the seal is our best lead."

"'Our' lead?" you ask, arching an eyebrow.

"Let us just say I have a private reason for being interested."

You nod politely, and let Bartleby continue, "On the other hand, you'd mentioned that the Pig's Foot Inn and Tavern is your friend's favorite watering hole, yes? Perhaps someone there can help."

The anticipation of many obstacles ahead begins to settle into your soul, heavy, as you scratch your chin in thought.

Where do you go?

To go to the Pig's Foot Inn and Tavern, continue to page 7.

To go to the supposed temple of Thomerion, turn to page 9.

Pledging to return once you learn more, you leave Bartleby on watch over Fedwick, and proceed out of the stone hut and toward the core of Whitetail. A few hours later, you swing open the tavern's oaken door, and a midday din drowns out its creak, assaulting you from all directions. A gang of card-playing orcbloods in one corner punctuates each bet and won pot with a shout and a slam of a gigantic fist, while a demure elven flutist's performance attracts both the stares and the coppers of several admirers near the front windows. Gnomes of various heights scrabble about from place to place, jabbering in their native language. Standing among all this and more, you feel lucky that even one table has a spot available. It's designed for a human's height—all the shorter ones are taken—but it will have to do. You cross toward the bartender.

"Josephine," you bellow, as a congenial blond lady behind the counter prepares your usual.

"Hello, friend," Josephine says, gripping your fist in welcome. "It has been several moons."

"My apologies. As of late, I have been preoccupied with a matter of grave importance."

"Grave?" Josephine's smile disappears.

You clear your throat, and dive straight into the questions. "Fedwick. When was the last time you saw him in here?"

"Fedwick... ah, he was in four afternoons ago. Sat in his corner, sippin' a cheap ale. Why?"

Your breath catches, but you say, "He is ill. I shan't say more than necessary, for foul play is clearly involved." Feeling cautious, you scan the room. A moment passes. "Was he here with anyone else?"

"Not that I can recall. Nothing seemed amiss as he drank, although he was very quiet, even for him. Then he just rose and left."

You nod, pull a silver piece from your pouch and slide it across to Josephine, who pockets it. She hands you a tankard full to the brim. "Should you discover anything," you grumble, "find me."

"Anything for you, good friend."

You shuffle toward and climb awkwardly into the seat you saw, within a relatively quiet nook, and stare down into the tankard. Vibrations send tiny waves of ale sloshing against the container's walls, and the reflection of your tired face repulses you, so you take several strong glugs, and pause to wipe your mouth against your arm. Your thoughts begin to turn inward, but then…

"They say she can work miracles…"

"What a bunch of rubbish. There's got to be some kind of rational explanation."

Bits of conversation from at least a pair of men, possibly more, meet your ears from the table behind you. That table juts up against the far wall of the tavern, and you recall seeing a hooded figure in the corner of your eye as you sat down, yet hadn't thought much of it at the time. You decide against turning around just yet, but your ears strain to discern more against the general uproar:

"What is she called again?"

"Demetria Argent, or so the legend says."

The image is now clear in your mind; at least one such person behind you could be trying to avoid detection.

What do you do?

To approach these people right here and now, turn to page 16.

To further research the topic on your own first, turn to page 59.

"I have made my decision. We go to the temple," you grunt, and then nod toward Fedwick. "Who shall guard him?"

Bartleby replies, "I shall assign the task to a fellow cleric of the sun."

After arranging as such, you fill your waterskins and pack a ration each, and are ready to trek to the warehouse. The cleric tells you it lies within an isolated valley, several hundred yards behind the town's westernmost grain mill. As you walk, he theorizes, "It's hard to tell whether anyone will be there, but be on guard."

You ask, "How did you discover this use of the warehouse?"

"A candidate for sacrifice cited it. He escaped one of their devilish rituals, even while barely alive."

You grimace, and your stomach turns a little.

"Needless to say," Bartleby continues, "We took him under our wing, and helped him recover."

"And this was not reported to the sheriff?"

Bartleby sighs. "Alas, it was. But Thomerion's followers are clever. They find ways to blend in, and cover up. Some even say their spies brainwashed the sheriff into believing the victim was insane."

Your companion halts. He cranes his neck, and points between two trees. "There," he whispers.

Together, you approach a vast, single-story structure overrun by vines. The surroundings have nearly engulfed it. Only the large double door at its front strikes you as having been at all maintained or used, since its western half stands ajar.

You and Bartleby exchange glances.

The cleric nods, and you push your way through the remaining foliage. Wishing that your pack would not make so much rustling noise, you lean over and peek through the gap. Most of what you see, one would most likely expect: Rotting crates, mold and dirt scattered about. You enter. A copper piece or two lay in cracks between boards, but retrieving them reveals their almost unusable condition. Lighting an oil lamp may otherwise have been called for here, but rays of midday sun pierce the roof

9

in so many places that you can see just fine, right down to the floating, dusty haze that tempts you to cough.

You tiptoe around a stack of crates and notice something different: a raised, rectangular slab of stone at the end of a makeshift corridor.

"Bartleby," you whisper as you tug at his sleeve. You point. "Ah," he muses, "Perhaps an altar of some sort?"

For now, it appears that no one's here but you two. You approach the stone, and note some permanent blood stains on its surface. "By the gods…" you mutter. Someone made a poor attempt to cover the marks with a pair of red and black banners.

"What's this?" Bartleby says.

He gawks at a massive book, which sits in the exact center of the altar's surface. You notice an icon burned into the cover: a hammer superimposed over the moon. Temptation to reach for it burns within you.

"By the gods," you grumble. "What is the Impactium doing here?"

Bartleby says, with a scratch of his head, "The dwarven holy verses."

"Indeed."

Only a few complete copies of the Impactium exist in the first place. The idea that the servants of Thomerion might be exploiting one makes your blood boil.

What do you do?

To examine the Impactium directly, turn to page 105.

To instead wait out the situation, turn to page 170.

You're no expert on the undead, but you do know they're almost never friendly. This skeleton's killer instinct may soon kick in, so you wield your axe with your free hand. The enemy shrieks and adapts an aggressive pose.

With a forward lunge, you swing your weapon at the creature's midsection, but it dodges, and slams its fist into your jaw. You struggle to maintain balance, as the blow carried more force than you expected from something with no muscle. Your enemy sidesteps and rears to strike again. You exhale in a strained, echoing heave.

Subdual tactics might be in order.

You let your weapon drop to your feet with a clang, grab the creature's legs with ease and yank, sending it crashing backward into the dirt. Stunned, it rolls onto its front in a weak effort to stand, but by that time you have already retrieved your axe and rent the skeleton's skull in two with one smooth arcing motion. The creature twitches once, and a violet wisp of life force drains out of it and disperses into the air.

You double-check that all your teeth are still present, and notice something tied to the pile of bones at the hip by a frayed string. It reflects your torchlight back into your eyes, forcing you to squint.

It appears to be a metal key of some sort.

"Hmph," you say to no one. You pocket the key.

"Find something?"

You jump halfway out of your armor and whirl about, only to find Bartleby standing nearby.

"Do watch where you swing that torch, if you please," he jests.

"Thank the gods," you grumble while reminding yourself to breathe. "I thought we'd been separated for good."

"As did I. You disappeared when you touched the book. As I mimicked your touch, it sent me here as well. A repeatable, self-resetting teleportation trap."

You arch an eyebrow. "And that means?"

"That we are dealing with something, or someone, much more powerful than ourselves."

You meet that observation with sober silence, and begin searching the chamber. Bartleby lights a small lamp, and follows your cue to help find a way out. The room stretches wide; it takes you a full minute just to scan the length of one wall. While far from natural in formation, the piles of chipped brick and random stone used as foundation for this cavern don't strike you as any form of sophisticated architecture, either. Further, you ponder why the church of Thomerion would be luring dwarves into their clutches. *A forced mass-conversion, so as to expand the congregation? A grudge of some sort against dwarves as a whole?* Your brow twists into a frown.

"Here," Bartleby shouts. You turn and cross toward the cleric, and see that he has found both a heavy metal door and, a few feet away within the perpendicular wall, a dark archway, under which the floor slopes downward. The archway leads to an open cavern.

You show Bartleby the key, in an open palm.

"Fascinating," he says.

"Quiet," you grunt. You step up to the door and listen, but all that meets your ears is your own faint heartbeat. Pulling on the latch reveals that the door, as expected, is locked. You ponder your options.

Could this door have a trap in it as well? Yet, who knows what we could find elsewhere…

What do you do?

To test the key in the door, turn to page 62.

To investigate the cavern, turn to page 41.

Something about this creature seems approachable, so you figure it could be all the better to refrain from knee-jerk hostility. You say slowly, "Can you understand me?"

It shrugs, and clatters about some more.

"How did I get here? Do you know if there's a way out?"

Its jaw begins to flap, and only sometimes corresponds to the ethereal moans and cackles it emits. A few specific syllables give away that the creature speaks the language of the underworld demons. By combining what little of that dialect you know with pantomime, you get the message across. The skeleton saunters toward an archway, which leads into a dank tunnel.

"Many thanks," you express to the best of your ability.

The creature inserts himself between you and the archway.

"Why?" it asks.

"Why?" you repeat. "Why what?"

It stands, silent.

You growl, "I'm not telling you anything!"

The skeleton whirls about and shrieks, "Then you may not pass."

With a lurch, it flips a stone lever within the wall, and an immense porticullis drops out of the ceiling, closing off the tunnel. Just as quickly, the creature assaults you, its bony fists pushing and striking with fervor.

"Curse you!" you shout. You draw your axe, just as a flash from behind you illuminates the entire chamber. A ray of focused energy envelops the skeleton, dissolving it, and within seconds nothing remains of the creature's bones but a pattern of chalky dust on the floor. You turn to see Bartleby behind you, who lowers his sun god talisman.

"Be careful where you point that thing," you grumble.

"A little gratitude would be appropriate," the cleric replies.

"I thought I'd lost you for good."

"As did I. After a few moments, I realized the only course of action was to attempt to follow you. Lo and behold, handling the book sent me here. Some kind of self-resetting teleportation trap."

You both glance about the narrow radius of illuminated ground.

13

"But now what?"

"What's over there?" Bartleby points to the closed passageway.

"Feel free to take a closer look. I'll be over here."

Perpendicular to the porticullis stands a large metal door with an obvious keyhole. You pull on the handle, but the door is locked. Perhaps the skeleton guarded both passages, you wonder.

You step back toward the pile of dust, and kneel over it. A small, disfigured hunk of metal sits within. Although a few untouched millimeters of its surface area reflect your torchlight, Bartleby's divine blast has rendered the teeth and shaft of the key useless.

You stand and ask the cleric, "Any luck?" as he attempts over and over to lift the barrier. You assist, but even with your combined strength, this porticullis is just too heavy to move. You flip the stone lever back to its original position, but that has no effect at all. And since both the blockage and door are made of metal, you don't see yourself chopping through either anytime soon.

A feeling of doom settles into your gut as you step up to the door for several moments. You listen at it, but hear only the voice of regret speaking within you as to why you never learned to pick locks.

Few options remain. Your shouts for help boom against the walls and the door. Nobody comes, first for hours, then for a full day, by which time you have consumed your limited rations and water. Days turn into weeks, and you have long since finished searching for secret passages or any form of salvation when your starved, dehydrated bodies give up the fight. Perhaps there is some slight solace, your final clouded thoughts tell you as your eyeballs roll backwards in their sockets, in the possibility of being raised again, if only to serve your captor as the next undead guardians of Thomerion.

Your quest has ended... or has it?

Making sure not to turn your back to the skeleton, you skim along the wall with your free hand as you shift slowly away. The creature just watches you. After what seems an eternity, you detect an opening behind you, the ground beneath which slopes downward. With one last hesitant glance at the undead, you slip into the tunnel.

Moisture drips from hundreds of stalactites here, yet the air feels dusty. Whereas the previous area seemed hastily constructed, this one seems merely connected to. At the same time, the cracking, ancient coffins that jut out of natural cubbies in the rock indicate extensive use of the space. All of the coffins are sealed tight.

You exhale through irritated lungs, and feel your chances of finding any form of friendly life down here--let alone the parties responsible for your capture or Fedwick's illness--start to fade.

A burst of white light meets your eyes, but just as quickly dissipates. You turn and take a few cautious steps back toward the mouth of the cavern, and a familiar profile steps into your torchlight.

"There you are!" Bartleby chimes.

"By the gods," you say, "I thought we were separated for good."

"As did I. You disappeared upon handling the Impactium. I figured I could only do the same, and the trap cast upon it sent me here."

"So..." you exhale, "What now?"

"Well," Bartleby replies, "you won't have to worry about that skeleton following us. It's a pile of dust. Although... I shudder to think how many times I'll have to use that energy blast in a place like this."

You nod, and turn toward the back end of the cavern.

The cleric asks, "What have you discovered?"

"Not much. Let's take a closer look."

Turn to page 41.

Your family may have taught you to play it safe, but your peers taught you to take a chance now and again. You figure that the worst that can happen from talking to the men is that they're out for themselves, and refuse your involvement.

You stand, turn about, approach their table, and put on your best authoritative voice and face, to compensate for your lack of height.

"Gentlemen," you bark, "You'll pardon me, but what are these miracles of which you speak?"

The hooded figure sits across from a muscled human in moss-hued clothing, whose longbow lies lengthwise across the table as if it were not an obstacle. This man's style reminds you of a band of rangers that patrols the prairie just outside Whitetail. You can discern far less about the hooded man, who glances at his companion and then back at you in evident shock. But then, he half-smiles.

"It needn't be of concern to a sharp gentledwarf like yourself, now need it?" he says, following that up with, "Nice axe, by the way." To his companion he jibes under his breath, "Seems like a popular place we found here, eh, Zander?"

You catch Zander shooting a glance at Josephine, who nods as if to say 'he's all right.' Zander turns back and says, "It's all right, Mikhail. Let's hear him out." The ranger's voice is rougher than you expected, and he gestures toward you. "Have a seat."

You nod your thanks, and pull your stool up to the new table. Mikhail bites upon a piece of chaw, his gaze unwavering.

Zander explains, "We seek someone with the power to destroy a cursed magical artifact once called the Black Rose." At this, Mikhail pulls a corner of his cloak aside, letting you catch a glimpse of a goblet, made of translucent crystal in the hue of midnight itself. "We have tried to physically shatter it, hired friends to cast spells upon it, everything, but to no avail. Something beyond our means protects it."

Mikhail says, "A collector previously owned it, and then a different collector after her, but its evil energy gradually corrupted their

16

flesh, turning them each into undead as hideous as Zander's mum-in-law, before anyone could figure out what was going on."

Zander frowns, and asks, "What was it again, that the church found, somehow invisibly burned upon their foreheads?"

"The seal of Thomerion."

The two men reel in surprise, as they hear you say these words at the same time as Mikhail. A moment passes. Zander looks at you askance, but before he can ask, you explain about your quest to remove the seal from Fedwick. He now smiles at you in unspoken openness toward teaming up.

"What could your friend have had to do with the Black Rose?" Mikhail muses.

"We shall find out, it seems, by killing two birds with one stone," Zander rejoices.

"Well, just be sure those stubs you call legs can keep up with the rest of us! Ha!" Mikhail jests.

You raise your tankard in salute, and mention, "I overheard something about a Demetria Argent."

Zander says, "She supposedly lives in a mysterious cavern outside the City of Storms. Word has it that she will only grant her services to those who pass her tests."

You huff into your beard, unintimidated.

"Shall we prepare to depart?"

"We should round out the party," you suggest.

You lead your team back to the stone hut. Bartleby accepts your invitation to tag along, and with a quick stop at the church arranges for a brother clergyman to watch Fedwick while you are away.

Your team rents some horses from the local stable. You stock some supplies, and soon you clomp along the rough road northeast of town, a day and a half's journey ahead of you on the way to the City of Storms.

Primarily populated by folk of the fairer races, your destination has earned its moniker from weather whose tumult threatens the foundations

17

of many a treehouse on a regular basis. Yet the people stay there, in no small part, to honor familial tradition, as well as to maintain the town's status as an integral hub of commerce.

For hours, you ponder these and other geographical insights, and wonder whether your newest companions will say anything at all, whether to each other or to you. The greatest tidbit they reveal is Mikhail's demeanor itself; at around high noon he pulls back his hood in order to wipe his brow of sweat. His pointed ears, sandy hair and angular face indicate he may have some elf relatives nearby. Bartleby says little throughout the day as well, although his face reflects an increasing weariness.

Similarly, your backside has stiffened by the time the sun sinks beneath the horizon, and in retrospect, you wish you had stopped more often than to just refill your waterskins from a stream.

Zander points toward a clearing in the wood many yards off the path. Mikhail nods. This will be your camp for the night.

"Who shall take which watch?" the ranger asks.

Mikhail raises his hand. "First watch," he says, sounding fatigued.

Most elves you've known get tired of always keeping watch, a side effect of how they need less rest than other races. Your charitable side urges you to give your companion a break, or at least help with the other shift. Then again, the chance to sleep straight until sunup sounds quite appealing in its own right.

What do you do?

To relieve Mikhail of first watch, turn to page 28.

To volunteer to take second watch, turn to the second half of page 159.

To stay silent, and hope that someone else takes watch, turn to page 61.

It strikes you as impossible that normal animals could execute such rhythmic knocking. Any such being might not necessarily be hostile, but then again, you contend, an innocent traveler would have unusual difficulty navigating at this hour. Why here, and why now?

You stand, but refrain from calling out, and take a few cautious steps off the path. In front of you darts a gaunt figure, its silhouette cutting off your view of the moon for an instant, only to retreat once more behind some vast tree trunk. Your eyes dart about as you scan the scene, and your muscles pulse, at the ready.

The breeze sends a chill up your neck. All is quiet.

"Who's there?" you grunt.

A crunch of leaves telegraphs just enough; you whirl about and catch an arm in mid-strike, then wrench it behind the figure's back. It drops a shiv to the ground and yelps in pain, but you use your other hand to seal its mouth. While it struggles to get away, you assess by the distant firelight that the being seems human, even if only in the strictest sense. Short, bald and nearly toothless, it appears so deprived that you're shocked it had the energy to surprise you. You throw the being to the ground and sit on its chest.

"What are you doing here?" you growl.

"None of your business," it hisses. "Let me go!"

"Oh, but I'll make it my axe's business if you don't talk."

"Eep!" It looks both ways, and trembles violently.

"Okay, okay," it sputters. "I'm a messenger."

"For whom?"

"I am to meet with an elf…"

"An elf? Which elf?"

"I was not informed of his name!"

You grip his skull, and bring him to within inches of your gaze.

"Why were you to meet him here?"

"I… I…"

You feel your eyes and nostrils flare with anger.

19

"To relay information from the commanders of the Army of Thomerion!"

Your face flushes, and your head spins. "What?" you whisper.

You glance back toward the campsite.

Mikhail.

The next moment, the messenger strikes you a low blow with its bony fist, and as you keel to your side in agony, it wriggles to its feet and bolts toward the horizon.

Rarrggh. My guard has been down in more ways than one.

You pace your breathing and lie still as the blunt ache subsides. A minute passes before you stand, and ponder.

Your instinct was right, you tell yourself. Yet he 'charmed' his way into having you trust him. But, you reflect, you don't know all the circumstances. Is it at all possible for the messenger to have referred to some other elf? And what about Zander? Mikhail has likely deceived him for far longer than you know.

An Army of Thomerion? Something must be done about this…

You return to camp, and push on Bartleby's shoulder.

The cleric wakes slowly. "What is the matter?"

You explain what you have learned in hushed whispers. Bartleby scratches his chin. "Our personal safety may be an issue," he offers. "I would be willing to carry on with just the two of us. On the other hand, how confrontational do you feel at the moment?"

What do you do?

To wake Zander as well and confront Mikhail, turn to page 251.

**To put some distance between you and the spy
by continuing on with only Bartleby,
turn to the second half of page 232.**

You affirm to yourself your job as night watchman: If there's a threat, help protect the party. In this case, there's only noise. No threat, you repeat to yourself.

At least, not yet.

Still sitting, you watch for a while in the general direction of the knocking, which fails to repeat. The mild wind's whistle takes over your ears, and your heart slows again as it becomes apparent that, whatever the source of the noise was, it is now gone.

You grumble for a moment about letting yourself tense up over nothing, one of your most insidious habits. Then, the night sky calms your thoughts, and your gaze wanders toward various constellations. Orion, your favorite since childhood, stares back at you from the south. You imagine a hunter, cinching its belt and preparing for the next kill. Minutes stretch out into hours, and your eyelids begin to flutter.

A hand on your shoulder startles you awake.

You turn your head and glance into Mikhail's hood. Although his eyes remain shadowed, his nod indicates he's ready to take over.

You prepare your bedroll and retire for the night. Tiny, twinkling points of light from the heavens form the day's last images, still visible on the insides of your eyelids as you drift into unconsciousness.

You dream of the armorsmith back home, and, waking only once during the night, remind yourself to get re-acquainted with her sometime soon, the drunken rants you spewed on your one and only date together notwithstanding.

Turn to page 38.

Not wanting to take chances, you shuffle toward Bartleby and jiggle his shoulder. "Men! There's something here!" you bellow.

Mikhail groans, sits up halfway, and scans with drowsy eyes. Zander wakes with a start, and says, "What's happening?"

"There!" you point, only to look up, listen, and realize there is only quiet; the depths of the night display little activity of any kind.

"The woods are as empty as Zander's head…" Mikhail moans.

"There was a knocking," you assert. "It sounded purposeful."

Zander stands and dusts himself off. "Well, whatever it was now knows we're here. We shall investigate, just to be safe."

Bartleby now sits up, and considers the exchange, but says nothing. Mikhail appears more alert. "Don't bother," he grunts.

Zander says, "It will only require a moment."

Mikhail grumbles, "Then the three of you go waste your time. Just watch out for mice as they skitter about the forest floor."

Bartleby shouts, "How dare you speak to us that way!"

Zander says, "Enough!" He casts a stern glare at his elf companion, who lies back down within his bedroll. "To each his own."

The three of you huddle just off the path. Bartleby lights an oil lamp; you enter the wood, and each scan in a different direction. A squirrel darts up a tree, and a ruffled owl perches, watching you.

You examine a gigantic oak, then its neighboring maple. Little about the trees stands out. Bartleby raises and lowers the lamp to discover every inch of possible secrets. Zander kicks through a tangle of moss. All in all, you spend a good while here, and find nothing. The three of you stand, stare at each other, and listen. Still no knocking.

Zander purses his lips at you. "Perhaps Mikhail was right." You frown back at him, and cross your arms.

The cleric defends, "I grant him the benefit of the doubt."

Zander gestures for the group to return to camp. You take a moment to get reoriented, find the fading embers of the fire again, and settle back onto the ground as Bartleby blows out his lamp. Your companions nod you their goodnights, but uneasiness creeps into you yet again. Something feels different.

Mikhail did not move or say a thing when you returned, although his bedroll appears crumpled, and for some reason has been moved to the very edge of the fire's radius of illumination. You stand and look closer.

"Mikhail!" you shout, "He's gone!"

The bedroll sits empty, beyond the hooded cape stuffed within.

The other two men approach. "Do you suppose he was kidnapped?" Bartleby muses, "Was this all a ruse?"

Zander shakes his head. "This appears to have been his choice. If there had been a struggle, we'd have heard it from the woods, or see blood nearby. Furthermore, he took the rest of his supplies with him."

You blink. "But surely there must be a reason for this," you say. "At least, beyond how he seemed rather wearied by us, if you follow me."

"Ever since I have known him," Zander says, "he has been a test of my patience."

"How long have you known him?"

"We met at a banquet a few years ago. The more we conversed, the more we found we had many of the same goals. It seemed a natural alliance at the time, but perhaps no longer…" He retreats into thought.

Bartleby says, "Let us rest. The heavy dew may allow us to track his footfalls in the morning, should we desire to pursue him."

You warn, "Fedwick's fate approaches ever nearer, while we propose to dally about chasing wayward elves?"

Zander ponders, "He still has the Black Rose. Without it, I stand to gain little by continuing on. This is not to say I would not help you on your quest. But Mikhail must be found first."

What do you do?

If you can afford to help find the elf, turn to page 136.

To continue on with only Bartleby, turn to the second half of page 93.

23

"Sir," you implore, "Where can I find the hall?"

Natar smiles. "You can find an agent of the city watch within a multi-level treehouse four paths to the south. He will tell you more."

"Thank you," you say, bowing in gratitude.

"Wait 'til Helmina finds out someone listened to me for once," he says. Natar turns back to his fields and, for a moment, you wonder just where he'll sleep tonight.

Finding city hall requires less than five minutes, and you couldn't have missed it if you tried. Made of the finest cherry wood, sanded and polished to a shining finish, it puts every other building you've seen thus far to shame. Stately ivy crawls up the sides, and an approach path, lined with stones, welcomes you.

You climb the provided rope ladder, and ring a bell just outside the main door. An instant later, a short elf in a black tunic bolts out of the door, past the two of you and almost over the railing. "Goodness!" he chirps as he replaces his spectacles, "We don't get out-of-towners much around here."

You adopt a humble tone, "We are sorry to alarm you, but..."

"Alarm me?" the clerk interrupts, "By the gods, you've rescued me from the verge of tears, I've been so bored. So, please, enter!"

He leads you to a set of short stools within the compound, sits behind a large desk, and faces you.

"Now," says the clerk, "How may I help you?"

"We seek the assistance of one Demetria Argent," you say.

"We have been told she is capable of miracles," Bartleby adds.

The clerk scratches his head, and replies, "She is quite intelligent. But then again, would it have killed her to show up for our meeting?"

"She was already supposed to have arrived?"

"When the sun was at its highest point."

"Perhaps," you theorize, "we are too late."

"What do you mean?"

You relate that Argent might be in danger, and also that you left a spy behind, one with a concrete connection to an army of Thomerion.

24

"I would wager," the clerk offers, "that these two facts are connected in some way. In fact," and with this he pounds his fist on the desk and stands straight as a pole, "this warrants immediate action."

"Wait, please," you blurt, "I have not explained…"

"I shall deploy a task force to find Demetria, and take her into protective custody."

"But, we need…"

The clerk keeps speaking, each sentence quicker and higher-pitched than the next, and his hands flail about in wild circles.

"If we have enough men involved, this will all boil over in due time. But where to keep her? The prison won't do. Ah! There's a perfect chamber for her in the back of this hall."

You and Bartleby exchange dubious glances.

"Oh, and since the two of you are now classified as informants, we'll need to do the same for you, as well."

You stand. "Now, wait just a minute…"

"No buts about it, my friends. What you've described, the City of Storms considers a dire emergency." The clerk puffs out his chest.

Bartleby asks, "And, if we were to refuse protective custody?"

"You would be in violation of local codes, and then, oh, then we would be able to make use of the jail." The clerk nods with fervor.

You grumble to yourself. Bartleby emits a defeated whoosh.

The chamber the clerk locks you in offers comparative luxuries, but the irony of the situation still frustrates you to your core. You could break out, but your status as a labeled fugitive would not help your quest. During the first day or two, you take some solace in that, should the city's overzealous personnel actually find Argent, she will come to you rather than the other way around.

She never does.

Better opportunities await you. Try again!

When a woman speaks with conviction, your mother taught you long ago, you had better listen. You approach Helmina.

"I always have to remind Natar that I know what I'm talking about," she grunts, "and you won't be sorry for listenin'. The friend's name's Sonoth, and you can find him two lanes east of here. He raises pigs, so there's no mistaking his property. Phew!"

You thank her, and she returns to sweeping the walkway.

You find Sonoth's house within minutes, and rap upon the door while holding your nose. A wizened elf emerges.

"May I help you?"

"Good day, sir," you say, "We're interested in meeting Demetria Argent. Helmina told us she was going to stay here."

The man thinks for a moment. "Ah, yes," he replies, "Demetria sent me a message detailing some kind of vision. She mentioned something about a cursed goblet."

You arch an eyebrow, as a weight settles into your chest.

"But, oddly," Sonoth continues, "She hasn't shown up yet."

"Is there any other way we might find her?" Bartleby asks.

"I do know where she normally lives. Come, I'll show you."

Bartleby places a comforting hand on Sonoth's shoulder, and guides him across his yard and into the forest path. The old man points a gnarled finger toward the northwest.

You spend much of the journey listening to Sonoth's mutterings, and his relative lack of agility makes the going slower than you'd hoped. The sun hovers just over the tops of distant trees when you find a large boulder, which anchors a curtain of ivy. You push aside the ivy, and reveal a dark tunnel leading into the ground.

You look at Sonoth. "Argent lives in here?"

He shrugs, and shudders. "Don't ask me why."

Turn to page 126.

"I shall notify His Highness," you tell the messenger, "but is there any chance that the army generals can hold their own for a while?"

The boy nods in comprehension. "We shall see…" he says with fear in his eyes, and runs off. You turn toward your hut, but hesitate. You rehearse a little act within your mind for a moment, and enter.

"Did I hear somebody outside?" Grindle asks.

"Merely a merchant boy," you lie, "trying to sell me something."

True to plan, your friend looks much better. "We are not out of the woods yet, so to speak," Wyver cautions.

You remain silent, but feel warm, as shame flushes your cheeks. As time passes and the spell approaches completion, dreadful images flit through your mind, of innocent citizens suffering, houses burning, all as part of an invasion you knew was going to occur.

It was only a matter of when, you remind yourself.

Finally, Wyver retracts his hands, and lets their glow dissipate. Ever so slowly, Fedwick begins to stir. He tips his head to the side, opens his eyes, and mutters, "What happened?"

Everyone cheers and applauds. You embrace your friend, and help him to sit up. As awkward as it feels, you then follow Wyver as he exits the hut. "Thank you," you say.

"I have done what I can," he notes, "It is time for me to depart."

"You had best hasten," you suggest.

Wyver blinks. "Why?"

"You would kill me if I told you. You will find out when you get there. Just, hurry." The king nods, and rounds up his bodyguards. As he rides off, you watch with mixed emotions, wary of an uncertain future.

You have revived Fedwick!

But is there more to the story?

Read through The Seal of Thomerion again to find out.

You say, "I will watch first if you could use the respite."

Mikhail pauses. "I insist," he replies.

Bartleby arches an eyebrow, and looks toward the setting sun.

You note the strain in the elf's voice. "Why is it so important?"

"I could ask you the same."

Zander snaps, "Just when I think I've seen it all, now I've seen people argue over watch as if paid for it in jewels by the wagonful. Well, there's no such extravagance on this trip, gentlemen. Just the cold ground and the need to keep an eye on everyone. You take first shift," he gestures toward you, "And Mikhail has second, for once."

The elf's gaze bores holes in you for a moment more, as you shift your weight and look away. When he catches Zander's glance in turn, though, Mikhail shrugs listlessly, lifts his hood back over his head and slips away to help set up camp. Zander ties the horses to trees and starts a campfire, before retiring to his bedroll. All the others soon snore mildly.

You nibble on jerky and berries to keep your energy up, then examine and clean your axe as your mind wanders. Memories replay themselves: Fedwick pushing you aside just in time to avoid an ogre's strike; Fedwick joining your siblings and parents at last year's summer solstice feast. You struggle to keep from panicking, and realize for the first time that he is not just like family to you. He is family.

At that moment, a rustling meets your ears from deep within the wood. Just as you dismiss the sound as that of nocturnal wildlife, you hear three knocks, which ring hollow as if on tree bark. You can't see much of anything beyond the firelight very clearly.

What do you do?

To do nothing and hope whatever it is goes away, turn to page 21.

To investigate alone and let the party sleep, turn to page 19.

To wake everyone else, turn to page 22.

Saul smiles smugly, turns over the jack of hearts, and places it in the only remaining spot. The final grid looks like this:

You have lost.

Turn to page 201.

You take a deep breath. Against your better judgment, you lower your offensive stance. Bartleby pockets the sun talisman clerics such as he often use as weaponry.

"First," you grunt, "who are you?"

The youth looks up.

"I will not utter another word until you pledge."

Annoyance bubbles up in your chest, and comes out in your tone. "Fine. We will let you go once you have answered our questions. All of them."

"You will be held to your word."

You glance at Bartleby. He shrugs, then gestures as if to give in.

"We will hold ourselves to our word," you vow, "Now, who are you?"

The youth half-smiles, a creepy countenance if ever you've seen one, and stares back into space as he speaks. "My given name was Crolliver. I am of the fourth order of the servants of Thomerion, and as such no longer have an official name."

Bartleby says, "The lowest of the orders. You are treated as a lackey, I presume?"

Crolliver purses his lips, but says nothing.

You continue, "What are you doing here? What were you doing to the Impactium?"

"The volume you saw on the altar has been modified with a magical trap. I was to remove the trap and return the book to my superiors."

"A trap? What was it intended to catch?"

"If I tell you, they will kill me."

You clench a fist. "Damn you!"

Crolliver stares straight ahead, unafraid.

Bartleby nudges you, and you shift to the side as he approaches to within inches of the youth.

"Look at me," Bartleby commands. The youth cooperates. His mouth twitches. Standing still, your companion whispers some foreign words, his pupils turn pale white, and he stares into the youth's eyes. A few seconds pass, before Bartleby shakes his head and turns away.

You glance back and forth between the two men. You place a hand on Bartleby's shoulder, and ask, "Are you all right?"

"Yes," he replies, blinking with force. "That spell reveals existing magical effects. He's under some kind of mental surveillance, whereby..."

Suddenly, Crolliver begins to choke and twitch. He gasps, sways, and struggles, hands at throat, his lungs drawing no oxygen. You and Bartleby reach forward in apprehension as the youth falls to his knees.

"As.... I.... suspected," he croaks, "The eyes of Thomerion... are... everywhere..."

The youth collapses onto his back. You clench your fists and loom over him in panic, sensing your only investigative lead slipping into the void beyond. Bartleby puts a hand to the youth's neck.

"He's gone," says the cleric.

"By the gods," you grumble, scanning the area.

You both stand and wait, and barely breathe. Many moments pass. "And yet..."

You turn to Bartleby, who finishes, "We have been spared. So far."

You scratch your beard, and slowly return to your rational norm. "It seems..." you grumble, "we have arrived back where we started."

The cleric shakes his head. "Not entirely."

"What do you mean?"

"When I searched this man for magic," he says, with a gesture, "A faint vision came upon me. I yet ponder its significance, or even whether I am sure that I witnessed what I thought I witnessed. But, there it was. A rank of undead soldiers."

Your eyes widen. "Soldiers? Doing what?"

"Filing, then marching. One carried a battle standard. Into it was sewn a swordfish upon a white circle, with a jagged spear through both."

31

"That symbol represents the militia of the tiny fisherman's community of Sungaze, on the northwest border!"

Bartleby scratches his chin. "That is odd, indeed."

You frown. "At this point, I do wish we had discovered something that could help Fedwick. At the same time, something is happening that is clearly bigger than any one dwarf."

"Should we, for now," Bartleby ponders, indicating the door, "investigate where Crolliver was headed?"

"Aha!" you grunt, feeling optimistic. But then, a second thought strikes you: If even the Impactium was a trap, who knows what dangers may lie underneath the warehouse?

What do you do?

To open the hatch, turn to page 179.

To travel to Sungaze instead, turn to page 35.

"We shall decline," you say to the woman, "but wish you good day."

Crolliver frowns and asks, "Are… are you sure?"

The woman's face falls, but she thereafter shrugs, turns, and sits in the dirt beside a ragged beggar. The two of them have begun conversing casually by the time you leave the scene.

You note the youth's morose look as you trek, and argue, "Shall we look at it this way? Perhaps the gold we saved will come in handier than any form of knowledge."

Crolliver ignores you, stolidly marching forward.

Turn to page 213.

You didn't come here to mess around. This person must not realize how much trouble he's in, given the circumstances.

You growl to him, "Do you think we're dim? There are lives other than yours at stake here!"

Bartleby lays a hand on your shoulder. Of the youth he asks, "Shall we get to the point? We seek someone with the power to undo a curse associated with the Church of Thomerion. If you have that power, you will help us. If you don't, you will lead us to someone who does. The consequences of disobedience are dire."

Sunlight glints off the cleric's holy symbol as he palms it, prepared to release its destructive energies at a moment's notice. The youth glares at Bartleby for a moment, then hangs his head in submission.

"Perhaps this can be talked through," he mutters.

"The time for talk has long past," you bellow. "You attacked us on sight!"

Without turning, the cleric cautions, "Do try not to let your emotions get the better of you."

"Am I not allowed a word in edgewise?" you harrumph.

"Just stay focused," he replies.

The youth glances one more time at each of you. "I cannot help you. But I know someone who can. With your permission, I shall lead the way." As a precaution, you retrieve some thick rope from your pack and help Bartleby bind the youth's hands. The youth frowns, but cooperates.

As you head back toward the entrance, the creaking of the warehouse's wooden panels hides your grumbles about your quest companion's pedanticism, while you remind yourself that at least your skill with an axe will never fail to rank superior. The cleric does not even turn about.

You emerge into the sunlight, and interrogate the youth as you walk into town. "Tell us, what would one such as I have done to earn a price on my head?"

"It suffices to say," he says, "that the past returns to haunt you. You are familiar with the Battle of Bladepass, in 1326?"

You blink with force. Confusion floods you. "A mere trifle," you say, "A small dwarf militia pushed back an oncoming corps of orcblood raiders in a matter of hours. 'Twas hardly integral to the larger war at the time, and was forgotten by history almost as quickly as it occurred."

"So you think."

You squint, suspicious. You process this information, while dodging the odd looks of a few passersby on this dirt path, which keeps your thoughts aimed inward for quite some time. You decide to question further, but look around you and notice that you now stand somewhere within the town graveyard. Dozens of tilted headstones cast long shadows in the dusk.

"Why have you led us here, of all places?"

The youth raises his bound fists above his head, snaps his fingers and shouts, "Thomerion shall prevail!"

At that moment, deep from within a half-dozen graves burst just as many bony hands, which quickly claw at and break away the soil around them. You ready your axe and shield, as panic pulses through your muscles. Scraggly heads, with stretched white skin and bloodshot eyes, and then partially-clothed bodies, follow each undead hand. Within moments, the zombies surround you. Behind them, the youth laughs, turns and breaks into an awkward run, toward the forest.

"By the gods…" Bartleby grumbles, "What now?"

What do you do?

To fight through the zombies to catch the youth, turn to page 92.

To run for your lives back toward town, turn to page 94.

"If the battle standard is any indication, we'll learn more in Sungaze than we ever could here," you postulate. Bartleby nods.

You hustle back to the core of Whitetail. You arrange for the rental of horses, and memories resurface from the only time you have ever visited Sungaze. Buffeted by coastal winds and edged by a pristine pink-sand beach, it struck you as having more than earned its moniker. As you ride along the northwest trail the next morning, you recall even more:

Tourists of all races have morphed Sungaze into a cultural melting pot, yet it manages its traffic well, under the leadership of the half-elven mayoress Titania Vermouth. While you never met her directly, a speech of hers stirred within you a call to action, even as you knew and cared little about the topic (poverty within unmapped rural villages) beforehand. At the time, you overheard an observation that she rarely leaves the area, due to extensive involvement in the affairs of her people.

Yet, as the sun hits its highest point on your first day of travel, an ornate carriage approaches, manned by a thin gentleman in black and pulled by a single white horse; as it passes you think you see Vermouth herself sit within it. Neither reinsman nor occupant acknowledges you in any way; the lady, in particular, instead stares slantwise toward the woods. By the time you have processed this, the carriage is already well on its way in the direction from whence you came.

You glance at the cleric. Bartleby seems to think nothing of it.

Suspicion crawls over you. Whatever the reason for travel, a small entourage usually accompanies important authority figures, if only for protection's sake. Time, however, is of the essence, and Vermouth might not appreciate being questioned by someone whom, to her, would just be a random hotshot with some fancy armor.

What do you do?

To continue on your way to Sungaze, turn to page 40.

To turn around and catch up with the carriage, turn to page 58.

35

After you place the seven of clubs, Saul deals the three of diamonds, thinks for a moment, and places it above the two sevens. The grid now looks like this:

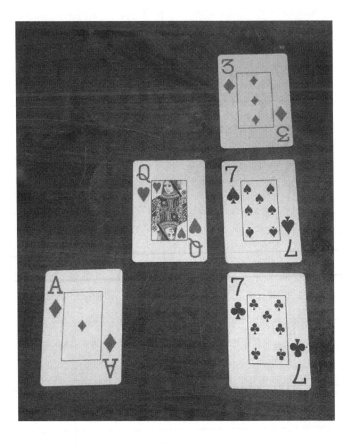

He then deals the ten of hearts. Only two spots are of much help.

Where do you place the ten of hearts?

To place it above the queen, turn to page 52.

To place it below the queen, turn to page 185.

You bellow, "We have reason to believe the church of Thomerion is up to no good. You see, we came from Whitetail, where…"

The gate guard cuts you off with a snap of his fingers and a glance at the tower guards, who nock arrows in their bows and fire. You fumble to ready your shield, but pain overtakes you as you realize that one such projectile now protrudes from your blood-stained armor. You failed to see any of it coming.

Glancing to your right as you fall to your knees, you note that Bartleby got off easy, with a shot to the skull. You keel over and look up one last time, as a pair of youths in black and red robes exchange nods with the guards and saunter past the gate toward you. You can only wonder how and when Sungaze fell to their power, as the taller of the two bends over, holds out his hands while muttering something incomprehensible, and puts you out of your misery with a shock of violet energy. Perhaps, however, as a newly recruited undead warrior, you can at least carry their battle standard in the end.

Cruel fate has taken your life. Rise again!

"If Argent is anywhere nearby," you shout, "It doesn't matter how we get to her!"

You grip your axe in both hands and proceed to where the ladder is concealed. With three furious chops, you bash a huge gap in the wood, then kick the hanging chunk of door off its only connected side and step inside the closet. You feed the ladder out into the open, where your companions begin to set it up, but hear the voice boom once again, "You do not pass!"

Everything fades to white.

Turn to page 65.

It is morning. The clouds continue to gather as you embark upon the final leg of your journey to the City of Storms, but so far they retain any precipitation. The winds are even calmer here than at home in Whitetail, and an eerie stillness settles over the wood.

"Where is this compound located?" you ask your party.

"A passageway leads to it," Zander informs you, "from a wooded outcropping just east of town. We are to recognize it by a gigantic boulder of gray and green."

You arch an eyebrow. "How do you know all this?"

Mikhail grins with pride. "The elven community has eyes and ears everywhere." He accompanies this with a grand gesture of his hands.

Several more hours of travel pass in silence, until you enter the city itself, which strikes you as even more sparse and agrarian than you remembered. Considerable distance separates each dwelling, and some have fallen into relative disarray.

"Hark!" a hoarse voice rings from nowhere, startling you. You look up at a grand oak, and there, a wizened female elf leans upon the wooded girders of a two-room house. Her many wrinkles, you'd approximate, belie just short of three centuries of hard-earned wisdom. She gazes down upon you with twinkling green eyes.

"Good day, stranger," Zander calls in return.

The woman raps her knuckles upon some tree bark with enthusiasm, and says, "Haven't seen folk like you around here in quite some time... what be your business here?"

She seems innocent enough, you think. You say, "We seek the assistance of Demetria Argent."

"Ah ha!" says the woman, stroking her stubbly chin, "A friend of mine, she is."

Your eyes widen, as you feel your chances of discovering a cure for Fedwick brighten.

She continues, "I take it you require her assistance? Many people seek her for her knowledge."

Zander speaks first, "We have two concerns, namely..."

"There is where you are at fault," the woman interrupts. Your face falls once more. "Not many know enough to come even this far in search of Demetria Argent. In that I am impressed. But, I can tell you something about her you would never know, not until you reached the back of the compound in which she hides."

You stand and wait, curious, for many moments. Bartleby clears his throat. Zander asks, "Ah… madam, do you intend to share with us this supposedly valuable piece of information?"

"Supposedly?" the elf adopts a look of genuine offense. "Not only is it truly valuable, but furthermore, one can expect to make at least a decent living guarding it." He grins.

"We have gold," you offer, excited.

Mikhail raspberries. Zander crosses his arms. You notice.

"When it comes to saving Fedwick," you bellow, "No price is too high!" You huff into your beard. After a moment, it sinks into you. You speak the truth. He is that important.

Bartleby's eyes widen, and he raises a fist to his chest. Your adamancy seems to have really sunk into him, at least.

"Then," says the old elf, "Make me an offer, young dwarf. But be warned, I am not cheap."

What do you do?

**To give in to your companions' wishes,
turn to the second half of page 189.**

To offer the old woman five of your own gold pieces, turn to page 49.

To argue that everyone should pool their money, turn to page 42.

Not one to be distracted by passersby, you quell your suspicions with the idea that even the busiest of mayors must have to meet with superiors every now and again.

"Staying focused on the task at hand..." you grumble to yourself.

"Pardon?" Bartleby asks.

You scratch your beard. "It is nothing..."

As the hours stretch onward, the number of travelers in either direction dwindles to near none. Once, a young woman passes by in a hurry, stopping just long enough to cast a glance that implies she thinks you're insane.

"Madam?" you shout, but she is gone.

Finally, you round the top of the last hill before the coast. Your position now affords a view of the majestic ocean, as well as of much of the town of Sungaze, with no more than three-quarters of a mile to go before the front gates themselves.

The gates are shut tight, and multiple guards stand in each of two watch towers.

You and Bartleby exchange glances.

"Quite the welcome," the cleric says, "for a tourist town."

"Shall we speak to them?"

"I don't see why not. We need to learn more."

You close the distance, and beckon toward the gate guard. A stout human, he frowns and crosses his arms when he sees you.

"Halt!" he shouts. You both comply. "State your business."

There are only two ways to explain it.

What do you say?

To cite your search for the servants of Thomerion, turn to page 37.

To explain your need for an experienced healer, turn to page 146.

You examine the cavern beyond the archway. Two other tunnels lead off from here, one to your left, and the other to your right. The ceiling of the one to the left is quite low, and may become lower within, but your torchlight doesn't illuminate far enough in to tell for sure. The tunnel to the right, in comparison, appears easily passable; its width and relative smoothness invite you into the depths of its darkness.

Finally, as you raise your torchlight as high as possible, you notice some kind of nook, carved out of the far corner of the wall many yards above your head. A faint glow emanates from the nook. While you didn't prepare for this trip to the degree that you have spikes, crampons and such in your pack, a quick inspection of the wall reveals just enough decent footholds and handholds to make you think you could both manage the climb.

Bartleby clicks his tongue. "Bizarre," he muses.

"Where do you think we should go?"

"I have no preference," the cleric says, "Except to say that we have time to explore, should divine providence shine upon us."

You nod pensively.

Where do you go?

To explore the squat passage in the left wall, turn to page 50.

To traverse the wide passage in the right wall, turn to page 71.

To climb to the nook in the upper corner, turn to page 53.

You feel your brow twist into a frown, and your breaths get quicker and huffier.

"I cannot believe my ears," you complain to the group, "We've come all this way, and the moment something positive develops, you think of your pocketbooks first. What else are we going to use our gold for? In truth, now?"

Mikhail snickers derisively and says, "Oh, I don't know. Food?" Zander looks up at the old woman and, in a diplomatic tone, says, "Pardon us for a moment."

The ranger addresses you. "It's hard to say," Zander says, "We may need to pay Argent herself for her services. We must be prepared for anything. But frankly, this old coot isn't what I mean by that."

Mikhail says, "I've run into these types before. Wrinkled, feeble, they can do little physical work, so they play tricks on passersby. They're swindlers, to get more to the point of it."

"So you don't trust her," you counter, "So, her information might be worthless, and we're out a few coins. What more harm can she do than that? We move on from there, lighter in heart for having tried."

"Lighter in heart?" Bartleby repeats.

You ignore this and give the argument one last heave-ho, "What do you say, gentlemen? I will pay you back at another time."

Mikhail and Zander exchange wary glances, then a few words under their breaths. You can't make the words out, but it doesn't take long for them to come to agreement.

"No," Mikhail says to you, "And that is that." With pursed lips, he pulls his hood over his head. The two men march onward and begin to search for the passage to the underground labyrinth, leaving you and the cleric standing near the treehouse.

You stand, stunned. You feel as if your values have been questioned to their core, as if teamwork just doesn't mean what it used to. You turn, and stare, morose, into the green expanse of the forest floor.

The sound of tinkling metal meets your ears. You glance over your shoulder to see Bartleby counting coins. Your heart lifts.

"Shall, say, fifty gold be sufficient?"

You step toward the cleric and slap a grateful hand on his shoulder. "You are a saint!"

"Don't let it go to your head," Bartleby says, his tone serious, "But I changed my mind because I begin to see within you things I would never expect from a military man. One sees such waste of life, the cavalier use of conscripted flesh as meat shields, in the thick of it all. I cannot help but think sometimes that one such person is to another no more than a tool, a mechanism by which to reach an end goal." The cleric pauses, and smiles at you, "Perhaps I was mistaken."

You smile back. For a moment, pride swells in your chest, then you think better of it, and clear your throat.

"Well, just don't think your quest partner's going soft on you," you mumble.

"I won't," Bartleby says with a chuckle. He finishes counting, puts the money in a small burlap sack, and hands the sack to you.

You turn toward the old elf and wave the sack.

The woman shakes with excitement, and says, "Would you toss that up here? My body isn't as young as it used to be, and I prefer to avoid climbing the ladder when I can."

You exchange glances with Bartleby, who shrugs. Worse things can occur than if the old elf were to just run off with the gold. You take two steps closer to the treehouse and shove the sack just high enough into the air, from where she snatches it with surprising agility.

She opens the sack, and counts and admires the coins, holding one at arm's length now and again, then reeling it in to within a few millimeters of her ancient eyes. She squints and winks, ponders and examines, and mutters an 'ooh' or 'aah' every few seconds.

You clear your throat, and shout, "Ma'am, that information?"

"Oh, oh, yes…." the woman splutters, "We did make a deal, didn't we? Well, I stand here on divine authority…" with this she adopts a mysterious tone, "…and thus swear to you the following is true: Demetria

43

Argent, even if found, will only grant one request to each party that finds her."

You scratch your beard, and process this information.

"Go on," Bartleby requests.

"You said, as I recall," continues the elf, "That you have two concerns with which you need assistance. You will need to address one at a time, or else incur Argent's wrath."

Your eyes widen, and your pulse quickens.

"And believe me," the elf says, "You wouldn't want to do that."

Bartleby shrugs again, and says, "The solution seems simple enough. We split into two groups."

"Very possible," says the elf, "But Argent will watch you. If at any time or in any way either group interacts with the other, she considers them both to be one party, together. These are her rules. I know not why she enforces them."

"Is there anything else we should know?"

"Only that challenges await you. I wish you luck."

"Thank you, ma'am." The two of you wave pleasantly as the old elf retreats into her treehouse.

Your party reunites near the supposed entry point, and you inform everyone of what you have learned. Mikhail adopts a look of intrigue, while Zander crosses his arms and stares at the ground.

The ranger asks as an aside, "Therefore, if we are to believe that crony, the question becomes: How do we handle this?"

You grumble, "The Black Rose has already done its worst work. I should think saving Fedwick would take higher priority."

Mikhail looks at you. "Do not be so sure."

You frown. "Pardon?"

Mikhail nods. "Parts of your skin are beginning to turn black and flake away. A pile of campfire ash's got nothin' on your neck!" He indicates a patch of skin, and indeed, as you run your fingers over it, you can tell something about you is changing.

44

Zander clears his throat. "We may have neglected to mention that the two collectors who were corrupted by the power of the Black Rose were dwarves. It appears your exposure to the artifact, even just by proximity, has also begun the same process."

"By the gods," you shout, "But… but why dwarves? From among all of us, why only me? How is that even possible?"

Zander replies, "Panic will not help. Only action."

You push back against a wave of fear. Without yourself around in a coherent form, Fedwick's existence would make little difference. Yet, saving both you and him at once seems ideal.

After considerably more time spent searching, Zander announces that he has found the entrance. He leads you to a large boulder, and pushes aside a large swath of ivy, to reveal a passage. It seems appropriate that one group finish their business, while the other waits outside.

Who will go in first?

**If you and Bartleby go in first to attempt to cure
your transformation, turn to page 126.**

**To have Zander and Mikhail go in first to address
the Black Rose, turn to page 265.**

Wary of your need for self-protection, you reluctantly admit to yourself that you will have to do without, or perhaps brush up on your hand-to-hand skills when you get the chance. You present your axe as potential collateral, and pat its handle with affection.

"He'll take good care of ye, Ol' Rusty," you speak to it.

"A beauty, she is," the fisherman says, taking it gingerly and examining the blade. "She would cut right through any of the saplings in my neighbor's field."

You cross your arms.

"That is," he stammers, "Uhh... if I were to use it for that purpose." He stares at the ground, but holds your axe close to his chest.

The fisherman leads you several hundred yards along the shore, until you reach a battered wooden canoe. Several of its planks have warped, the mooring hook hangs by a thread, and it contains only one oar.

"I'm to lend you my only weapon for this?" you groan.

"We had a deal," the fisherman insists.

Bartleby urges, "Come. It is all we have."

You climb in, and with some effort, push off from the shore. You take turns at the helm, one of you rowing while the other uses some prominent shoreline landmarks to keep your path straight. Glancing into the water as dusk approaches, you note that a school of gigantic rainbow struggles against the waves, and your stomach rumbles. Some jerky from your pack sates your hunger. Eventually, the sight of torchlight from a handful of Sungaze port guards in the distance distracts your body and energizes your soul.

"Put out your light," the cleric whispers. You comply. Bartleby stops rowing, and you float in complete silence for what seems an eternity.

Finally, the distant light goes out.

You take the oar, and row with vigor. Soon, your eyes ache for more light than the full moon alone can provide, and you lose certainty of just how far away you are from port.

At that moment, your vessel comes to a jarring halt, with a creaking crash of wood against wood. Your arms flail outward, and you catch a plank sticking out of the pier, but Bartleby's luck fails him; he splashes into the water with a shout. He slowly stands within the shallows, appearing unhurt but dripping and frowning fiercely.

Together, you tie the boat to the pier. The cleric takes a moment to look into the horizon, as the stiff breeze whips his soaked hair into his eyes. He pats the pockets of his tunic.

"Well, that is an unpleasant surprise," he intones.

"What?"

"In the spill, I seem to have lost my sun talisman."

You grimace. "No sense in looking for it now. The waves may have already carried it away. But, are you saying we plan to enter Sungaze completely unarmed?"

"After all this, do you wish to turn back?"

You sigh, and concede, "The clues have led us here."

Feeling around by hand as you delve farther into the city, you find an isolated alley, and hide yourselves in some old, near-empty crates.

"Déjà vu, all over again," quips the cleric, as you drift into sleep.

Dawn forces your body awake despite overwhelming fatigue. You poke your head out of the crate and scan the area, surprised that no one has yet confronted you. The main avenue appears deserted, as wisps of dust and leaves circle in mini-tornadoes, bothering only a rat or two.

"Somebody must be here, somewhere," you muse. When you look into windows, you realize that the town's population has been largely locked down; women and children sleep or play in listless stupor. One man presses his hands and face against the glass as you peer in, staring back at you with desperation, although he says not a word.

"Fear rules this city," the cleric says.

"Where do we even begin?"

"Someone with some authoritative connection to Thomerion must be here," Bartleby theorizes, "I can feel it."

From behind you, within the nearby street, comes the quiet gnashing of bones, as well as the stamp of many footfalls. The noises sound coordinated and simultaneous, and grow louder over time. As you press your back against the wall, your worst fear is confirmed: a full troop

47

of skeletons, organized in rows six across and four deep, files past you, marching in double-time and led by a gigantic orcblood.

Behind the troop follows, to the best degree his withered body will allow, a one-eyed fellow dressed in black and red robes. A black weasel with deep mats in its fur rides on the man's shoulder. The man holds his hands extended outward, and controls a thin cloud of white energy that hovers around and through all the undead. One of the skeletons begins to turn out of formation, but the crony closes his fist and stares intently at the dissenter. It falls back in line.

"Losing your touch, are you, Termulus?" the orcblood grunts over his shoulder.

"Shut your mouth," the necromancer snaps. "Without the Black Rose, I am lucky I can handle this many at once."

Black Rose? You scratch your beard in thought.

"This shall become much easier once we arrive at the training grounds," the orcblood says.

"It had better. After that, I will need rest."

You wait until the troop is out of earshot, and say, "We shall need to catch the crony alone. But, when, and where?"

What do you do?

To confront the necromancer near the training grounds, turn to page 150.

To follow him to his resting place, turn to page 147.

"Please, go on ahead," you instruct the rest of your party while glancing inside your coin pouch, "and I'll catch up to you."

The ranger nods, and leads Mikhail and Bartleby deeper into the wood. You watch after them for a moment as they begin to search for the entrance to the labyrinth.

The old woman clears her throat.

"I'll pay you what I can, madam," you call up. You take a small sack from your pack, place five gold pieces in it, and beckon.

"My knees are going..." she croaks, "and I prefer to climb the ladder as little as possible. Could you kindly toss that up to me?"

You arch an eyebrow, but comply. The old woman catches the bag, but fumbles it to the wooden floor. She bends over, retrieves it and examines the contents. She takes one coin out of the bag and allows the light to shine on it. She stretches her arm out long, then holds the coin within inches of her eyes, and squints. A minute of this passes.

"Ahem," you grunt, "Pardon me, but about that information?"

The woman glances in the bag again, then back at you. "I thought you were handling platinum pieces! This offer is an insult!" She begins to shuffle toward the main door of his treehouse, taking the bag with her.

"Hey!" you shout, "Come back here!"

The old woman enters, and slams the door.

You growl and admit to yourself that maybe this was a waste of time. You hear Bartleby call, "We've found it!"

The injustice of the situation tears you in two. The idea of letting the elf traipse away with your gold makes your blood boil, but embarrassing yourself by making the group wait even longer hardly seems a better alternative.

What do you do?

To cut your losses, turn to the second half of page 154.

To climb the ladder and demand your gold back, turn to page 106.

Whoever told you to avoid getting dirty as a child can bugger off. Something about the low tunnel intrigues you, even as it may involve getting on hands and knees.

A few hundred yards in, the passage, otherwise plain, lowers and narrows to where you would be surprised if a gnome could squeeze through. You attempt to turn around, but fail, wedging yourself in between crags of crumbly dirt. With a wrench of your shoulder, you face forward again and shout, "Can you hear me back there?"

The cleric lags behind. "I can," he replies, "but I begin to doubt the wisdom of this choice. We have no idea to where this leads."

"We had no idea to where any of it led," you grunt, "So kindly refrain from whining."

"Yes, sir," your companion mumbles, "Whatever you say."

As you crawl ever forward, the passage widens again. You go a few more yards more, and reach a small earthen chamber. Bones and a few remnants of wooden coffins jut out from within the walls here as well, but in a more haphazard fashion, as if they long ago served as an extension of the original crypt.

"Fascinating," Bartleby mutters as he pushes past you to examine the far wall. He handles its rough surface, finds a broken relic of some sort, and pulls at it. It stays entrenched.

"Are we at a dead end?"

"Hard to tell..."

With his next step, the cleric trips and stumbles to the ground. His shout of pain nearly bursts your eardrums. You close the distance, and see a monster-sized femur that juts out of the floor where he stepped. The next moment, you hear a deep rumble from the squat passage. As you look up, a choking cloud of dust and detritus emerges from the passage and into where you stand. You cover your mouths and noses and take shallow breaths until the air clears.

"A cave-in trap!" you grumble.

You roll back Bartleby's right pant leg to reveal a disgusting patch of purple and red on his ankle.

"I've... got this..." Bartleby grunts, breathing heavily, "... under control." He sits and pulls himself back against the chamber wall. Through gritted teeth, he recites a prayer, and holds his hands out over his ankle. The skin there flashes white for an instant, and over several minutes thereafter, the purple patch fades to a normal pink.

The cleric attempts to stand, and wobbles a bit.

"It seems I'm losing my touch," he groans.

You scan the ceiling and floor. You wrest several coffin pieces from their places in the wall, and find nothing behind them but more dirt, bone, and stone. With no other alternatives, you move to the entryway and dig by hand. After a few hours, you begin to feel that you're making progress, when a vague light-headedness creeps into you. Your breaths become shallow and quick, and you turn toward Bartleby to find that he's sweating profusely, ready to pass out.

"Airtight," he whispers, "We've... used... what little oxygen... was in here..." Even the torch you took into this place is now not much more than a bundle of faint, flickering sparks.

You claw and scratch at the blockage like an enraged badger.

There must be a thin spot somewhere, you think, *somewhere that if I just... break... through...*

A lightness purer than angels conquers your mind, and your final thoughts are hopes that, as you learned from legend, your ghost can pass through the very walls that killed you.

Your travels cease here, but don't give up.

After you place the ten of hearts, Saul deals the three of spades, thinks for a moment, and places it in the bottom-middle position. The grid now looks like this:

He then deals the eight of diamonds, and there are only two spots left to place a card.

Where do you place the eight of diamonds?

To place it to the left of the ten, turn to page 168.

To place it to the left of the queen, turn to page 64.

Your wonderment about the glow from the upper nook nearly overwhelms you, and you point toward it.

"Let's see what's up there," you implore.

Bartleby nods. "That option spoke to me as well."

You tromp toward the wall below the nook, and grip and pull against the stone, letting your weight stand on a large crag.

"Seems safe," you grunt, "I'll head up first." Bartleby nods his agreement.

The climb exhilarates you, employing muscles you had almost forgotten you had and skills that last saw action in your army years. Only one obstacle presents itself: the final few yards requires a tough stretch of the arms and a huge pull, up and over the lip of a small outcropping. With a tremendous heave, you find yourself on flat ground again, breathing heavily. You look about.

The area is little more than a chamber of ten feet by ten feet, forged naturally and of the same materials as the rest. The source of the glow, however, stands in the far corner: a statue of a succubus, made of reflective, silverish metal. Its face is twisted into an evil scowl.

"By the gods," you whisper, moving closer.

Its mouth hangs agape. Its wings spread to a majestic distance. The statue's eyes are made of the purest ruby you've ever seen.

"Those alone have got to be worth several hundred gold each," you marvel. "Although, if there were a way to take the whole thing..."

"What are you talking about?" you hear Bartleby call.

You stand on tiptoe, and stretch as far as you can, but the statue is too tall. Your reach falls just short.

What do you do?

To call down and ask Bartleby to help, turn to page 70.

To repress your temptation and climb back down, turn to the second half of page 195.

The sun has climbed only a hand's breadth into the sky by the time you reach the City of Storms. Light rain pelts the ground, but the wind is still. Passing through the town gate seems a formality here, for the watchwoman pulls double duty as a cattle rancher, and is busy preening her herd. One mottled specimen moos as you pass, and you reach between the slats of a fence to scratch it between the ears.

Zander informs you that Argent's compound is on the far side of town, so you trek along several dirt streets, and observe as you go the considerable bubble of space most residents grant themselves. At one point, after you pass one treehouse, you estimate that a quarter mile passes before you circumnavigate the next. Miles turn into more miles. The ranger leads you over a knoll and through a sudden turn to the left, and confusion sets in as the trees become thicker, even though you never recognized whether you passed the northeast city limit.

"The entrance should be somewhere nearby," Zander says. "Look for a large stone with a symbol of a bow and arrow etched into it."

As you and Bartleby search, questions swirl in your mind. After a few minutes, you're unable to focus on much else.

"You appear distracted," the cleric notes, as you kick aside a stone and stare toward the sky.

"The note I found on Mikhail…" you say, "It was from an…"

"Orcblood general," the cleric finishes, "Yes, I read it over your shoulder."

You arch an eyebrow. "Did the squirrel's message include the details?"

Bartleby nods as he examines the trunk of a large oak. "Sufficient detail. It will be taken care of."

You scratch your beard. "The orcbloods have their own god. Why would they send a servant of Thomerion?"

"These concerns," your companion chides, remaining focused on the foliage, "must be left to others, should we wish to save your friend."

"The messenger said something about an army of Thomerion."

Bartleby turns toward you. "An army?" Alarm tinges his voice.

54

You cross your arms.

The cleric places a hand on your shoulder. "We are but three men. We could turn back now and take more direct action, but at what point does this become bigger than us? We must prioritize."

You nod, pensive. "You speak wise words."

"The Ambrosinian government, while often slow to act, is one with which I have established an unusual rapport. I was once, after all, a chaplain in the castle temple."

"Impressive. Of this I was not aware," you marvel.

"If I say something is true, they believe me," your companion continues.

This argument seals the deal and reaffirms your focus. The situation affords neither the time nor the need to think further about Mikhail. Yet, there his betrayal remains, in the back of your mind...

"I have found it, gentlemen," Zander calls from several yards away. You rejoin the ranger, who shows you the boulder, and takes a few steps to the side. He pulls aside a tangle of moss to reveal a hidden path, behind the stone, made of worn, smaller stepping stones, which descends into the earth.

You light a torch, taking care not to set any foliage aflame, and proceed with your party into the tunnel. Zander takes the lead, while Bartleby brings up the rear, with you in the middle. The passage feels dusty at first but turns mustier the deeper you go. You step upon stair after stair, and ponder the motivation behind this living situation.

We have not yet met a guard or other resistance, you realize, *so maybe there's not so much for Argent to hide.*

Silence prevails, beyond the occasional drip of moisture from a stalactite. It begins to feel as if you could have read the dwarven holy verses from cover to cover by now...

Finally, you see a faint light ahead. As you press forward, the passage opens up into a large square chamber, hewn of stone. Torches on the walls illuminate the area, so you quell your own flame. Wooden doors sit in the exact centers of each of the side walls, and a large metal double door is set into the far wall. The area stretches maybe thirty yards in both directions, and the ceiling looms the height of maybe four dwarves overhead.

Bartleby and Zander disperse, and search the area.

"Look at this..." the cleric intones. He indicates a nook in one wall, into which has been built a large hourglass. It seems connected to something within the wall, and Bartleby attempts to manipulate it, but to no avail. Shiny silver sand fills about three quarters of the bottom half.

As you explore further, you note something more about the ceiling. Chipped into the stone in the exact center, disrupting its otherwise perfect flatness, is a small indentation, covered by a thick sheet of glass.

A copper key sits upon the glass, in plain sight.

Then, a female voice from nowhere booms throughout the chamber, "Pass the test, or face my wrath. You get one chance."

You hear the mechanical sound of gears and clashing metal, and before any of you can react, a massive iron gate falls within the passage you came in through, shutting you in. Then, the hourglass slowly turns over. Its sand rushing through to the bottom, counting down to what appears to be your deadline.

"Wonderful..." the ranger groans.

"What do we do now?" the cleric asks.

You hold a hand to your chest, to manage your breaths and keep from panicking. It seems a good time to delegate.

"Everybody, examine a door. Then, we meet in the middle and confer."

"Agreed," Zander says. Bartleby nods with force. The others disperse, and you head toward the door to your left. You find that it's secured tightly. In place of a keyhole, someone built a large peephole into the center. You look through it while standing on tiptoe, and see inside a small closet of sorts. A large, transparent tank-like container has been secured to the far wall, and a transparent tube snakes out of the container, toward you, and through the stone. When you back off a step, you notice that a section of the tube, curved upward and molded into the shape of a funnel, protrudes from the wall.

You return to the peephole once more, and note that inside, some kind of lever mechanism is attached to both the tank and the door itself. Finally, a braided metal wire pokes up several feet out of the ground and into the chamber. Suspicion rises within you.

You glance at the others, who appear ready. The party reconvenes.

Zander says, "My door appears to be our overall target. It's locked, but I surmise the key above us fits its keyhole."

Bartleby says, "Mine has no keyhole, just a peephole. Within the chamber behind, a braided wire runs into a closed box, and against a wall therein stands a tall ladder."

You shake your head. "I find this a mite hard to believe. Can't we just smash in the door hiding the ladder, with Ol' Rusty here?" You reach over your shoulder, and pat your battleaxe.

"It doesn't appear all that strong," Bartleby says, with a shrug.

"What? The door, or the axe?"

Bartleby frowns. "The door!"

Zander shouts, "Enough! Which option seems prudent?"

What do you do?

To figure out the puzzle the hard way, turn to page 89.

To cut down the door on the right, turn to the second half of page 37.

Something funny's going on here, you tell yourself. You spur your horse forward until it's alongside Bartleby's and explain what you thought you saw. "Let's look into it," the cleric agrees. You turn about and break into a brisk trot until you once again share the path with the carriage. The reinsman turns to frown at you.

"Good day, Miss Vermouth," you chime.

Vermouth does not turn, but mumbles, "Good day…" Her head lilts, and her skin appears far paler than a typical half-elf's.

Bartleby asks, "May we be of assistance?"

At that moment, the driver cracks the reins and kicks his horse, prompting an alarmed whinny. Vermouth yelps as the carriage lurches forward, but you are too quick for them, as you steer your mount into an interceptory position. Bartleby remains behind the carriage.

The pride of working together once again to cut off escape routes settles into your chest as you bellow, "Might we ask, why do you need to run? Where are you taking the mayoress of Sungaze?"

"This is official business," the reinsman bellows back, "Yield!"

Bartleby says, "Perhaps the lady can speak for herself…"

You wait in silence, but glance inside once again from this closer perspective. Despite Vermouth's half-hearted attempts to hide them, her hands are bound by iron manacles.

"By the gods," you shout, "Why is she…"

The driver growls at you, stands and draws a broadsword. Vermouth screams and pulls her knees toward her chin as two males in black and red robes burst out of the carriage's rear compartment. Each brandishes a talisman with the combination of skull and dagger upon it.

The eyes of all three flare with murderous intent.

What do you do?

To assist Bartleby with the robed men, turn to page 78.

To fight the driver first, turn to page 77.

You assert that you don't need to make friends with the very first people you come across. Just hearing this new name should be enough.

Miracles, eh? Legends? I'll see about that.

You chug the rest of your ale and emerge from the tavern. The best place to research legends, you reflect, would likely be the Ambrosinian library, within the royal grounds, so you begin your trek in the direction of the castle's grand spires. Little of note occurs along the way, beyond the shouts of a few merchants hawking a velvet cloak here or a mystical wand there, but even those folks back away when they see the resolve in your eyes.

The drawbridge lay flat, and snappily-dressed couples locked in dainty conversation file in and out. When you approach, the gate guard barks, "State your intent." You stand straight, hands behind your back.

"I intend to peruse the royal book depository," you grunt.

"You are to respect the integrity of the grounds and all written materials, and will be watched at all times by royal personnel, who are instructed to enforce this rule at all costs. You are to keep your weapon sheathed at all times, and are to refrain from making sudden moves that may be interpreted as threatening or hostile. Are these clear?"

"Yes, sir."

The guard pauses, and looks over you.

"You may pass."

You begin to ponder upon how security has increased from the last time you were here, but are waved along to prevent traffic backup. You enter the library through a vast door just a few yards into the grounds.

Dozens of tomes of all ages, thicknesses, and types now flank you. Some sit on warped wooden podiums older than you. You clomp down an aisle, scanning the titles for relevance, then test the steps on a ladder intended to reach upper shelves. The leather bindings on some books squeak with newness when you handle them; in other cases, it would be a miracle if all the pages were present. Light chains lock down most volumes, valuable as they are. The establishment imposes upon you a deep-seated feeling of awe and respect.

You turn a corner, and catch the eye of the gnome bookkeeper, who seems busy transcribing something, but offers a polite nod in your direction. Her green hat wobbles and nearly falls off her head.

"Pardon me, ma'am," you grunt.

The gnome looks up. "How can I help you?"

"I seek information about a certain Demetria Argent."

The gnome clears her throat, and emits a weak giggle. "In that case," she chirps, "you might want to speak to the halfling."

You frown, and cross your arms. "What halfling?"

At that moment, a short someone whizzes by you, lugging a huge tome, open to its very middle. He marches up to the librarian, jabs a finger partway down a page, and shouts, "See, you old fart! I told you genies can't bend their own rules. It says that if you wish for more wishes, you could rip a hole in the fabric of the universe!"

The gnome rolls her eyes, and replies, "Fascinating, Grindle… just…. fascinating…"

"Still," Grindle rambles on, "One day I'm going to jaunt on out there and find me one of them buggers! All you have to do is rub the lamp…" His voice rings with excitement, and he closes the book with a whump. The title reads, 'Legends of Olde, Heroes of Anew.' Only when Grindle turns does he notice you standing in the same aisle. "Oh, hello!"

You nod calmly.

"What would you wish for, good sir," he says to you, "if you could have anything you wanted granted by a genie?"

He seems harmless enough, if a bit energetic. On the other hand, everyone with half a brain knows genies don't exist.

How do you respond?

To refer to your need to heal a dying friend, turn to page 155.

To cite a desire for endless riches, turn to page 72.

You gaze into the twilight as your three companions discuss watch duties. Mikhail ends up with an extended first watch, with Zander on second, and Bartleby on stand-by. Not a twinge of guilt weighs upon your heart as you climb into your bedroll.

That night, a vision comes upon you. You see yourself standing within your stone hut, with Fedwick on his cot. You try to step toward him, but your legs feel useless, as if they stick you to the floor. You begin to hear an intermittent thumping sound, which comes in pairs.

The pulse-like sound grows louder, each iteration a bit bolder. You gaze at Fedwick, but he does not stir. Powerlessness drowns you, and you clench your hands over your ears. You scream. Just as the pounding climaxes, ready to pierce your very core…

"Gaaahh!"

You sit up, breathing hard, and wipe your brow. Zander turns toward you, and crouches. His demeanor calms you. "Are you all right?"

"'Tis but a musing of the gods," you grunt, "have it meaning or no." You recline once more, and rub out a twinge of pain in your hip.

"Sometimes, dreams have meaning," the ranger offers, "My grandparents preached that the discussion of dreams fosters any positive change that may await on the horizon."

"And…" you wonder aloud, "What about negative change?"

"Ah," he replies, "There is one of the great mysteries, indeed."

This sinks into you, heavy. Several moments pass.

"Should we fail," you whisper, "to where would we turn next?"

Zander says over his shoulder, "You will find a way. The Black Rose? The lives that it maligned, they are gone. We do what we can about it, and little more. But in you, I see a unique fire that drives you, the fire of friendship."

The wind howls, a chill omen of much to come.

Write down the keyword FIRE.

Turn to page 38.

Feeling bold, you point at the keyhole, and ask of Bartleby, "Shall we?" He looks over his shoulder once, but acquiesces, and keeps his talisman at the ready.

You inch forward, insert the key into the door, and take a deep breath. With some effort, you turn it. The door moans in a struggle of metal against aging metal as you pull it open.

Behind it lies a hexagonal chamber. A lighted oil lamp sits on a well-polished desk in the corner, and sparsely populated bookshelves line the walls. You notice a larger version of a now-familiar circular emblem etched into the stone floor: a skull, pierced by a dagger.

"I see you defeated my guardian," utters a calm voice. You whirl about. From within the room's darkest shadow steps a stout human male with salt-and-pepper hair and wearing black and red robes.

"Who are you?" you grunt. "And why do you entrap people in this place?"

"Not so fast," the robed man replies, approaching the far wall.

He flips the lever implanted therein, and the metal door, seemingly of its own power, closes and locks behind you. You inspect it only to find that there is somehow no keyhole from this side.

You turn back toward the man, and scowl. Bartleby folds his arms.

"What do you want from us?" you ask.

"It is you who should ask yourselves what you want from me." The man's even tone belies the oddity in his statement. "For you see, I am a bishop of the faith that will soon be your salvation. Some call me Richard the Redeemer. Others, Thomas the Tempest. My specific name matters not."

Dubious, you continue to listen as the bishop paces the floor.

"What is important is that the Church of Thomerion seeks people like you. Determined, courageous, strong of heart and will. At a glance I can discern the spark within you. Most whom we encounter do not make it this far."

"Enough babbling," you say, "A friend is at death's door by the hand of your church, and…"

"Ahh, then he, too, shall soon know the glory of our army."

You blink. "Army?"

"But you, my friends," the bishop continues, "You can have it easier. For you see, the living are almost as useful to us as the dead."

A moment passes.

Is this person insane?

"I'll make you a bargain. Join us," the man hisses, "And your friend will yet live."

You shout, "Now, wait just a…"

"I have the power to remove the seal and the disease."

Bartleby places a placating hand on your shoulder, and asks of the bishop, "And if we refuse this bargain?"

"This chamber is rigged to be filled with toxic gas upon my command word."

You assert, "Preposterous! You would die as well!"

"You, my friends, are the ones who fear death."

Legitimately joining the Church of Thomerion wouldn't stand as a long-term plan, but there's a chance that this death threat isn't the bluff that it seems on the surface.

What do you do?

To agree to the bargain, to gain an insider's track to a cure for Fedwick, turn to page 131.

To take down the bishop right here and now, turn to page 135.

Saul turns over the jack of hearts, and places it in the last spot. The final grid looks like this:

You have lost.

Turn to page 201.

When your vision clears, you find yourself out in the open, near the gigantic boulder. You look about, and notice Bartleby nearby.

"We've been expelled from the compound, somehow," you remark.

"Shall we try again?" the cleric asks.

You proceed back into and through the tunnel, to find that the giant porticullis still blocks your passage, only this time, you are on the other side, looking in. You shout through it, and garner no response. Argent has made it crystal clear she wants nothing to do with you. You could try to break through the barrier with your axe, but hold off, since it might get you in even greater trouble.

Your party heads back to town and investigates the supposed temple, an abandoned warehouse, after all, only to search among dusty crates for hours, but find nothing of value or consequence. On the way back to your hut, Bartleby recites a prayer to the patron god of mysteries, as deducing what to do next sinks into your soul as the greatest conundrum you've ever faced.

Minutes turns into hours, which turn into days of sitting within your hut, planning, and discussing possibilities with yourself. But for every one that you come up with, you find an equally compelling precedent telling you not to trust that it could ever work.

You ask random strangers on the street what they can do to help, but nobody can. Time runs out for Fedwick far faster than you'd anticipated. Perhaps, over time, you console yourself, the gods can forgive your inaction. If only they'd been kinder in the first place…

Don't let evil win. Read another path!

"Unless I am desperately needed elsewhere," you say in your most humble tone, "I would like to go to Managhast. A friend has been inflicted with the seal of Thomerion, and the fruit could save him, as well as hundreds more, before they become part of the undead army."

"Well said, my friend," Bartleby chimes, clapping a hand on your shoulder. You look up at the cleric. It occurs to you that he has never before so directly called you a friend. And yet, now is the time when fate dares to send you in different directions.

You take his hand, pull him toward you and embrace.

As the two of you separate, Bartleby glances at Vermouth, who smiles warmly. "I will watch over her like a hawk."

"You had better," you grunt, "Or you'll have to answer to me."

The cleric chuckles, and retrieves his horse from the nearby wood.

Vermouth describes the general location of Managhast, a few days' journey off the west coast, and says that her brother, Saul, has access to a ship and will be glad to take you there if you mention her. "He can be found in Fort Remnon. You must act quickly. Good luck to you."

You watch as Bartleby assists the mayoress in mounting, then follows suit. Vermouth clutches him around the waist and waves at you as the pair gallop down the hill due south, shrinking in size until they appear no larger than a brown dot.

The sound of pained whinnies leads you to your own horse, who has laid itself down upon an expansive patch of moss. Its rear right leg shines with blood and purple bruises. You mutter curses, regretting the timing of the cleric's departure. As it is, you'll have to walk.

It deserves better than to be eaten alive…

You take a pocketknife from your pack. After comforting the creature for a moment, you feel around its neck for a major artery, gently slit it and turn away, so that it may bleed out in peace.

Two losses in one, you reflect. *How many more must I endure?*

You repress a lump in your throat, hitch up your pack, and take a step forward.

Over time, the emerging sun's warmth soothes your nerves and your heart. The few souls you pass on the path, true to Vermouth's description, seem oblivious that anything awry has occurred behind you. You attempt to inform many that they head into a besieged city, but most ignore you. Thoughts of powerlessness rage inside you.

Night has arrived by the time you reach Whitetail. You visit your hut, clear Fedwick's forehead of sweat, and test his pulse. It is persistent but weak. You thank the universe for the opportunity to chance to sleep in your own bed.

The next morning, you purchase vials, rations, an extra waterskin and a map, then return to your hut and slip the cleric attending to Fedwick a couple gold pieces, all before the sun has risen a hand's breadth into the sky. You hold your head high as you exit the west city gates.

The going poses little challenge for the first two days, but not long after you enter the deserts thereafter, your lips chap and your throat scratches like a feline upon a post. You drink, but your water does not sate you. Cracked soil, dotted with the occasional cactus, surrounds you.

People come to and fro on this route every day, you assert.

As you scan the area, however, no sign of civilization shows. You stop, and double-check on your map where you think you currently are. Even your light clothing now weighs you down. Your head swims as you glance sideways at the cruel orb that is the sun. You figure there is no other place to go but forward, and note something in the distance.

What appears to be a small conglomeration of tents stands about a league away, their front flaps flittering to and fro in the breeze. Standing in their exact center is a sizable pond. Fedwick's plight resounds within you, reminding you of the possibility of a mirage.

What do you do?

To visit the oasis, turn to page 181.

To continue on your journey to Fort Remnon, turn to page 180.

Upon further observation, a blond troubadour of about forty years stands out as the group's leader, as he frequently indicates specific points on a weather-beaten map in his hand. You approach and begin a bit of small talk, and within moments explain your situation, while trying to remain as low-key as possible. You point toward Vermouth.

The performer shakes his head. "I don't know," he says, "We don't want to risk any trouble."

"At least let her speak to you," you implore.

He cooperates as you lead him to Vermouth; they begin negotiating in hushed tones. Temptation to listen in strikes at several points, and once, you note that they smile slyly at each other.

They turn their backs to you for a brief moment. Then, the leader removes his cloak and helps Vermouth put it on. They wave the rest of both groups toward them, and upon the leader's command, two other performers lend you and Bartleby their coverings as well. You drape the luxurious maroon fabric over your shoulders.

"Thank you," you say.

"Go through first," the blond replies, "And we shall soon follow. Once our business in Koraxon is complete, we shall spread the word in Ambrosinia about the plans of the church of Thomerion."

"Our gratitude knows no bounds," Titania says from underneath her hood.

The three of you take a place in line. Just a few parties now stand between you and the orcblood border patrol.

"What did you say to him?" Bartleby asks Titania.

"I told them I would pull some strings and arrange a royal concert. They'd never earned a gig that big in their lives, he said."

You chuckle. "And, could you do that?"

"Not in a lifetime."

You laugh out loud, hearty and deep.

You now approach the border pass itself. The biggest orcblood shouts, "Halt! State your business."

"Our business is commercial," Titania says with confidence. "We seek gems in the mountains of Koraxon."

"If this is true," the guard replies, "Then why do you carry no mining equipment?"

To this, none of you say a thing.

The orcblood steps closer. "And, your voice. It is familiar."

You feel a bead of sweat collect on your brow.

"Remove your hoods," the guard orders. He casts a menacing gaze first toward you, then the cleric, and back toward the mayoress, and flexes a fist as you hesitate. Another tense moment passes.

"Did you hear what I said?"

Suddenly, the brute reaches toward Vermouth and wrenches back her hood, virtually stopping your heart. You are about to shout an order to retreat when, by the evening light, you note a very different countenance than the one you expected: Titania's face appears rounded, older, her hair a mix of splotchy red and purple, with silver at the roots.

The orcblood grunts, backs down, and scratches his head.

"Are you satisfied?" Bartleby asserts. "Manhandling a woman as if..."

"My apologies," the orcblood mumbles, "Fine. Go on through, then. You may pass." He hastily addresses the next party.

You focus on slowing your breathing and pulse as you proceed through the bottleneck, but wait until the orcbloods are well out of sight to request an explanation.

"In addition to the cloak, the band lent me a quick-change disguise potion," Vermouth says, "but, goodness, remind me never to imbibe one for fun. Bitterest thing I've ever tasted."

"I hope it wears off eventually," Bartleby remarks.

"You would," she flirts.

You arch an eyebrow.

Write down the keyword CLOAK.

Turn to page 174.

"There's something up here that I want. I shall need your help."

"One moment," you hear, followed by shuffling.

You wait for a few moments, and then glance over the edge.

Bartleby stands below you, hands frozen to the stone. He looks straight into the wall, and squeaks, "This doesn't come naturally to me."

You grumble, "Well, why didn't you say so earlier?" You remove your pack, anchor yourself against it, reach down and grip his hand. With the cleric's left hand assisting the pull, together you begin to haul him over the precipice. A thin sheet of stone underneath his step gives way, but you brace harder and keep hold.

"One... last... try..."

He pushes up to just above the overhang, and crawls forward. Finally, you sit and rest. Bartleby cleans his flushed face, but soon sees the statue, and stands.

"Amazing," he comments, "even if suspicious..."

You frown. "Just do it."

Bartleby shrugs. He embraces your legs and hoists you up on his shoulders. You pluck the rubies from their place, and pocket them. The cleric sets you down just in time to dodge two jets of noxious green gas, which burst from the eye sockets and begin to fill the room.

Thinking quickly, you run toward the entry gap and launch yourselves from the precipice. You use your shield to absorb part of the impact, but Bartleby lands hard, skids and bumps across jagged stones and dirt and crashes into the far wall. You help him up, and look to see the fumes ballooning out into the primary cave space.

"Are you all right? Can you walk?"

"There's no time to worry. Let's go!"

You dive toward the wide passage opposite the cove, where a wind current disperses the gas, keeping it away from your tender lungs.

Write down the keyword RUBY.

Continue to page 71.

Hearing mild snoring and an occasional rattling from within, you step into the wide passage. Within one wall is a decrepit prison cell, secured by rusted bars. The area reeks of mold, and flies have nested in a far corner, around a small mass of what once might have been meat.

"Psst...."

You raise your head. The sound came from further within the tunnel. You continue forward, and scan more cells similar to the first. Within the fourth cell lies a shirtless goblin in maroon trousers, who looks up at you. Splotches of dirt mar its craggy green face.

"What the devil?" you exclaim.

The goblin holds a finger to its mouth, and points farther down the hall. You turn, and see yards away an enormous black hound, asleep. Gore-splattered fangs protrude from its jaws, and with each strained exhalation, a string of spittle hanging from its lip grows by a bit more.

On the wall behind the dog hangs a golden key, on a brass hook. The goblin points at it, then at the lock on his cell door. His intent sinks in, but so does a memory of being called to restore the peace after goblin thieves ransacked the local merchant's guild two years ago.

"Who are you to ask us to release you?" you whisper. "A monster, just as the rest of this place seems to be filled with."

"Searching for treasure, I was! And captured, I became. But in exchange for letting me keep my life, I offered to work as a slave."

Bartleby asks, "To whom did you make this offer?"

"A bishop of the Church of Thomerion. He works down here, and I saw him stash a wand in a secret location. It controls minds, it does!"

You and Bartleby exchange glances.

"I'll lead you to it! If, please," it begs, "you let me out..."

What do you do?

To attempt to get the key and recruit the goblin, turn to page 233.

To refuse his pleas and find the wand yourselves, turn to page 231.

71

You paste on a smile and blurt, "Why, I'd wish for a dragon's lair's worth of gold pieces. Who wouldn't?"

Grindle grins wide, his eyes beaming. "My thoughts exactly! I like you already." An idea seems to come to him, as his mouth twists into a big 'O.' "And, speaking of money, perhaps," he says, pointing at you, "you would like to help me with something."

You pause, and ask, "Such as?"

"You may not believe this," Grindle says with a flourish of his hands, "but you should, for it is truth. I was not long ago all set to participate in a royal audience, an opportunity to speak with his highness King Patrick, so as to ascertain funds for the development of a new and wondrous invention!"

Skepticism begins to bubble from within, but you maintain a polite demeanor. "An invention, you say? Of what sort?"

"A steam-powered flying machine."

You blink. A moment passes.

"What?"

"I know!" Grindle's voice arcs into a high register. "Perhaps the greatest invention of all time, just short of being ready to be placed in the capable hands of the populace, but by your best guess, would you say I received the funding?"

You cross your arms.

"I did not."

You let your jaw drop with fake drama. "No! In truth?"

"Absolute truth, swear on my grandmama's makeshift grave." He jerks an open hand straight up to seal the oath. "Just like with everything else, King Patrick felt he needed evidence, a working prototype, before acting upon the device's potential. He just can't see that he's putting the cart before the horse!"

"Please, listen," you interject, "I seek information about a Demetria Argent, so unless you know something about her…"

"No, no, no. Hear me out. Hear me out," Grindle begs. "For you see, I've deduced from extensive research, in-depth interviews and a rash

72

of sheer luck that…" He pauses, and glances over his shoulder. "King Patrick is not the true ruler of Ambrosinia."

You huff into your beard, and grunt, "You spout nonsense."

"You want Demetria Argent, you say? I can lead you to someone else, someone who will one day single-handedly transform this country and all who live in it into harbingers of technological and philosophical greatness! Someone who can spread happiness and health, prosperity and wealth throughout all corners of the land!"

Health? At this word, your ears perk, and your impatience fades.

"I saw him," Grindle whispers, "I saw the true ruler."

You scratch your head. "Explain."

"Let us walk as we talk," Grindle offers.

You exit the library, barely keeping up with the halfling, who skips across the cobblestones with unbridled energy. Outside the castle grounds, Grindle waves and smiles at a gaggle of merchants, then turns about and addresses you while trotting backward.

"I ventured out within the southern forest one day, to gather spices, but became hopelessly lost. At the cusp of dusk, in climbing over a hillock, my foot became caught in vines, and I wrenched my ankle something fierce."

You grimace, but continue to listen.

"My cries of pain must have echoed throughout the wood, for within a few moments I saw a human, clothed in bear's hides. Streaks of dry blood decorated his temples and forehead, and he used a spear as a walking stick. I was not sure whether he was ally or enemy. He held a finger to his lips, and I could not help but obey his request for quiet. He bent down toward me and held his hands over my foot, and I felt a rush of energy come from him and into me. Within seconds, I felt good as new. It took a moment to recover, and a desire to thank him overwhelmed me, but by the time I stood and turned, the man had disappeared."

A powerful healer, indeed, you reflect.

Grindle pauses to hitch up his knickers, and reaches up to place a hand on your arm.

"This, my friend," he continues in a serious tone, "Is how this all ties together: The man had the royal birthmark. You are aware of how, without exception, all descendants of King Jeremiah the Third, for three generations straight, have a large, somewhat trapezoidal imprint running from their cheeks to their necks, on the right side?"

"Indeed," you recall, "it is hard to interact with King Patrick without noticing it."

"I suspected his true lineage, and so questioned many who knew the royal family, even some cousins, aunts and uncles. It took some coaxing, but they shared just enough for me to piece together that King Patrick must have an older, long-lost brother, to whom the throne should have passed when their father died."

You nod. "Young Wyver. They kept it quiet, but he contracted pneumonia and gave up the ghost when fourteen years of age."

The halfling stops, stands on tiptoes and stares you right in the eye.

"So you say. My theory is that, for whatever reason, he faked his death, and became a man of nature."

You arch an eyebrow.

"My mission," he booms, insofar as a halfling can boom, "Is to find him again, and persuade him to take the throne."

"So that you can complete your invention?"

"Exactly!" Grindle leaps over some stones in the road, diverting the attention of a pair of merchants and a few nearby children.

Your shock at this being's ways of thinking nearly exceeds the bounds of verbal description. If you play along, though, you tell yourself, you may be able to employ the druid in question to heal Fedwick.

What do you do?

To dismiss Grindle and try something else, turn to page 81.

To team up in an effort to find the druid, turn to page 83.

If the gods test me, you think, *I had better take the high road.*

You thank the boy, and hustle back into your hut. "King Wyver, your highness," you shout.

"Do not interrupt," he chides, without breaking stature.

"You are needed at the castle. The undead attack there as well!"
"What?"

The others in the room glance at each other nervously, and at you.

Wyver says, "May I remind you that if I leave, the unfinished magic will leave Fedwick in such a vulnerable state that he…"

"I am aware," you assert. "Go."

"Are you sure of this, my friend?" Bartleby asks.

"Yes. Every minute counts, and I daresay Fedwick himself would advise the same. He was that kind of person."

A moment passes. "Your country thanks you," the king says.

Wyver retracts his hands, and the glowing aura disappears. Fedwick turns white as a ghost, and convulses, first mildly, then violently. You stand over him, helpless. No one says a thing.

You look up, and note that His Highness has already left the premises. You kneel and embrace your friend, attempting to calm him in whatever way you think your touch might get through. "Forgive me," you whisper. Soon, he lay still. You feel for a pulse, and do not find one.

No further attacks from undead occur near or at your home, and by the end of the day, the scuttlebutt is that the capital is safe. Wyver arrived in time, you hear, to reorganize his personnel and push back the invaders, for now. Casualties were numerous, but could have been far worse.

A loyal servant, to the end, you reflect. *But, at what cost?*

You helped save Ambrosinia!

But is there more to the story?

Read through The Seal of Thomerion again to find out.

After you place the seven of clubs, Saul deals the three of diamonds, thinks for a moment, and places it above the queen. The grid now looks like this:

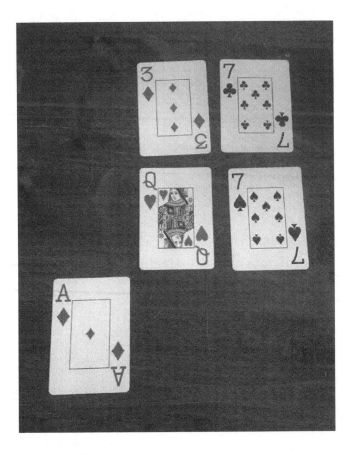

He then deals the ten of hearts. You rule out the positions at the middle-left and bottom-middle, as they don't help, but the ten works well with the queen, in either of two different places.

Where do you place the ten of hearts?

To place it below the seven, turn to page 216.

To place it to the left of the three, turn to page 200.

If you turn your back to a fighter with a blade, your father used to preach, you might just find that blade in your back. Anticipating a mounted duel, you taunt the driver with a scowl. At this, he launches himself from atop his perch and knocks you both to the ground. Your horse rears, whinnies and flees into the woods. Meanwhile, scuffling breaks out at the other end of the stopped carriage.

You're still catching your breath as, a yard away, the driver stands and swings his sword. By pure reflex, you back up a step and raise your own weapon in defense, and the driver's blow snaps the axe's haft in two.

"Ol' Rusty!" you shout, though there is no time to lament.

Out of the corner of your eye come several blinding flashes of light, followed by the thud of a collapsing body. Single-minded, you tear your shield from your back and charge the driver's midsection. Both of you collapse into a heap once again.

You sit on his chest and rear back a fist, only to feel your arm caught by something. You struggle to disengage the grip of a robed hand for a moment, before you feel dark energy pulse through your entire body, causing pain on a scale you never before imagined possible. You roll onto your back to see all three men glowering at you.

The driver licks his lips, savoring the prospect of murdering a curious dwarf, for whatever purpose that may serve. Whether or not Bartleby suffered the same fate, at least you'll shed the mortal coil knowing that you were correct: something was more than a little fishy about this "royal" carriage.

Your quest has ended... or has it?

"Help!" the cleric shouts.

Thinking quickly, you steer your horse toward the rear of the carriage, where the men have almost pulled Bartleby off his mount. You draw your axe, and with a plunging underhand swing, bury its blade in the chest of the taller of the robed youths, who screams and collapses.

The momentum, though, causes your horse to collide with Bartleby's; their legs entangle and they throw you both to the ground. You roll with the fall and stand, but Bartleby now lies sprawled out, a few yards away, his limbs spread in an awkward pose. You frown.

Was he knocked out?

You can scarcely afford to ponder, for the second robed youth approaches from your left, channeling magical energies into a ball of deadly power. You pull your shield from your back and adopt a defensive stance. An impulse to retrieve your axe burns within you, but doing so would paint an even bigger target on your back, even if for an instant.

"Behind you!" rings a female voice.

You whirl about just as the robed youth charges, to find the swordsman driver in mid-swing. By some miracle of reflexes, your shield deflects the blow, and you use the opening to clench the driver around the waist and swivel in place by a half-circle.

The youth fails to react in time; his spell discharges into the wrong target, and violet sparks shoot through the driver's body from hair to boot. You let go so the energy has no chance to jump to you, and a memory of war flashes through your mind.

Yet another pathetic meat shield.

One enemy remains. The rage in the youth's eyes has doubled. He throws his head back, roaring a challenge. He draws a dagger…

At that moment, a familiar face barrels out from behind the carriage, locks the youth in a strangle-hold, and twists his head in a neck-breaking display of force. The sickening crunch is a fitting exclamation point to the battle.

"Bartleby," you cry, "Thank the gods you're all right."

"We men of the cloth can handle ourselves hand-to-hand..." he brags, "...now and again." He sees you arch an eyebrow.

"Don't let it go to your head," you grunt, with a chuckle.

"Indeed, well fought, gentlemen," Vermouth calls.

You walk back toward the carriage, open the side door, and assist the mayoress out into open ground. Bartleby retrieves your axe and helps place Vermouth's hands on a nearby tree stump, where with a mighty swing you break the chain binding her manacles.

"Thank you, thank you, thank you!" she blurts.

"What did these... monsters want from you, Miss Vermouth?"

"I would have shouted for help the moment I saw you," she explains, "If not for their threats of torture. For, you see, the Church of Thomerion has set into motion a collaborative plan, along with the Koraxon military, to invade the whole of Ambrosinia, and in time, take over the capital, Whitetail, itself."

Your eyes widen. Bartleby reels in shock. A moment passes.

"Go on," you implore.

"They sought from me a keyword, by which to employ a cursed goblet called the Black Rose. I overheard from my captors that this item, once activated, allows the possessor to control any and all undead who were once marked with the Seal of Thomerion."

That explains quite a bit, you think, scratching your beard.

Bartleby asks, "Does anyone else know the keyword?"

Vermouth shakes her head.

You ask, "Do you know where we can find this goblet?"

"Since Sungaze has already fallen, I imagine the Black Rose is on its way to Koraxon, and to the hands of the orcbloods' general, Grekk Del Arken. Without me, however, their plans are at least stalled for the time being."

"We shall hide you," you offer.

Vermouth shakes her head again. "They have their ways. If they found me once, they could find me again..." Her voice trails off. Bartleby stands, and squints into the horizon.

"You appear to be brewing a plan," you observe.

"What if…" the cleric explains, "We have the mayoress activate the Black Rose herself, and command the undead to step down? The invasion can be prevented from the inside out."

Your pulse races at the chance, your adventurous spirit refusing to be quelled, as it were. But you also frown, as more questions bubble up from the worry in your core.

"Has Sungaze requested any help from Ambrosinia?" Bartleby asks. "Surely the king could mobilize troops to address the issue."

"All communication routes were cut off. Besides, even if we were to get through, King Patrick has proven mulishly stubborn, acting only after he sees that trouble is afoot in his own lands."

You flush with apprehension, knowing your plight has become tiny in perspective, but manage to ask, "Madam Vermouth, do you know if the seal and the disease associated with it can be removed?"

The mayoress puts her hand to her chin. After a moment of thought, she muses, "I would visit what is called the Tree of Purity, whose berries I've been told have supernatural cleansing powers, on the island of Managhast. Should you choose to go there, tread lightly. The occupants are friendly to no one but their own."

Given the length of a trip back, there isn't enough time to both save Fedwick and assist in preventing the orcblood invasion. Can you trust these two to complete the job on their own?

What do you do?

To stay with the party on their way to Koraxon, turn to page 157.

To steadfastly pursue a cure for Fedwick, turn to page 66.

"I am sorry," you grunt, crossing your arms, "but I find it hard to believe a word you're saying." A strong desire to head back home and reflect upon what to do next washes over you.

""Tis truth!" Grindle blurts.

"I wish you luck on your journey." You turn on your heel.

Grindle's face falls. "Sir," he calls, after you have taken two steps. "I would encourage you to open your mind," he says, "Open your heart, toward adventure, and the possibilities of an endless universe. Today, I pledged that, with or without someone to help me, I would seek my savior at all costs. May you find yours, as well."

You nod, respectfully.

"I anticipate, however," Grindle concludes, "that the journey will be difficult." The halfling turns and skips down the road, whistling a random tune. His words sink into you.

Open my heart? I did not know it was closed. Savior? I did not know it was I that needed to be saved.

You process these thoughts further, and realize that it was a certain open-heartedness, many years ago, that led you to become friends with Fedwick in the first place. You sat once, after a harrowing training session, and stared into the sunset, wondering about the purpose of war. Fedwick approached, sat beside you, and wiped his brow. He stared where you stared. Nothing was said, and nothing need have been said. In many ways, you remember as you enter your hut once more and sit in an ancient rocking chair, this dwarf gently forced himself into your life and 'claimed' you, even though you were not ready.

Having rejected multiple concrete leads, and now, diving within yourself in a philosophical sense, you become inclined to pursue a longer-term solution. Fedwick may die, you admit, but you get the idea that, to discover the cause, you must work from the inside out.

You trek toward a dwarven temple, and speak with some men of the cloth within. Over several weeks, they counsel and guide you toward a life of devotion to your god, and Fedwick's death soon appears to you as little more than part of the natural cycle of life, independent of the foul

81

play. Life seems worth living once again, that is, until even stranger things than an evil sigil start to appear around town. Rumors hold that men in black and red robes are coercing Whitetail officials into less than noble behavior. You emerge from the temple one afternoon to find the streets littered with detritus; merchant carts have been overturned, a patch of trees incinerated. Townspeople mill about in confusion.

Out of nowhere, a helmeted footman darts toward you and shouts, "We need help at the north gate! The undead attack!"

You ready what is now your primary weapon, a talisman of the god of the mountains, and follow the footman as quickly as your legs can take you. At your destination, a dozen animated skeletons are locked in bloody combat with twenty armed guards and conscripts.

You dive into the fray, and use your talisman to blast first one skeleton with divine energy, then a second. The remaining undead, however, begin to comprehend that you're a threat, and soon, four of them surround you, ready to pounce and use their short swords to turn you into a pincushion.

Whirling about from one creature to the next, you notice a distinctive dent in the skull of one particularly short skeleton.

It couldn't be.

Someone you once knew from the military had taken a major injury to the head, in a quite similar spot, during a skirmish. You look into the skeleton's empty eye sockets, and see someone there no one else could see.

Fedwick?

The skeleton shrieks, and strikes.

Better opportunities await you. Try again!

You decide to grant Grindle the benefit of the doubt.

"How would we find this prince?" you ask.

"I have two ideas. I'll explain on the way back into the woods."

"Just in case we need his help," you mention, "Let me introduce you to an acquaintance of mine." You lead Grindle back to your hut, explain your situation to Bartleby and invite him to join; he accepts with fervor. The three of you pack lightly, including a ration each and lamps.

"I thought of something else," you purport as you pass through the city gate, "You never did explain why you need my help in this quest."

"Ah, protection from those that would sooner eat me than help."

Bartleby arches an eyebrow. You remark, "And yet, you said earlier that you had wandered out here on your own, to gather spices."

"I hail from Fort Remnon, which is, as I'm sure you're aware, surrounded by arid lands with little threat from wildlife. My naivete triumphed over basic logic, but it shall stand as a lesson learned."

This fellow, you think, *becomes more perplexing by the moment.*

Many miles into the wilderness, the trees thicken, and vine growth slows your passage. Uninhibited, Grindle calls back to you,

"We go to the druids, or we make the druids come to us. As for the first idea, I've discerned that they often communicate with each other via the carving of symbols in the shadowed sides of trees. If we actively search, we might piece together something valuable."

"And, the other plan?" you ask.

Grindle stops and retrieves a rusty, dented whistle from a pocket. It appears to have survived a trip to the underworld and back.

"Trust me," the halfling chuckles, "This shall get their attention."

And possibly the attention of any number of other things…

What do you do?

To search for druidic runes, turn to page 87.

To have Grindle blow the whistle, turn to page 119.

83

You force your hesitation down and away, and clear your throat.

"M'lady," you bellow, "We seek a fellow druid. The nation is in grave peril, but this person may have the power to…"

"And why should we help you? You slay our brethren, the wolf, who you surely could understand has value to us."

Grindle shouts, "Hey! That thing was about to eat us alive!"

"It was my companion," she mourns, "He acted only out of instinct. We were hunting together…" Her face drops, and she kneels.

"Let me handle this," you placate. Bartleby arches an eyebrow. You trundle toward the druid, and lay a hand on her shoulder. "M'lady. We are deeply sorry. If we can at all make it up to you…"

The druid looks up at you. You smile, hoping against hope to project your sincerity. This remnant of mirth grows within, until it emerges as a tiny chuckle.

"We could always… turn it into a nice fur coat," you joke.

Bartleby slaps his forehead. Grindle groans.

"What?!?" the druid shouts.

"Heh… I didn't mean that, I…"

The druid leaps backward and incants several crisp, foreign words. Vines and branches of all kinds reach out from the woods, wind themselves together and envelop the three of you. You struggle, but fall on your face as the foliage hoists you forty feet into the air, closing at the top like a net. Grindle shouts as he trips and his shiv drops through to the ground below. As you sit up, the druid snaps her fingers, and the vegetation mutates into solid stone. Even your axe couldn't sever it now.

"May this give you some time to think about your actions," the druid seethes, before leaving your sight. Several moments pass.

"That's rather an understatement," Bartleby grumbles.

"Might you handle this predicament better than the first?" Grindle asks, with a sigh.

Somehow, you don't think you can.

Your travels cease here, but don't give up.

You wait patiently, until Bartleby points at Grindle, and whispers a few words. The halfling points at the cleric, then back at the druid, and shrugs and nods. He steps forward, and you breathe a sigh of relief.

"My dear friend," he intones, "may I say, what a lovely bauble you wear there. Is that amethyst?" He turns to wink at you, then back to the druid.

The druid balks, then blushes, and handles the delicate necklace to which Grindle referred. It consists of a leather cord ending in a stone inset in copper, but you hadn't even noticed she possessed it. "Yes," she says, "it is indeed amethyst, but it is not just a bauble. It is magical, and grants the power to turn plant matter into stone."

You whistle.

"How did you acquire it?" the halfling continues.

"It was a gift, from our tribal leader. He once fancied me, although that time has long past. I know not from where he acquired it." She arches an eyebrow. "Why do you ask?" Her voice sounds softer.

"Out of curiosity, and because it suits you so well," Grindle says.

You and Bartleby exchange glances.

"My thanks," the druid purrs.

The halfling has her in the palm of his hand now. "What are you called, m'lady?"

"I am Roghet, master to the stag and cousin to the oak. My starsign is that of the crab, but those who know me would tell you I do not fit the sign."

"You mentioned your leader," Grindle notes, "Would this person happen to have a large birthmark, one that stretches from his cheek to his neck?"

Caution tinges Roghet's smile. "How do you know that?"

"He assisted me not long ago, and I wish to thank him in person."

You arch an eyebrow.

Lies of omission seem to be quite the habit with this bloke.

Roghet ponders, and turns back to your group with a smile. "I am sure he would not mind speaking with you for a moment. I will lead you to him, that is, if you do one thing for me."

"Anything," Grindle replies.

"Help me bury Midnight." She indicates the wolf corpse.

Your jaw drops, and a rush of remorse floods your heart. "Madam, if we had known he was your..."

"You need not explain," Roghet objects, "Wolves are naturally aggressive, and our tribe is still figuring out how best to calm them, to train them. That a few will fall is to be expected. And yet..."

No one says a word for several minutes, as the party digs an improvised gravesite. Roghet picks up the wolf, and sets it within.

"May the earth be your protector, and the winds carry your spirit to divine paradise." She reaches for a flask at her waist, wipes a little oil on her finger, and anoints the creature upon the forehead. All four of you fill in the hole. You wipe your brow, and stand.

"Now come. This way."

The dwarf druid beckons, and together you trek over hills the size of gladiatorial stadiums, around trees wider than the reach of four men, and even across a river colder than the arctic winds. At one point, a crocodile approaches, but Roghet incants a strange series of words that calm the beast into a dreary-eyed stupor, and you pass easily.

Deeper into the wood, exotic species of plants, sprouting spiked blue fruits and striped flowers the likes of which you have never seen before, surround you on all sides, as a white-crested eagle calls out from its perch high above. The utter majesty of this territory makes you long for simpler times, or at least times in which you felt a connection to something greater than yourself. *Is that what this quest is about?*

Turn to the second half of page 138.

Choosing to err, if indeed you err at all, on the side of caution, you wave off the halfling's preposterous whistle plan.

"Put that thing away," you order. "We shall look for druidic runes."

Grindle's face falls, and he turns the trinket over and over in his hand for a moment. With a final shrug, he pockets it. "Suit yourself," he chimes, "I'm bound to have some other use for it sometime."

Leaves crunch underfoot as you wander about this shallow valley, examining the trees above, below, and from every which angle you can manage. Many hours pass, and your feet and legs begin to ache from the acres' worth of exercise. A sunbeam blinds you as you round a corner to face westward, but as you squint, a strange contour in the bark of a mighty maple jumps out at you.

"It's high time we give this up," Bartleby groans as he sits upon a log, "There must be something they know that we don't."

"Not just yet," you say, "Take a look at this."

As the others converge toward you, you indicate two pairs of symbols, arranged in rows: an arrow points southwest, below which has been etched a thin groove with a single bend that doubles back upon itself, much like a serpent. To the right of these you find another arrow, this one pointing straight ahead, accompanied by an imperfect circle.

Where do you go?

To head southwest, per the serpentine line, turn to page 96.

To head west, via the circle, turn to page 99.

Thinking fast, you pull Titania through the first archway you see, and take shelter behind a large wooden structure within a tiny, dimly-lit room beyond. The clomps continue from the adjoining space, and you hear grunts, but as of yet, nobody has bothered you. You wait.

In the several minutes it takes for the noises to subside, however, you notice that your pack and axe begin to feel heavier, and that the object you hide behind seems bigger and more ominous than when you first entered. You circle around to look at it.

Before you stands a grand water clock. Its myriad mechanical features glint at you from within a tall casing protected by glass. You feel an eerie energy emanating from it, and upon a closer look, you note that the hands whirl about, counter-clockwise, at a rapid pace.

"What's happening to us?" Vermouth says at a high pitch. One glance at her explains all. She has shrunk to almost half her normal height, and her few facial wrinkles have given way to rosy cheeks and a flawless, fair complexion. If you were to meet her today, you'd guess that she's about eight or nine years old.

You glance at a partial reflection of yourself in the clock's glass. Although as a dwarf, you have far more years on you than Titania, similar changes have occurred; your muscles aren't as developed, and a deep scar from a wound you remember taking in battle has disappeared.

"We need to get out of here, now!"

You grip the girl by the hand and hustle clear out of the tower and into the streets. Bartleby is nowhere to be found. Looking over your shoulder as you hide behind boulders, you ask, "Are you all right?"

Titania fights back tears, and says, "I... think so."

A consequence of your both growing younger hits you.

"Miss, why are we here? In Koraxon? How did we even get here?" Your memories seem to have regressed along with your bodies.

"I wish I knew," she replies.

Don't let evil win. Read another path!

88

Second thoughts flood your mind. "If the disembodied voice is any indication," you postulate, "It appears that Argent is somehow watching us. It might be best not to take shortcuts, after all."

"Then," Bartleby asks, "What do we do first?"

"Thinking backwards from the door with the ladder behind it, the chamber with the funnel is probably our starting point. The lever may have something to do with opening the door."

Zander steps towards your door and peers through the peephole. He invites Bartleby to do the same, whose face lights up as he steps away.

"I've got it," he offers, "Fill the tank with water from our skins using the funnel. It should raise the lever."

Zander counters, "The lever looks too heavy for that, and we might not have enough water to fill the tank. If instead, we use some of my spare rope," he indicates his pack, "We could make a loop, snake the loop through the tube and pull the lever directly."

Bartleby says, "A ridiculous plan, if I've ever heard one."

"And just as likely to work, if not more, than yours."

You try to ignore your companions' petty competition, and to focus on deciding which option is more practical. Nevertheless, your breath escapes you in a frustrated huff. Decide!

What do you do?

To attempt to manipulate the lever with rope, turn to page 254.

To attempt to fill the tank with water, turn to page 255.

The sorceress sits in the remaining chair, leans forward and speaks in a low voice, imparting an air of confidentiality.

"I propose the following. I discovered, long ago, a quite miraculous potion recipe that, if I have interpreted the ancient texts correctly, should serve to both dissolve the Black Rose and heal your friend." Argent says these last words directly to you.

Bartleby asks, scratching his head, "How can it both destroy and cure?"

"This particular mixture, when imbued with divine energy, serves to neutralize evil, whether that evil takes the form of an artifact, a disease, or anything else. It has thus been called the Bard's Brew, since it is a jack-of-all-trades, of sorts."

You feel your face brighten, and you sit straight up in anticipation.

"I must inform you, however," the sorceress continues, "That the ingredients are quite a challenge to come by."

Zander implores, "Can you help us find them, Demetria?"

Argent chuckles. "Given the circumstances you have just divulged, I would feel safest if I remain here. If you bring the ingredients to me, however, I shall mix them in correct proportion and in the proper order. One tiny mistake, and the entire recipe is ruined."

You wonder out loud, "What exactly do we need?"

"Ah..."

Argent stands, swivels on her heel and approaches her desk, from which she retrieves a small, dusty tome. She opens it to near the very back, clears her throat and reads slowly, glancing at you between each item:

"Two ounces of the blood of a monk of the highest rank. A flawless pearl, at least an inch in diameter. And finally, a feather from a gryphon's wing."

You arch an eyebrow, and look about. Excitement at having a concrete solution by which to cure Fedwick mixes in your chest with sober trepidation. Bartleby crosses his arms, and stares. All four of you take some final sips of tea, as this may be one of your last moments of true rest for quite some time to come.

After another moment, Zander stands. "Demetria, we shall do our best. We thank you for your hospitality and your help. If you'll excuse us, our window of opportunity narrows by the day."

"Of course. Good luck, gentlemen."

The three of you retreat back into the outer section of the compound.

"You do not know how truly you speak," you say to the ranger.

The cleric lays a hand on your shoulder. "Fedwick may live yet," he offers, "if we each pursue one ingredient and agree to convene here later."

Nothing guarantees one's safety when travelling alone, but it seems you have little other choice. As for which choice is best for whom, you're aware of a monastery somewhere to the northeast, but you would need help to find it. A pearl

of the required size is exceedingly rare around these parts, but not unheard of. And gryphons... you groan as you recall... one can find their nests all over the southern mountains, but they're not known for their cooperation with humans.

Which potion component will you seek?

To acquire the abbot's blood, turn to page 110.

To search for a sizable pearl, turn to page 128.

To hunt down a gryphon feather, turn to page 129.

Your chest tightens as your only tangible contact with the Church of Thomerion begins to fade into the distance beyond.

You utter a primal roar, rear back with your axe and unleash a mighty swing at the nearest zombie, which connects at the base of its neck. Its head, still groaning, bounces off a gravestone and lands in a thick patch of thistles. The remaining zombies close the distance with alarming speed. One envelops Bartleby from behind, its claws closing down upon him in a vicious bear grip.

The cleric reaches over his shoulder, hooks the creature by the armpit and throws it across himself, body-slamming it into the cold ground. He pins it there with one hand, extends his sun talisman and concentrates. An instant later, a piercing beam of energy blasts forth from the item and incinerates the zombie's skull.

"Impressive, friend," you marvel.

"One to one, now," the cleric counts. "Care for a tie-breaker?"

You chuckle, and just as you turn around, a zombie sinks its teeth into your arm. Pain crackles through you, and you grit your teeth.

"Let's finish this," the cleric says.

You retreat a few steps, as Bartleby closes his eyes and clutches his talisman. White light coalesces around it, and forms a halo so vivid you can see little else. Suddenly, the halo bursts out in all directions, radiating in a wide circle that smashes into each and every enemy. Their charred, broken remains now litter the ground around you.

"Show-off," you grunt. Bartleby laughs. More undead begin to break through their caskets, but more slowly this time.

"This could be endless if we let it. Let's just get that lackey."

Bartleby nods. You rush through the remainder of the graveyard, hurdling gravestones, but halt abruptly, as two dozen zombies now stand in a rough line ahead, spanning the property's entire breadth. More catch up from behind. Your heart beats a mile a minute, and doom settles into your soul. Crolliver has disappeared entirely.

"Do what you did earlier," you order, "Do it again."

92

Bartleby hangs his head, and shows you that the talisman itself couldn't stand the impact of the explosion. It sits in several dark, splintered pieces within the cleric's palms.

"Oh," you mutter, "Oh. Oh, my."

The undead close in, and you chop a few more up, but as the blade of your axe gets stuck in the backbone of one, the creature twists about, wrenching it out of your grasp. Before you can retrieve it, other zombies pile onto you and the cleric. You collapse under their weight, and your skin burns from their bites and powerful punches. As you meet your end, you wonder aloud what could have been done differently, if only fate had granted you a second chance.

Cruel fate has taken your life. Rise again!

"Time is of the essence," you assert once again. "We may need to part at this time, if we are both to accomplish what we desire."

Zander frowns. "I thought," he grumbles, "that we were a team."

You stand, stoic. "We were."

The ranger retrieves his bedroll and pack, and begins to walk. "Good luck to you, then."

"Would you help us in one small way," Bartleby calls out, "How do we find Demetria Argent, once we arrive in the City of Storms?"

Zander remains silent, and continues forward.

"Come," you plead, placing a hand on the cleric's arm, "We've upset him. It's of no use."

"But, I don't think we can…"

"Someone in the area will know something. It is guaranteed."

Turn to page 124.

Your instinct tells you this can't end well. "There's just too many of them!" you shout. You and Bartleby run toward the graveyard entrance, just avoiding the grip of two zombies. The whole of them pursue you at first, but soon straggle behind, tripping over their own tatters and fighting amongst themselves. You stop to catch your breath.

"We need to find our way back to town," you assert, "From there, we should develop a secondary plan." Bartleby nods his agreement.

While tromping across the grasslands, you grasp at whatever ideas flit through your mind. Reporting the incident to the authorities seems logical, but since you're unharmed, strikes you as rather secondary. You investigate the Pig's Foot Inn and Tavern after all, but at the late hour at which you arrive, only a few discombobulated drunkards and a blind beggar remain at the tables. The bartender shouts his last call.

"Perhaps we should call it a day," Bartleby suggests, "and reconvene tomorrow morning." You nod your agreement.

"Now that I think of it," the cleric continues, "why don't you stop by the temple of the sun when it's convenient? Perhaps something about the spiritual surroundings could inspire us."

Feeling your heart lighten, you accept Bartleby's invitation, and shake his hand. You part, and while slowly returning to your hut, you acknowledge the information you've gleaned so far with a sober heart: *What could have been so important about the Battle of Bladepass that it haunts Fedwick and me to this day?* You fall backwards onto your bed, and stare at the ceiling's irregular texture for many hours.

The next day, you breakfast on flatbread and a large orange, splash your face with water from your basin, and turn to assess Fedwick once again. Paler than yesterday, he seems at once both peaceful and in complete conflict with the world.

We'll figure this out, you reflect. *Even if it doesn't make sense.*

A knock sounds. At your prompt, the now-familiar attending cleric enters and bows. You leave Fedwick in his care once again.

The sight of the sun temple's marble archway punctuates your uneventful walk. At the apex of the arch, a golden face radiating beams in twelve directions watches over all who pass under. As you enter, you note the white altar standing between two alcoves. A single brown-robed someone kneels within the shadows of a pew and prays quietly.

Bartleby emerges from an alcove. "Quite glad you could make it," he says, clapping you on the shoulder. "I wasn't sure if the dwarven gods would frown upon your being here."

"Oh, they probably do," you jest. "But, what now?"

"The sight of the Impactium, as well as its aftermath, got me thinking," Bartleby muses, "What if we could lure those responsible for Fedwick's suffering to us, instead of the other way around?"

You scratch your beard. "In what sense?"

"Fight fire with fire. Take something valuable from the church of Thomerion, and set a trap to catch those who want that item back."

"You would stoop to their level?"

"Believe me, I had the same misgivings. And yet..."

At that moment, the robed worshipper stands and exits the pew. He approaches the church's prayer box, and deposits therein a slip of parchment. Limping, he passes under just enough light to expose a face you recognize, marred by missing patches of hair and a gigantic bruise that disfigures his left cheek.

You tap the cleric on the shoulder. "Bartleby," you whisper, "That appears to be the very same Thomerion devotee we captured." The youth does not turn, but shuffles toward the entryway without a word, and is now almost out of the temple. He now paints a pathetic picture. At the same time, your experiences in the graveyard are still fresh in your mind.

What do you do?

To take revenge for being attacked by zombies, turn to page 112.

To have mercy and offer to heal the man, turn to page 115.

To call it even and let him leave the temple, turn to page 197.

95

"Let's head this way," you decide, pointing to the tilted arrow by the strange curve. Your trek quickly reveals the meaning of the rune. The woods open up into a valley, through which runs a river of considerable width. You glance downstream, and note its many curves.

Bartleby approaches the bank, his boots squishing in the damp grass, and squints into the flow. "The river must be low from the lack of recent rain," he observes, "and, someone constructed a path of stones here." Looking closer, you see them too; their jagged surfaces lie less than a foot under the surface.

Grindle chimes, "Anyone up for fording the thing?"

Adjusting your pack, you cautiously step into the knee-high liquid. Just to be safe, the cleric lifts the halfling onto his shoulders, and the two of them take up the rear. The river chills your legs, and you sneeze, but maintain your footing. Each step requires you stop and reassess your balance. About eight steps remain, then seven, now six.

Bartleby notes, "We're almost there. No turning back now."

At that moment, a gurgling growl meets your ears, followed by a sharp snapping sound. You whirl to your right, to find a crocodile swimming in your direction. It licks its scaly chops and flaps its jaw at the sight of you, while its short legs pump to close the distance.

Instinct takes over, and you shove forward, only to slip and send yourself face-first into the water. You flop onto your back, and as Grindle tries to position himself between you and the beast, Bartleby fumbles to ready his sun talisman. You push to righten yourself, but the haft of your axe catches underneath a stone, and you grumble a curse.

The halfling stabs at the creature, but his momentum carries him too far forward, and he loses control, sputtering. Even at the river's shallow depth, it begins to carry his small body away into the distance.

The cleric focuses for an instant, gripping his talisman with a shaking hand. A burst of white energy erupts from it, but sails over the crocodile's head, scorching a patch of cattails on the opposite bank.

"By the gods!" Bartleby shouts.

Your flailing has closed the distance between you and safe ground, but the crocodile cuts you off. It pins you to your side with a forceful leap, and its jaw clamps down upon your torso. Control of your limbs disappears into the icy blue, along with copious amounts of your blood. The cleric approaches with a shout, but retreats when the creature glares at him, his face marred with a look of fear and abject horror.

Your last thoughts run along the lines of how every man, even a friend, has a point where he must save himself above others. Perhaps you should have thought of that far earlier.

Your quest has ended... or has it?

Exhausting yourself doesn't sound all that entertaining right now, and yet, better to err on the safe side, you reflect, by designating someone of size and strength at least equal to those of the druid.

"Bartleby," you call, "Would you mind taking this one?"

"'Twould be my pleasure," the cleric says with warlike fervor, taking his place on the far side of the stump arena. He points at Darby, and winks cockily. You sit among the growing throng of spectators.

Darby hands both men a staff. "Are both combatants ready?"

They nod. Wyver frowns in concentration. An eager grin emerges upon the cleric's face.

"On my mark," Darby shouts. "Three. Two. One,"

The tension burns in your veins like lava.

"Begin!"

Both men lurch forward to make the first move, their staves clashing in a stalemate. Bartleby twists the knot of arms and wood sharply to his right, but Wyver compensates, keeping his feet planted. Not a drop of worry crosses the druid's brow. Wyver draws back, and the two circle each other for a moment.

"Go, Bartleby!" Grindle calls out. "You've got this!"

"Wyver will pound your man into the ground," Roghet growls.

"Did someone ask your opinion?" the halfling says.

The dwarf's face falls, but she quickly turns back and resumes cheering for her tribal leader.

Wyver swings his staff's end in an upward arc; it crashes into Bartleby's jaw, and the cleric reels backward. He shakes off the blow and counters with a solid shot to the druid's gut. Now having turned in a complete circle, the combatants tie themselves together in a breathless tangle once again, and shove and strike repeatedly, with no end in sight.

You realize you've been chewing on your fingernails, and spit out flecks of dirt while keeping your gaze locked on the action.

Wyver moves in for a jab, which Bartleby dodges. The opening allows the cleric to hook his opponent's near leg with his staff, which throws off the druid's balance. The cleric leans forward with all his weight, and Wyver's feet slide across the wood, breaking off massive splinters; the pair now dangle at the very edge of the arena. A druid spectator gasps.

Wyver reaffirms his grip, steps over Bartleby's staff and swings his own weapon across his body, smacking the cleric in the back. Your combatant sails off the front end of the stump, but catches just enough of Wyver's outstretched limbs that they collapse together within a pile of ivy.

The match is a draw. A cacophonous roar erupts from the crowd, in congratulation to both sides, for a fight well-fought.

The men stand, and brush themselves off. "Not bad, for a man of the cloth," Wyver jokes, extending his hand.

Bartleby laughs, and they shake. "Nor you, for a man of peace."

Wyver turns toward you. "I like how you think. As pledged, I shall return to claim the throne."

Turn to page 109.

"I don't know what it could indicate," you say, "but I think we should pursue the westbound path."

Bartleby says, "No objections here." The halfling nods his acceptance as well.

The trees and grass begin to thin as you trek in this direction, spanning outward into a beige, sun-beaten prairie. Wisps of cloud drift by overhead, as a field of wheat stalks adjacent to the path dances and bends in the breeze. The path takes a sudden downturn. Many yards ahead and just to the north, you see a circular door, built into the ground at an awkward angle.

Grindle begins to skip down the hill. You struggle to keep up without letting the tall vegetation smack you in the face. The halfling stands over the door, and knocks upon it three times. "Come out, come out, wherever you are!"

You chide, "Quiet, small one."

Grindle sulks, and steps off the hatch.

You approach, and look about you. The three of you are the only signs of life out here, beyond the high-pitched trill of a far-off tanager. Without a word, you attempt to lift the hatch, and find it unlocked. Underneath it lies a series of ancient steps that descend into the ground. Not a glimmer of light escapes the passageway.

You call in, "Is anyone there?"

The only response you hear is the echo of your own voice.

You stand, and frown. "What do you think, gentlemen?"

What do you do?

To explore the passageway, continue on to page 100.

**To declare the situation a waste of time,
turn to the second half of page 264.**

"Someone must be here," you insist, "He or she must be busy at the moment."

Bartleby protests, "This could be their home. Would you appreciate it if a group of strangers burst into your hut back in Whitetail?"

You glare at Bartleby, and cross your arms.

"Besides," Grindle adds, his eyes darting about, "I was pretty sure druid healers didn't live in random holes in the ground."

"It's all we've found so far," you counter. "We're going in."

The others roll their eyes, but acquiesce. You pull a torch, flint and steel from your pack, light the torch and begin the descent.

The halls here appear to have been carved out of the natural soil, equidistant and precisely straight, down to the millimeter. You've traversed only a few hundred yards when the path curves to the right. Ahead from there, the floor has changed. Instead of dirt, the entire area is covered with dead grass, moss, and other foliage. The radius of illumination fails to reach far enough to tell where this passage leads. You extend a hand out to your side, instructing the group to halt.

In the direction from which you came, you hear muttering. Judging by its low-pitched repetition and tenuous tempo, you'd guess someone down here is incanting a spell. The voice sounds alternately phlegmy and tight, dry, as if constricted.

"How did anyone get behind us?" the halfling whispers.

Bartleby moans, "That doesn't sound like someone we want to meet, if you ask me."

Your instinct pulls you in two directions at once.

What do you do?

To turn around and follow the voice, turn to page 143.

To continue in the same direction, turn to page 104.

"The small one shall compete," you bellow. The murmuring among the surrounding druids intensifies.

Grindle's jaw drops. "Me?" he says, "Why me?"

"Trust me," you reply, "You can do this."

The halfling glares at you with his hands on his hips. "That doesn't answer my question!"

You chuckle and take a seat, feeling tempted to pull something from your pack on which to munch while you take in the show. Bartleby nudges you with his elbow, and smiles.

"Is this in return for not telling you the whole truth earlier?" the halfling cows, barely gripping the staff as Darby hands it to him. "I think we're more than even." Wyver, also now armed, takes his position. His shadow darkens the whole of your companion.

Darby grumbles, "Are both combatants ready?"

Wyver nods with force.

Grindle gulps, but readies himself.

Darby counts off, "Three. Two. One,"

The tension of the moment dances off your skin like snowflakes. "Begin!"

Wyver swings first, his staff bearing down upon the halfling's legs, but Grindle jumps a yard into the air. The druid recomposes himself, steps forward, and strikes again, but his target ducks, barely in time; the halfling's hair flaps to one side from the breeze.

Grindle forces a half-smile. "Can't catch me!"

He takes short stabs at the druid, followed by roundhouses, but Wyver parries them all with nary a caught breath. "Hold," the prince commands, "A wolf!" He points over Grindle's shoulder.

"Where?" Grindle shouts. He whirls about, just long enough for Wyver to bury the end of his staff between the halfling's shoulder blades and push. You smack your forehead as your combatant flies forward and lands face-first in a pile of clover. The observing druids erupt in raucous laughter and cheers.

You feel your face fall along with your spirit. Only Roghet moves to help the halfling up. "Thank you," Grindle says to the dwarf as he brushes foliage off his tunic. Roghet blushes, but says nothing.

"Pathetic," Wyver groans. He jumps off the stump-arena.

Bartleby defends, "He did the best he could."

"I speak about you."

You reel as you look up to find the druid's gaze boring into you.

"I..." you sputter, "What could you possibly mean?"

"It speaks volumes," Wyver continues, "that you would endanger the life of the smallest among you, even one that I have encountered before and helped at the time, for little more than your own amusement. Or did you really think he had a chance against me?"

"Endanger?" you counter, "Your weapons were harmless."

"But you had a concrete goal in mind, did you not? I cannot help but wonder if you would do the same to protect yourself in a potentially lethal situation. You are careless, and it is for this reason that I cannot accompany you back to Whitetail, after all."

Roghet squeals and claps her hands. The three of you look at each other and then back at Wyver in shock.

"Surely, you must reconsider," Bartleby implores, "Did we not make clear what we are up against?"

"May the gods' favor shine upon the royals as they battle," Wyver says, "Meanwhile, our society shall persist in peace. Come, friends."

The three of you watch as the druid encampment flows out of the clearing and disperses among the surrounding wood.

Grindle frowns at you. "I've never been so humiliated in all my life," he mutters. "Good day to you, gentlemen." While the halfling's words sink to the pit of your stomach, he turns his back on you and sets out toward the path back to town.

You call, "Forgive me, Grindle...I..."

Bartleby puts a hand on your shoulder.

"Not you, too," you grumble.

"Let him be. It is what it is."

You dislodge a rock with your toe, and look up to the heavens. Several moments pass before the halfling fades out of sight.

Bartleby says, "The important thing now is that we start over."

"Let's check one thing," you suggest, "when we get back to Whitetail." Your guilt softens a bit, but far from completely, as you trek. The first building you enter is the Pig's Foot Inn and Tavern, but the two men from whom you heard the initial lead are nowhere to be found.

You retreat to your hut and retire after much contemplation. Sleep comes in fitful bursts, marred by the knowledge that your actions so far have resulted in so little.

You meet up with Bartleby again the next morning, and decide to investigate the supposed temple, a warehouse-like structure west of town, after all, but you find little there but old crates filled with useless junk and a whole lot of dust. Now that both leads are dead, the idea that your timing, in tandem with one frivolous indulgence, will kill Fedwick begins to eat away at your sanity.

Weeks pass, during which you ask various strangers for anything helpful, and never come an inch closer to self-forgiveness. Bartleby attempts to intervene, but you push him away, enraged. One afternoon, you feel a twinge of pain in the back of your head, followed by overwhelming relief, as if something there snapped in two.

Within your hut, you place two fingers on Fedwick's jugular. His heartbeat runs cold and slow as molasses.

I deserve the same fate, you conclude. *Worse.*

You retrieve a large paring knife from your basin, and turn it over and over in your hand. The blade glints in the noontime sun, invites you, speaks to you. The handle sprouts two eyes and two legs, and jitters and twitches in an effort to bury the business end in your heart.

Am I seeing what I think I'm seeing?

You look around you one last time, cackle quietly, grip the knife with white knuckles, and comply with its wishes.

Better opportunities await you. Try again!

103

The voice chills your spirit, and something within begs you to think twice. "Perhaps you're right," you whisper to the group, "Let's keep going, and maybe we'll find another way out of here."

Grindle and Bartleby nod, and you begin to push your way through the weird grasses spread across the tunnel. Just when you feel you're making progress, a lack of ground betrays your next step; your momentum carries you downward and through the façade of foliage. The drop seems to take forever, but you finally hit the hard ground shoulder-first. As you roll to your back, burning lances of pain shoot throughout the whole of you, radiating out from what you're pretty sure is a dislocated scapula.

You look about. Bartleby took a similar spill, and sits in the pit beside you, blinking hard as blood trickles from his skull.

"I'll go get help!" Grindle shouts from above, having stopped short. You look up. You lie about twenty feet down, and that the smooth stone walls bear few, if any, viable holds. The halfling, carrying the party's torch, dashes out of sight. Within seconds, you hear a high-pitched scream, followed by a sickening, biological crunch, like that of bone being twisted out of place. A voice croaks from within the dark:

"What have we here? Intruders?" The same voice replies to itself, "Why, yes, indeed, my friend. These will make an excellent stew later, or perhaps we can trade them for more treasures."

"We shall have to deliberate." The voice snickers and fades. You hear light footsteps, then all is quiet again. You check your pack with your good arm. While you have rope, you did not think to include a grappling hook of any sort. The prospect of escaping seems unlikely.

The cleric groans, "I shan't say I told you so, but…"

You nod, and lay back upon your hip, to stare into the void.

Don't let evil win. Read another path!

Suspicious circumstances aside, you feel you must spare the holy verses this sacrilege. You step up to the altar and lay a hand on the book's leather cover...

Suddenly, your vision warps, and then fades to black. A moment later, you realize you're sitting, and feel raw dirt wedge itself underneath your fingernails as you push yourself up. Complete darkness shrouds the area, and you cannot tell whether you were ever unconscious for whatever reason, or if so, for how long.

"Bartleby?" you whisper into the void. The only response is a hollow clattering from a few feet away, which sends your pulse racing. You whip off your pack and fumble within it, feeling for the rough texture of flint. It's near the bottom. You also grab a small torch, and with a strike of the flint on the ground, light a faint flame.

You raise it just in time to illuminate a filthy, graying undead skeleton, wearing tattered leather armor. It stands and turns toward you, but stays where it is, its limbs swaying slowly. Its neck emits a loud crack as it tilts its head and flexes its jaw, apparently curious as to why you are here. Cautious, you grip the axe at your waist.

What do you do?

To try to communicate with the creature, turn to page 13.

To attempt to slash the skeleton to shards, turn to page 11.

To instead find a way out of the area, turn to page 15.

The woman has clearly stolen from you. Surely you have time to call out the elf's ridiculous lawlessness by confronting her.

You close the distance between yourself and the treehouse, and with a quick double-step upon the first hempen rung, you confirm that the ladder will hold your weight. No reaction escapes the house.

One rung after another, you ascend into and through the foliage. On two occasions you remind yourself to not look down, and yet do so after the second time, and your stomach turns.

You reach up one final time, and your hand hits a wood panel. You pull yourself up, step toward the door and rap with force upon it.

"Hag!" you shout. "Do you realize what you're doing? I have half a mind to have you thrown in the town dungeon!"

Silence. A moment passes.

You test the door, and find it unlocked. You push the door open, and see beyond it a wood-walled chamber, decorated with banners and abstract sculpture. The old woman is nowhere to be seen, although a back door appears to lead to another part of the treehouse. Most everything here is splayed with a spectrum of greens, ranging from kelly and olive to a hue reminiscent of the darkest jungles of the earth.

"Squawk!"

You jump, whirl about, and find yourself face-to-face with a caged parrot of some sort. Its orange feathers contrast with just about everything else. It shifts its weight around as it stands upon a peg and shouts at you,

"Squat man lost his gold! Squawk!"

And there it lay. Underneath the parrot, on the floor of the cage, unsullied and arranged in a neat pile, sit your five gold pieces.

This is pure insanity, you think.

You feel your pulse race and your face flush with unadulterated rage. You glance about one last time for the parrot's guardian, clamp both hands upon the cage's front door, undo the latch and reach inside. The parrot flaps its wings in alarm and attempts to scratch at you, but you are too quick. You wheel about, the coins now in your possession, and have

106

almost made it to the door when you feel a sharp point pierce the back of your exposed neck.

You reach behind you with your free hand, grip the parrot with all your strength and wrench it off, its serrated beak tearing a wide gash in your skin as it goes. You launch the bird against the back wall and, as it recovers, you slam the door behind you.

You descend the ladder and sit on a large stone. Breathing heavily, you console yourself that at least now that that ordeal is over, you can move on. By the time you are ready to stand, however, the wound has begun to burn and swell in such ways as you were not aware lacerations could. You place two fingers to it and press until it stops bleeding.

It is nothing, you assert as you tromp through the wood and rejoin your group. *Already well under control.*

Bartleby welcomes you first. As you pass, he says, "I was going to ask how things went with the old elf, but I can't help but notice the purple wound on your neck."

Purple?

You avert your eyes, as if nothing has happened.

"Let's have the others take a look," the cleric says. "Gentlemen!" he shouts, in the direction of Zander and Mikhail, who close the distance. Your elf companion winces upon taking in the sight. Zander struggles to keep himself composed.

"What?" you ask.

"We need to find help for you as soon as possible," the ranger states, placing a hand on your shoulder.

You arch an eyebrow. "Why?"

"That's the bite of a Venusian firebird, and its cure requires a specific spell be cast upon it every three hours for at least a week. Unless of course," he continues in a low tone, "you prefer that its poison consume you from the inside out within hours, until there is nothing left of you but a quivering mass of dwarven jelly."

You turn toward Bartleby, who answers your questioning gaze, "I cannot do it alone, but the elven clerics here are quite capable."

"We could ask Demetria Argent to help," you beg, "That is, after all, why we are here."

"We don't know how long it will take to find her," Zander insists, "or even whether she can help if we do. Your friend, Fedwick, was it? In truth, he seems to have the better of it now."

Your eyes become large as plates, as the gravity of the situation settles into your chest. The others help you find the nearest healer's residence. The first half-day of recovery is not so bad, physically. Soon, however, you begin to feel as if your veins might combust, your dizzied mind becomes incapable of any rational thought and your muscles convulse uncontrollably. The poison has affected every inch of you, and while magic keeps it from killing you outright, you couldn't bother to save Fedwick now, even if you had the willpower of the gods themselves. Mikhail and Zander proceed toward finding Argent on their own, and pledge to you that they will notify her of your plight, should they succeed.

With further treatment, the symptoms eventually fade, and the physical anguish changes to mental. Your companions haven't returned for you; you presume they fell victim to something within Argent's compound. You ask around town, but no one can help. Little recourse presents itself, and fifteen days have now passed since your friend was diagnosed. Powerlessness and regret take control of you, but it is not until you trek back to Whitetail and into your stone hut that you break down completely.

Your tears wet the gritty floor, for Fedwick's chest no longer rises, nor falls.

Your quest has ended... or has it?

The surrounding druids murmur amongst themselves. Roghet turns away, and wrings her hands.

"But…" she sputters.

"I promise you all," Wyver interrupts, "These days, these years among you, this debt which I carry, they will not be forgotten. You have saved me. It is now time to repay you, by saving Ambrosinia itself!"

The encampment cheers even more loudly than before. Wyver approaches Darby. The old man's eyes become wide as plates.

"Watch over them for me."

"Are you… sure of this," Darby croaks, "my friend?"

The leader looks into the old man's eyes, and retrieves from the pocket of his tunic a circular talisman with a large fang inset within. Wyver gently sets the item into the hand of Darby, who grips it with care.

"No," Wyver answers, "But until now, has that ever stopped me?"

His followers laugh and nudge each other knowingly.

"Shall we depart, gentlemen?"

"What is our plan?" Bartleby asks.

"If you wouldn't mind making a small side trip," you request, "A friend of mine could use your healing abilities, your highness. After I escort you to the castle on the way, I shall press ahead and meet you at my home later. It is a stone hut with a hooked chimney, a quarter-day's distance east of the capital."

The prince gladly agrees to help you, as time will allow. The four of you gather your supplies, and begin your trek. Looking over your shoulder, you ponder upon this culture, perhaps more in touch with what's really important than the barbaric chaos in which you were raised.

At that moment, out of the corner of your eye, you think you see a regretful scowl flash across the face of one certain female dwarven druid, just before she turns and retreats into the shadows.

Turn to page 203.

"I don't yet know how I shall present the problem," you admit, "but I choose to pursue the abbot's blood."

Zander and Bartleby accept your decision. The ranger volunteers to get the gryphon feather, which leaves Bartleby with the pearl.

"Gentlemen," you continue as the group exits the compound altogether, "We shall next meet here, then?"

Zander says, "Let us designate a day by which we should assume the worst, if one or more of us has not returned by then."

Bartleby offers, "Four evenings after the morrow?"

You observe, "Zander has the longest quest. Better to make it six."

The others nod their agreement, and you shake hands with both.

"May the fortune of the gods shine upon us," you pray. You turn your back quickly, and frown in contemplation.

Where to begin?

You'd estimate that, of all demographics within Ambrosinia, the elves of the City of Storms know the most about monks. You ask around the city's cultural centers, at a makeshift library, the merchant's guild, and even a boarding house, but you fail to find even one soul that has ever traveled to the monastery. A kind old lady spends an eternity trying to recall the way, only to forget the question after her pet ermine skitters at her for food.

You thank her, turn and shuffle down the road for many yards, staring at the ground.

It makes sense that a monastery would be secretive, even mysterious, but this is getting out of hand.

"Well, bust my britches and call me shorty," rings a familiar voice.

You turn to find a fellow dwarf, slightly taller than you but with craggier features and thinning hair, standing near a tavern door. He smiles at the sight of you, approaches and slaps your shoulder.

"Paddy?" you marvel. "Padeeno Coberfitch?"

You look into the dwarf's grey eyes. Much has changed, but there it is, the same steely gaze that you remember boring into you when you were at less than your most disciplined, the gaze of the man who mentored you in your early years in the militia.

"It is indeed you!" You cry out in joy, and embrace your visitor. He returns the affection, with some hesitation, and clears his throat.

"Better to not let the townsfolk think I've gone soft," he grumbles.

"Pshaw," you reply. Paddy laughs, a hearty chuckle from deep in his chest. You continue, "What have you been doing all these years? I had thought you had retired to the glorious beaches of Sungaze."

"I had," he replies, "And this is the proof." He jiggles his large belly in both hands, and laughs some more. "Yet, I have returned."

"For business? Pleasure? Family?"

"Business, I am afraid. This is merely one stop on my journey to the Blue Eagle Cloister, where my assistance has been requested."

You rejoice, "I happen to be headed there as well! What would they need with an old fuddy such as yourself?"

Paddy pauses, and answers, "Our spies have caught wind of bandits' planning a full-scale attack upon the monastery grounds, to occur on the morrow."

Your smile vanishes.

"King Patrick will not devote royal troops to the issue. I have already asked, but he has encouraged me and others to form a counter-force, consisting of anyone willing to participate."

"Who has joined thus far?" you ask.

"Oh, some hill-hobbits, a few centaurs from surrounding prairie..."

"I must join you."

Paddy reels. "But, your life will be in danger, son. We've already been through too much of this together. I would prefer..."

"I will not take 'no' for an answer."

Paddy glares at you for a moment, and twists a lock of mustache hair between two fingers. Then, he bursts out in his loudest guffaws yet.

"Ha! I taught you well. Then, come."

Turn to page 163.

Huffing fast and hard at the sight of the youth, you give in to the spark of rage he planted within you, letting it grow large.

"This time, I shall do what I should have done the first time," you shout as you tromp toward the lackey. The cleric grabs your arm and twists you about.

"He is of no danger to us any longer," Bartleby says, "Perhaps he has visited the temple to make amends."

You wrench free of your companion's grip. "I care little for your objections!" You turn, close the distance and cut off the youth just as he recognizes you and begins to run. He puts up his hands in supplication. You launch a hard kick into his gut, and he collapses, unable to breathe.

"I surrender," he wheezes from the floor, "No… tricks…"

"Not good enough," you yell. You think you see a portion of Fedwick's ill countenance flash through your mind. A blood vessel pops somewhere in your head, just before you straddle the cur and smash your fist into his nose.

"This is unacceptable!" Bartleby yells. "This is a place of worship, not battle!"

"So was the warehouse. You said yourself to fight fire with fire," you growl.

"But what does revenge accomplish?"

You barely hear the cleric's pleas now, as you are too busy reducing your target to a bloody pulp. For lack of an answer, Bartleby begins to panic, glancing back and forth between the two of you, but then locks his jaw, takes a step back and incants some mystical words. You look up long enough to note the concentration in his eyes.

The fact that he is casting a spell at you, on the other hand, is a mere afterthought.

Suddenly, you lose control of your muscles. You still lean over the youth, stuck like a statue with one leg sprawled to the side and an arm on your knee. You can still breathe, but try as you may, nothing else cooperates.

The cleric bends forward, gazes straight into your eyes, and says calmly, "I will not be a part of this any longer. You are no better than the people you claim to fight."

You watch, helpless, as Bartleby helps the youth onto his feet and casts a healing incantation upon him. He, in turn, sets his hand upon your scalp for a moment, and you feel something burning there. The pair of them then turn and retreat to the inner recesses of the temple, leaving you there to stew.

Somehow, this is the biggest betrayal of all.

Eventually, the paralysis spell fades, but leaves you exhausted. You summon enough energy to drag yourself back to your hut, and stare down at Fedwick once more. You think you hear an unfamiliar, high-pitched voice echo something unintelligible, but soon deduce that it comes from within your mind.

Is this rage sending me over the edge?

Later that night, stinging lances of pain shoot through your forehead. You glance at the bottom of a silver cup, where your reflection reveals the combination of a skull and dagger branded right between your eyes. Sweat has accumulated in every wrinkle, and your eyes run bloodshot.

Hrmph.

You cross your arms, and blink forcefully.

They say, if you can't beat 'em, join 'em.

Your travels cease here, but don't give up.

You glance at your companions, who smile knowingly. Without a word, you leap onto the stump and put up your fists in a mock fighter's stance. "That's the way," the druid says, and Darby hands each of you a padded staff. The spectators' murmurs intensify.

"Are both combatants ready?" Darby shouts.

You nod, and growl. Wyver bares his teeth.

"On my mark, then. Three, two, one…."

The rush of your military years resurfaces, and flushes through your veins like invigorating ice.

"Begin!"

You strike first, a wide arc at Wyver's neck, which he parries with some difficulty. He steps aside and brings his staff down upon your shoulder. You wince and drop to one knee, but push off from there and charge Wyver's midsection. Your weapon connects with his sternum, and you hear the air whoosh out of him as he grunts in pain. The commotion in the crowd ebbs with the action, loud, then quiet, then loud again.

"Are you going to let him get away with that?" Roghet shouts.

"He'll get away with that and far more!" Grindle taunts.

Roghet raspberries in the halfling's direction, but he waves it off.

You now both breathe heavily, and circle each other for several moments. Wyver's fierce jab breaks the stalemate, but you twist out of the way and counter with a backhand strike, which the druid catches in a bare hand. You shove away from his hip, neutralizing his staff as well, and become entangled in a net of wood and sweaty limbs.

The crowd cheers voraciously, and someone within utters a series of primal yelps. A breeze cools your brow as the two of you separate.

It's time to finish this, you think. *But how?*

What do you do?

To keep attacking Wyver's chest and head, turn to page 217.

To attempt to trip him with a leg sweep, turn to page 219.

I would not want to be in his position, you reflect. While your feelings don't quite approach pity, the longer you watch the worshipper, the clearer the extent of the church's unhappiness with him becomes.

You whisper to Bartleby, "Let's see what we can do for him."

Bartleby nods and remarks, "I hoped you'd say that."

The youth has partially exited when you call, "Sir,"

He halts, pauses, and says over his shoulder in a hoarse voice, "What do you want with me now?"

"The time for fighting has passed," the cleric says.

"Of course," you add, "We still have unanswered questions."

The worshipper turns toward you and slowly shuffles back down the center aisle. When he looks up, first into your eyes, then the cleric's, his tears shine in the dim light.

"I thought I could make a difference," he says. "I thought that even if they didn't appreciate me now, they might appreciate me someday. That is all I ever sought. Appreciation, belonging, commonality. A sense of camaraderie. In those senses, the church of Thomerion is not all that different than either of yours, you should know."

You and Bartleby exchange glances.

"But," the youth continues, "no more. I will not stand for them. I came to this temple today to pray, to perhaps find a new direction."

You smile. "We can help you in that goal."

The youth reels. "You would do that? After what I did to you? Knowing who I am, who I was?"

Bartleby affirms, "Indeed."

Joy saturates the youth's countenance. "Bless you both! Bless you both, to the ends of the earth and back again."

The cleric leads you both to the inner recesses of the temple, where, with the help of a couple magical spells, he treats and dresses the youth's wounds. After just a few minutes, the youth looks a lot better, and his voice carries energy once again.

He stands. "Thank you, good sirs. Thank you so very much."

You nod curtly. Bartleby smiles.

"What can I do," he continues, "to return the favor?"

"As stated earlier," you purport, "we seek those responsible for inflicting the seal of Thomerion upon a friend."

"Ah, yes. I will tell you everything I know. Let us talk over a light libation."

You exit the temple. Not a cloud mars the sky, and the noontime sun warms your skin as the three of you trek to the Pig's Foot Inn and Tavern. The youth orders a brew for each of you, and you pull up some stools at a centralized table. The place seems quiet.

"First," the youth says, "I do not believe I have even introduced myself. I was once called Crolliver, though under the church's ranks I no longer had an official name. What is your friend called?"

"Fedwick, of the Canterbury clan."

"I know not specifically who harmed him, but I can tell you why. Bear with me, for some background is in order. All will be explained." He takes a large glug from his tankard. "Koraxon now seeks revenge for the Battle of Bladepass. Most people, including many historians, ignore this battle because they do not know what truly occurred there."

Crolliver's tone takes on a dramatic tinge. "But, in the thick of the fighting, as the momentum began to sway back toward the orcbloods, a dwarven lieutenant looted a valuable goblet from the corpse of a defeated barbarian. Some necromancer had forged it in the hue of midnight, and infused it with dark magic, but this magic was not to be discovered for many centuries.

"This lieutenant entitled the goblet the Black Rose, and thought little more of it than as a trophy. He passed it down to his daughter, and she sold it to a collector, and she to another, and so forth. As such, it has been touched by many hands. Its magic, however, eventually corrupted those hands, not to mention the bodies they were connected to, for the goblet had taken on a semblance of sentience, and rebelled against its dwarven possessors."

Your eyes widen. You and Bartleby teeter at the edge of your seats, listening intently.

116

"Only recently did the Church of Thomerion gain wind of the Black Rose's resurfacing, and so performed some research. They discovered that the item grants the ability to control all undead whom, in life, were at any point marked by the Seal of Thomerion."

Worry tinges your brow. *Fedwick...*

"What do they want with undead?" Bartleby asks.

"That brings me around to my original point," Crolliver replies, "The church has long sought to establish a theocracy in Ambrosinia, and has entered into an alliance with the Koraxon military. Once the orcblood generals have regained control of the Black Rose, they plan to stage a full-scale invasion, employing a vast army of undead."

You shudder at the thought, so violently that a few drops of your drink splash from your tankard onto the table.

"In fact," the youth finishes, "I am surprised they have not yet forced me to join that army's ranks, given the capabilities of some bishops regarding remote magic. I suspect your spells," he says this to Bartleby, "cleansed me of the mental link they implanted when I joined."

"They punished you," you comment, "but they would go so far as to kill you, one of their own servants?"

"The sacrifice of the one expedites the goals of the many." Crolliver recites this as if he has heard it many times over. He takes another drink. Several sober moments pass.

"What, then," Bartleby asks, "do we do now?"

Crolliver says, "A key superior is to rendezvous with the orcblood general Grekk Del Arken quite soon. I suggest we intercept the Black Rose, by traveling to Koraxon and disrupting their plans."

"Can this bishop," you ask as tension rises in your chest, "remove the Seal of Thomerion?"

"Indeed. We shall do what we must to ensure his cooperation."

A tinge of evil flashes through you. *Maybe revenge isn't so wrong after all,* you think.

Turn to page 122.

You whisper once again, "Try an old stand-by." Bartleby nods, holds the wand out over the slumbering bishop, waves it from side to side, and says in full voice, "Abracadabra!" Upon the last syllable, the chunk of wood explodes in his hand, catches the bedsheets on fire, and wakes the bishop. The cleric screams in agony, and clutches his arm, now blackened and disformed.

"By the gods," you shout, "A cursed keyword!"

"What is going on here?" the bishop shouts as he dashes from the burning bed and bolts toward the exit. The goblin attempts to stand in his way, but the bishop shoves his palm into its face, bowling him over. "How dare you!" the man shouts. He leaves the room and slams the door behind him, after which you hear the thunk of something heavy from outside.

The goblin stands and approaches the door as smoke begins to fill the bedchamber. You pulls open your waterskin and spread water upon parts of the flame, putting them out while other parts flare and enliven. Books alight, and the hellfire spreads further as the goblin pulls with all its might upon the doorknob, to no avail.

You search in panic, and manipulate objects within the room, but unlike in the hexagonal chamber, there appear to be no secrets or other ways out from here. Within moments, you can barely breathe, and one by one, the three of you pass out from lack of oxygen, saving you the agony of burning to death.

Cruel fate has taken your life. Rise again!

You figure the three of you can handle yourselves, should even the worst happen. As Grindle looks about with a cognizant eye, you nod toward him. "Have at it."

Grindle cackles with glee, raises the whistle to his lips and inhales. You cup your hands over your ears as he blows, but instead of a shrill blast, the instrument emits a gurgling coo, as if calling to pigeons. The sound carries a few yards from where you stand and then dies.

The halfling frowns, and pauses.

"Intriguing…"

He takes an even larger breath, and blows so hard into the whistle that his cheeks flush. This time, the call's volume sends it ringing throughout the wood, although it maintains its peaceful tone.

You stand, and wait. And, you wait some more. Bartleby shifts his weight from foot to foot. Grindle scratches his head.

You hear sudden rustling, and a wolf emerges from the brush.

"Well, isn't that dandy," Bartleby groans.

A growl rumbles from within the wolf's core. You wield your axe, but hold your action. The stalemate continues for what seems like ages. The wolf barks twice. Bartleby holds his hands out in front of him as if to placate the creature, which now stands mere yards away. The halfling, on the other hand…

You look about. "Wait," you say, "Where did Grindle go?"

You leap out of your skin as a familiar body assaults the wolf from underneath a patch of moss, and sinks a shiv into its flank before it can react. It howls in pain and falls to the ground. Shaking the camouflage from his hair, Grindle straddles the creature and finishes it with a slash to the throat. He stands, breathing heavily, and wipes a spurt of blood from his chin.

"Nice work," you exhale, stunned. You put away your axe.

A moment passes.

"Once again," the priest notes, "Not to complain, but we find it hard to believe you need protection out here. You've proven you don't."

119

"Gentlemen," the halfling protests as he cleans his blade with a large oak leaf, "Where is your sense of adventure?"

In an instant when the setting sun catches the shiv just so, you notice an insignia carved where the hilt meets the blade: An encircled red skull, pierced at a forty-five degree angle by a dagger.

By the gods…

You tackle the halfling, who looks up at you, bewildered. "Hey!"

You grip the cur by the collar, and your voice emerges as a guttural roar, "What is this?" You wrench the shiv out of his hands. "This is the seal of Thomerion! Explain yourself!"

"I…I…" Grindle starts shaking.

"What have you to do with them? Tell me!"

You feel a hand on your shoulder. Bartleby intones, "Peace, my friend. If he had wanted to harm us, he could have done so long ago."

You remind yourself to breathe, and look back and forth between the cleric and the halfling. While holding your face within inches of his, you warn Grindle, "If you run, I swear you'll have seen your last days." With great reluctance, you stand, and help the halfling up.

Grindle brushes himself off. "I once belonged to the church, but no more. That knife is my only remnant of those days. I had hoped the bishops would restore order within its ranks, but the infrastructure became more chaotic over time, until plans began being hatched."

"Plans? What sort of plans?"

"Plans to replace the king with a theocracy, designed to spread the church's chaos to every corner of the land."

Your eyes widen. Bartleby puts a hand to his forehead.

"I only overheard a few bits of conversation about the topic, and about the possibility of collaborating with the Koraxon military. After all, the church by itself is too weak in numbers to ever accomplish something so drastic."

Bartleby crosses his arms. "So, our deceptive little friend, what are you really after?"

The halfling traces a line in the dirt with his toe. "The truth is due. There is no invention. I seek the druid prince in order to bring him to his rightful place of power, for he, unlike his stubborn brother, will believe me when I profess to what I have witnessed, and mobilize troops to prevent the invasion."

You ask, "Why did you not just tell us this in the first place?"

"If you knew I was involved with the church, would you have chosen to associate with me? Earning trust is impossible around here."

His voice diminishes as he speaks, and gazes off to one side. You and Bartleby exchange glances. An unwitting smirk crosses your face.

"You have helped us," the cleric says. "That is enough."

Grindle exhales, and collapses with relief. "Oh, thank you, thank you, thank you for not killing me, good sirs!"

"I also thank you for not killing him," a calm voice intones. You look about. It sounded as if it came from within the wood.

A dwarf, dressed in furs and leather, peeks out at you from behind a large maple. Her dark brown hair drapes across her shoulders in thick braids. She strikes you as quite beautiful, even as her deep brown eyes squint at you in suspicion. She carries a spear, but little else.

"For," she continues, "nature determines our fate, not man."

Bartleby says, "Well, this is most fortunate. Perhaps you can..."

"What are you doing in our homelands?" the druid interrupts.

Any semblance of attraction to this person within you fades. *It appears we're hardly out of the woods when it comes to meeting hostile creatures here*, you think.

What do you do?

To attempt to explain yourself, turn to page 84.

To stall in hopes that someone else says something, turn to page 85.

"We shall have to be able to pass the border security," Crolliver notes, "but, I have an idea. Come with me."

The three of you finish your brews and exit the tavern. From there, you follow the youth to a modest home in the southwest quadrant of town. He implores you to wait outside, and enters.

You turn, and stare into the distance.

Bartleby lays a hand on your shoulder. "Have faith, friend."

You nod, and reply, "Earlier, you advised me to crowd out emotions with logic. When I was young, there was nothing but the fight, the war, which taught the same lesson. No more does my spirit embrace that wise practice, it seems."

Bartleby smiles, his eyes crinkling with understanding.

You ask, "Why have I changed so?"

The cleric pauses, then replies, "Because... that is life's journey."

You think of Fedwick once again, and your eyes begin to well, just as Crolliver bursts through the door of his home and steps toward you, carrying two well-maintained robes of black and red.

"I hope these fit," he remarks, "Either way, they shall have to suffice." When you put your robe on and attempt to walk around, several inches of cloth drag across the dirt. As you pull the hood over your brow, however, you feel sneaky, even a bit back-handed.

Your party stocks some supplies, and exits the city with a hearty salute to the south gate watchmen. The terrain challenges you on the two-day journey, changing from hills to steppe to craggy mountains. You regularly drink from your waterskin, even as regional breezes cool your brow. When you reach the official passage into Koraxon, you gape at the steep cliffs of granite that bar any other way through. Immigrants dressed in thick autumnal burlap choke the bottleneck from both sides, and keep a small corps of guards scrambling to address them all.

Crolliver cuts straight toward the scarred orcblood that appears to run the operation. A pair of peasants shouts at him, but the youth presses forward undeterred, even as the chief yells a call for order. He whispers something in the orcblood's ear, then points at you two.

The guard grunts, "You may pass," and your group hustles your way through the rest of the crowd and into Koraxon territory.

After you put a little distance between you and the border guard, you ask, "What did you say to him?"

"The secret phrase," he replies, "'Thomerion shall prevail.'"

"Bosom buddies indeed, the church and these brutes."

You exhale, and wipe your brow. The capital city of Vartzog now lies only a day's journey to the east.

As you trek, you look over your shoulder now and again, as the general populace begins to appear rather unsavory. A gang of stubble-chinned men mumble under their breath—something about dark runes--while leaning against some trees. Not long after you pass them, a cross-eyed gnome all in blue dashes past you at an insane clip, screaming and twirling about in full circles as he goes.

"Tell your fortune, gentlemen?"

You turn to find a fair-skinned, curly-haired human maiden speaks to you, smiling sweetly. She carries a black pack over her shoulder, rounded as though it could contain a crystal ball.

"Good day, madam," you chime, "We happen to be busy, but…"

"Your friend," the woman persists, "You seek to save his life?"

You halt, and turn. "How… how did you know that?"

"And you," she says to Crolliver, "Redemption will be yours. You can count on it."

The youth blinks, and stammers, "…Re…really?"

"More detail for only five gold pieces," the fortune-teller coos.

Bartleby says, "I don't know if this is wise…"

You scratch your chin.

What do you do?

To hire the woman, turn to the second half of page 227.

To politely decline and move on, turn to the second half of page 32.

You sleep fitfully that night, as your suspicions grow concerning the intentions of anyone you might meet from this point forward. By the time Bartleby wakes you, the sun has already risen above the eastern horizon, yet fog pervades your mind, and weariness swims in your bones.

"Bartleby," you muse as you prepare to depart camp, "perhaps this was the wrong decision. Could we ever guess what Mikhail could be up to?"

The cleric pauses before answering, "It may not be within our power to act upon. We are two men, doing what we can to save one."

Wise words, you reflect. *Yet, not particularly comforting.*

The rest of the journey to the City of Storms proves uneventful, although the black tinge of several patches of cumulus clouds in the distance puts you off somewhat. When you arrive, the distance between residences surprises you; your limited knowledge of the area hadn't included its apparent evolution toward agrarianism. As you don't know quite where to start, you approach a slender elf wearing a straw hat and tilling a turnip garden.

"Pardon us, good sir," you grunt. "Might you have a moment to spare?"

"Good morn to ye," the farmer wheezes, "How may I help you gentlemen?"

"Have you heard of a Demetria Argent? We have learned she is in the area. Would you know where we can find her?"

The farmer scratches his temple and says, "Why, yes, in fact. I understand she's to come out of hiding, to meet with the local council yet this afternoon. Something is to be discussed about 'an impending doom,' although I wouldn't read too much into that."

Bartleby asks, "Why not?"

"Argent has lost credibility with the locals as of late. Not sure if it's age, or what, but at least a few of her experiments have not turned out quite for the best."

You and Bartleby exchange glances.

"I think we shall still want to see her," you reply.

"Now wait just a tootin' minute!"

The sharp, high-pitched voice came from a nearby farmhouse. You see a portly woman, looking matronly in a plain white apron, hustle out from behind a hay bale and toward the three of you. She smacks the farmer on the tush with the bristled end of her broom.

"Helmina, now calm yourself," the farmer chides, coughing.

"Argent never had any such intention, Natar!" the woman corrects, "A friend told me that the old codger plans to hole up with him, on account of that her life was supposedly in danger."

"And you don't think," Natar counters, "that the city guards could provide her enough protection as is?"

"Oh, what do you know?" Helmina snaps, with a dismissive wave of her hands. She turns and sweeps a stone walkway.

Natar looks at you, straight-faced. "I love that woman," he says. "I'll just… keep telling myself that."

Bartleby snickers.

"Either way," the farmer continues, "What more would you like to know?"

Whom do you believe?

To ask Natar where to find city hall, turn to page 24.

To ask Helmina where to find her friend's home, turn to page 26.

You retrieve flint, steel and a torch from your pack, but wait until you have entered the passage to create a light source, so as to avoid setting any foliage alight. Bartleby takes up the rear, as you lead the way.

The dampness here seeps into your bones, and the tunnel stretches on for what seems like an eternity, but soon, you see a faint light ahead. Before you lies a large, well-lit stone chamber. You extinguish your own light, and search the area.

"By the gods…" you mutter when you discover a sizable hourglass, its bottom half filled with shiny silver sand, secured by a horizontal peg into a nook within one wall.

"Look up there," the cleric says, pointing out some kind of key, held in within the ceiling, but visible through a sheet of supporting glass.

You also discover two doors of ancient wood, one on each wall besides the one you came through. Within the far wall is a sturdy metal double-door, complete with a distinct keyhole.

A massive porticullis crashes down within the passage from where you came, causing you to jump nearly out of your armor. The sound of gears grinding meets your ears, and the hourglass slowly turns over, seemingly of its own power.

"Is this what Mikhail meant by passing Argent's test?" you ask.

Bartleby nods, "Perhaps, although it appears no one will be granting us guidance of any sort."

You examine the left door more closely, and note that it is locked tight, but has a peephole. Looking through it, you see a transparent tank of some sort, built into the far wall, which contains a lever. From the tank runs a tube that snakes along the side of the chamber and out the front, to form a funnel. You're surprised you hadn't noticed the funnel sticking out of the wall a few feet away.

Bartleby returns from the other door. "It's locked," he informs you, "But protects a ladder we could use to get at the key."

"Anything else?"

"A braided metal cord runs into the chamber from underground, and ends in an enclosed box connected to the door lock."

Braided metal cord? A memory resurfaces, something about an experimental form of explosive.

You look again through your peephole, which confirms what you'd thought: The wire Bartleby mentioned runs up and into this chamber, dangling loose.

"We need to get into here," you command, "and light the fuse."

"How do we do that?"

"This funnel... let's start there."

Bartleby looks through your peephole.

"Indeed. I think we could empty our waterskins into the tank, raising the lever in the process."

You glance at the hourglass, already more than half-drained. Bartleby pours first, while you stay at the peephole.

"It doesn't look good," you say, "That only filled the tank about a third of the way."

"Let's continue trying anyway."

You nod, trade spots with Bartleby, and begin pouring. You anticipate the click of a lever, a gear turning, something, anything, and hold your waterskin upside-down for ages to get every last drop out.

"Nothing?" you ask.

Bartleby's face falls. "You were correct. We don't have enough water between the two of us. It is not even close."

"What now, then?"

"We cheat, and break down the door to get at the ladder."

"Don't you think Argent would object to that?"

"How do we know she is even here?"

"We've come this far. Where else would she be?"

The two of you still squabble when the final grain of sand hits the bottom of the hourglass. You feel magic overcome you, and everything fades to white.

Turn to page 65.

"I would prefer to search for the pearl," you declare, "Would you gentlemen know of any good sources by which to find such treasures?"

"Do not waste your time with standard jewelers," Zander instructs, "for I have yet to meet one whose wares are of near the requisite size. I have, however, been told that, day after the morrow, the possessions of one of the collectors corrupted by the Black Rose will be auctioned off, and the proceeds are to benefit the merchants' guild of Whitetail. She evidently had no living relatives to bequeath her treasures toward."

"Sounds iffy at best," Bartleby counters, "wealthy and well-traveled though she may have been. You might have better luck harvesting one yourself, if you can find a prime bank of oysters not yet picked over."

You scratch your beard, pondering which plan might guarantee success, if either.

"That's settled, then," Zander says, "I shall take on the gryphon feather. You will pursue the abbot's blood?"

Bartleby nods.

Zander says, "Before we part, decide which course you are taking, if you could. There is a reason I request this."

You blink at the force in the ranger's tone, and wonder to what he could refer.

What will you do?

To attend the merchants' guild auction, turn to page 160.

To attempt to harvest your own pearl, turn to page 220.

"No rest for the weary," you preach, "Nor solace for the weak. I shall volunteer to acquire a gryphon feather."

Zander blinks at you and asks, "Are you sure?"

"Someone must do it."

The others commend you on your bravery, which comforts you little. Upon further discussion, you agree that Zander shall pursue the abbot's blood, which leaves Bartleby with the pearl.

The cleric says, "Let us meet again soon. Shall we convene just outside this cavern?"

You say, "In six days after the morrow."

Your companions nod, and you part. You return to your hut to prepare some supplies, including several suits of warm woolen clothing. You look down once again at Fedwick, and note that he smiles slightly, and looks a little less pale than before. You ponder for a moment.

Are you dreaming of a cure, friend? Have the gods told you how hard we're working to set you free?

You choose not to rest just yet. Instead, you trek southward until well after the sun has said its hellos to the moon. Just when you are at your weariest, fortune smiles upon you, for you discover a party of excavators on their way to the city of Bladepass. They refresh you on some of the inner workings of the mountain passages, and even lend you a primitive map. Among their ranks is a lute-carrying troubadour, whose melodies soothe you into a deep slumber.

The next morning, energy courses through your veins, and you feel like you could ride on the winds. But soon, as you travel, your ankles and calves scream for rest, as the inclining terrain challenges them with every step. When you reach the spot where the path breaks off into the wilds, you stare up at a vast cliff of granite with the heavy realization that the worst may be yet to come.

There it lay. You squint to see it, but a nest of straw, as big to you as a pebble at the moment, lay nestled, exposed within a tiny outcropping in the stone. You see in the cliff face beyond it some cracks that may make the area passable to a dwarf of your size.

You raise your chest, and exhale sharply.

Here goes nothing.

You round a corner, and find the entrance to the cave system, precisely where the map indicates. After you enter, though, the document's details become far less helpful. The passage seems to squeeze in on you from all sides. You push, hurdle, and scrabble your way through and around piles of rock, and at one point nearly slip into a crevasse, regaining your balance at the last instant. You wipe your brow, and wonder whether you may have gotten turned around at some point.

Finally, after passing a swath of stalagmites, you see light ahead. The tunnel opens, and you no longer feel so choked when you step out into open air and breathe in the sky's purity.

True to what you suspected from a distance, the nest lay untended. A circle of straw as broad as an outhouse stretches before you. It supports a single egg that could feed a family for a week, bone-white with purple specks across its surface. Brown feathers with white highlights poke out of the nest in several scattered locations.

You consider the situation.

Since I need to be sure the feather is from the gryphon's wing, a direct confrontation is in order.

A mischievous thought strikes you. Gryphons raised in captivity make superb mounts for knights, thus their eggs are worth a pretty penny on the market. You could not only cure Fedwick on this quest, but ensure a more than comfortable retirement for the both of you.

What do you do?

To take the egg from the nest, turn to page 186.

To just shout at the top of your lungs, turn to page 211.

You glance at the cleric, who frowns, but nods. Gritting your teeth in reluctance, you say to the bishop, "We accept your proposition."

"A wise choice," he seethes, drumming his fingers, "You will not regret it. But, seeing as how you are new, your loyalties may need a little… tweaking. First," he holds out his hand, and glances at the key you used to get in.

You hand it over. "I shall return," he says.

The man manipulates something hidden behind books, you hear mechanical whirrs and groans, and the metal door opens once again. Watching you carefully, the bishop slips out, and the door closes and locks itself behind him.

"What could he mean by 'tweaking'?" Bartleby muses.

"All I know," you reply, "is that Fedwick's life is still in our hands, not those of the church."

You realize you now stand in the exact center of the floor's gigantic Thomerion emblem. The eyes of the skull seem to gaze straight past you, at something upon the high ceiling, but following them reveals nothing of import, beyond a dusty lantern hanging from a rusted chain.

"What if we used that to burn this place to the ground?" you muse.

"You grasp at straws," the cleric says, "The circumstances require patience."

You throw your hands in the air. "Yes, but…"

A loud creak meets your ears once again, the door opens and the bishop reenters the study.

"Have you readied yourselves?" he asks.

Neither of you say a word.

"Thomerion shall prevail," he mutters as he raises a slender, unadorned wand. You feel light-headed for a long moment. As you look up, the bishop appears to you as nothing less than a good friend, someone you should help. Shock that you ever thought anything else ripples through you, and you humbly appeal to your master for your initial orders.

Over the next full day, church authorities shuttle you and Bartleby about from place to place within the city, where you perform tasks ranging from setting traps and barring doors to inflicting the Seal of Thomerion itself upon innocent victims, all while keeping as low a profile as possible. As the sun sets, you retire to a cot within the secret catacomb, thrilled to your core about the good your work will do for the church.

The next morning, the reality of the situation sets in, as the mental fog imposed by the wand's magic gradually lifts. You hadn't paid attention, for instance, to the fact that the bishop houses you in the equivalent of a dirty prison cell, barely fifteen feet square. As you twiddle the threads of the robes provided you, guilt floods your heart.

You turn to find Bartleby brooding. The bags under his eyes belie a loss of his usual composure.

"What have we done?" he asks as he holds his face in his hands.

You reply, "We didn't know what we were doing, my friend."

A goblin outside the cell barks, "Master is meditating! He requires silence!"

You wait several moments for him to pass, before whispering,

"We're now penned in by the likes of that creature?"

Bartleby replies, "It begins to feel as if this quest will end up doing more harm than good."

An idea strikes you.

"Not necessarily," you offer, "If only we could use that wand for ourselves."

Bartleby turns his head, and looks at you with wide eyes, as the life flows back into his face.

"Superb!" he blurts, "But, how would we go about attaining it?"

What do you do?

To attempt to bribe the guard to help you, turn to page 222.

To attempt to break out of the cell, turn to page 226.

132

The proper keyphrase hits you both simultaneously. Upon your prompt, Bartleby holds the wand out over the bishop's head once more, and intones, "Thomerion shall prevail." The bishop opens his eyes, and sits up. "What are you all doing here?" he shouts.

As the cleric waves the wand more, he tells the bishop that you are his close friends, and that he ought to do your bidding. "After all," he asserts, "nothing else has ever been true." The bishop smiles. "What can I do for you?" he says with a pleasant lilt.

As you guide him out of the catacomb and toward your hut, the goblin asks, "So, you are to heal a friend?"

"Yes," you respond tersely.

"Of the seal of Thomerion, I presume?"

"Yes." You walk some more, focusing straight ahead.

"I warn you, good sirs," the goblin continues, "you make but a tiny dent in the larger picture. Thousands more share your friend's plight."

You hesitate, and turn. The goblin nods.

By all appearances, Bartleby has the situation under control. You instruct him and the bishop to go on ahead.

"Thousands?"

The goblin nods again, and something clicks within you.

"Your master said something about an army. Is the church forming its new ranks from the dead, or the soon-to-be-dead?"

"I was only told so much," the goblin admits, "but, it does not sound good for Ambrosinia."

Minutes later, you reunite with your good friend with mixed emotions, as the bishop removed the seal quickly and easily. Fedwick even looks at a tad healthier than you remember, for all the rest he's acquired. You embrace, but hold off on sharing stories of what you've been through just yet.

As a group, you do what you can to stem this sect of Thomerion by escorting the bishop to local authorities, where they detain him on charges of attempted murder. Over time, the goblin becomes a worshipper of the sun god, and even works his way into society at large, becoming gainfully employed as a carpenter.

As weeks have passed in the process, however, the knowledge that something bigger occurs behind the scenes weighs on your heart and mind. Even as you keep the artifact that got you what you wanted, you can't help but wonder where you would begin to help, should this supposed army threaten the peace of Ambrosinia as a nation.

You have revived Fedwick!

But is there more to the story?

Read through The Seal of Thomerion again to find out.

The auction has yielded you nothing.

There should still be time to find one on my own... but not much.

You ask around town, and learn that the best place to harvest pearls is Ethias Gulf, to the north, but can't glean much more information than that. When you get to the gulf, you have no idea where to start, and no fishermen or other experts are around to help. After hours of hiking along the shoreline and searching by eye and hand alone, you find a few oysters, but they have long since been picked clean.

You camp alone halfway back to Whitetail, and spend the night staring at the stars from within your bedroll. You beg the gods for some kind of clue, and, as if in taunting response, you cross paths with some well-to-do women the next day, but their adornments contain specimens just shy of the required size. The rest of the six days your party allotted itself pass without improvement, and though you later attempt to meet the others nearby Argent's compound, they are nowhere to be seen.

Cheer up, you tell yourself, as you flex your fists, your breaths coming in furious heaves, *Maybe tearing some hair out will help...*

Better opportunities await you. Try again!

As you ponder, the bishop stands before you, his arms crossed, a cocky look on his face. You and Bartleby lock wordless gazes for a moment, in mutual understanding.

Together, you assault the bishop, who crumples to the ground under your combined weight. He struggles, but you sock him in the jaw, and he goes limp.

"That was easier than expected," Bartleby comments as he retrieves rope from his pack.

"Don't jinx us," you mutter, while helping him secure the bishop's arms and legs.

"We need to find a way out of here."

You examine the chamber walls, and find the lever the bishop had used to lock you in, as well as an entire bank of similar switches, some newer or older than others. You pull them one by one, although only the very last affects anything. You hear gears and machinery creak and groan, and an entire bookshelf lurches outward and shifts to the side. Behind is a passage built into the earth.

With some effort, Bartleby hefts the bishop over his shoulder, and you proceed through a dimly-lit corridor, which ends in an overhead door. You open the panel, and emerge into a familiar space: the back of the abandoned warehouse. The stone altar stands just yards away, much as before, although the Impactium is nowhere to be found.

You point out a nearby wheelbarrow. "Let's haul him in this," you offer.

The implement makes going back to your hut far easier. Back in the core of town, you dodge or ignore the stares of multiple passersby, and so shift to taking the back alleys as much as possible. Once, the bishop stirs and moans, but you promptly reacquaint him with unconsciousness using the handle of your axe.

By the time he next wakes, you have tied him to a chair, and loom over him, glaring. He faces Fedwick, who still lay in his cot. His eyes widen in cognition, but he does not struggle.

Turn to page 142.

135

"Fine," you grumble. "We track down Mikhail first."

"Thank you," Zander replies evenly, before retiring to his bedroll.

Bartleby takes over watch, but concerns about the sudden deprioritization of Fedwick disrupt your sleep, and the sun's beams wake you far too soon.

"Poor creature," you hear Bartleby say from a distance, "Would it be too much to ask that we take her with us?" You look up to see that the cleric refers to Mikhail's horse, left behind in the commotion.

"I'm afraid so," Zander counters, "Having to control the reins of two would slow any of us down."

"But they're not even ours to leave here," Bartleby argues, "Do you recall that we rented them?"

You listen, and frown.

"This path is heavily traveled, and the barding denotes the possessor. Someone will find it and take it back."

"You have more faith in the universe than I, then."

A moment passes, while Zander ties the spare horse to a tree, and both men prepare their packs. The ranger chuckles. "Surprising to hear that, from a man of the cloth."

Bartleby purses his lips, and says nothing.

The party sits and eats, but, once sated, Zander scans the land. Just as predicted, footprints stand out where Mikhail's weight crushed the wet grass, although you hadn't anticipated their southward bend. You've mounted, and are about ready to depart from the path and into the prairie when the cleric pulls you aside.

"One wonders," he says, looking over his shoulder, "whether that strange soul has had some influence on Zander over time."

"Mikhail?" you clarify, "Until now, he seemed harmless."

"Secretive, yet mirthful. Insulting, yet light-hearted," Bartleby comments, "If the world were ruled by that kind of dichotomy, we might all go insane."

The two of you turn and stare at the horizon as Zander leads.

The travel is smooth for the next half-day or so, although the ranger frequently orders you to halt, and reassesses the trail more often than you feel comfortable with. At this pace, you think, the elf will get to wherever he's going one heck of a lot faster than you.

You shake your head for lack of answers, and breathe deep. "What's this?"

Far ahead, you see an encampment of about a dozen tents and bedrolls, inhabited by a cluster of rough-looking humans and elves. Several busy themselves with skinning and tanning hides of various sorts, although one sees you and waves his arms in a frantic beckon.

"Let's help them," Zander declares, pressing forward.

"And, whatever happened to caution?" you grumble to yourself.

"Here we go again," Bartleby mumbles.

You both follow the ranger, who meets the trapper halfway.

"You blokes," the man barks, "wouldn't believe what happened just a short while ago. A crazed elf in a hood, it was. He just waltzed right through here, knocked me off my horse and rode off with it!"

Mikhail... the Black Rose...

"We can get it back for you, sir," Zander offers, "In what direction did this elf ride?"

"I was shaken by the fall," the trapper admits, "and by the time I stood again, he had already disappeared."

"By the gods..." Bartleby says.

"Did anyone else see where the bloke went?" the trapper asks his companions. Some ignore him, while others shake their heads and shrug.

"Mikhail's bound to stay one step ahead of us now," you observe.

"We shall do our best to find him," Zander asserts. Bartleby uses a minor spell to heal the trapper's bruises, and in return receives a mottled fur pelt.

"In case you get cold out there," a nearby woman says with a smile and a wink. She and the trapper clench hands warmly.

This lifts your heart. Almost as soon as you leave the encampment, however, Zander's face falls.

"What's the matter?" you ask.

"If Mikhail was indeed on horseback," the ranger theorizes, "we may now be at a loss. Look." He indicates a broad patch of mud, from which extend many different trails of hoofprints. Upon a closer look, two paths seem the freshest.

"Might an established civilization lie anywhere nearby?" you ask.

"Only Bladepass, which lies further southward," he replies. "I believe heading westerly would lead to Vagrants' Canyon, while to the east, we would meet the spot where the mountains cut through the prairie."

You scratch your head in confusion, as you know little about these lands or those that inhabit them.

What do you advise?

To follow the westbound prints, turn to page 145.

To follow the eastbound prints, turn to page 262.

As Roghet stops to consult a pattern of runes etched into a tree trunk, Bartleby closes the distance, and adopts a look of curiosity.

"Would you ever have guessed?" he inquires.

"Not in the slightest," you reply.

"Everyone, stay here until instructed otherwise, if you please," the druid requests. She glances at the sun, and retreats further into the wood.

Bartleby sits down on a mossy rock. Grindle leans on a large birch and cleans his shiv.

The cleric asks you, "Tell me more about Fedwick, if you would. Before you called for me, I had met him only in passing."

"Ah, Fedwick. He deserves such a kinder fate," you reflect. "For his role in my life is best described as impactful. Steadfast, humorful. His advances towards women,"--you stop to chuckle--"Daresay, not what you would expect. But, his personality is varied. He is as likely to indulge in anger as in mirth. We would get in trouble as children, with the neighbor farmers, with the elven minority, but then again, what child does not? The key was, we did it together."

Solemn, Bartleby puts a hand on your shoulder. "I saw a life in his eyes, my friend," he says, "even as they were closed. A life paralleled in your eyes. I've come to believe you want this more than anything."

You look aside, and nod. A moment passes.

Roghet reappears. "Come," she says.

The group pushes onward for many more yards, until you encounter a wide clearing, with an enormous tree stump at the very center. The foliage seems to be at its very tallest here, and molds the cloud-shielded sun's rays into a muted cylinder of light. As you look around this hallowed space, only the chittering of squirrels meets your ears.

At that instant, a dozen beings slowly emerge from the wood. They have bows drawn and arrows nocked, but have not raised the bows to fire. You grip the axe at your waist, but hold your action. By all indication, these druids don't know why you're here.

"Roghet, you know better than to bring outsiders here."

The authoritative voice belongs to a tall human male, who stands at the opposite end of the clearing. He wears a pelt of rich brown fur about his shoulders, and his temples are streaked with mud. A patch of bright red stretches from his right cheek downward. As he approaches, his countenance softens to that of sudden cognition.

"You appear familiar," the man says, at Grindle.

The halfling grins, hops excitedly, and counters, "As do you!"

"These men wish to thank you for your help," Roghet explains.

"Oh, but there is so much more to it than that!" the halfling shouts. "Sir Wyver, your highness. You must take the throne! I beg you…" Grindle closes the distance and begins kissing the druid's feet. Bartleby rolls his eyes. Roghet huffs.

By the gods. What happened to the subtlety that got us this far?

Wyver clears his throat, and crouches. "I recall healing you. I am glad to have been of service, but… what is this all about?"

"It's… a long story," you admit.

"Our small but affectionate friend here," Bartleby explains, "has uncovered a plot of grave import, on the part of the church of Thomerion."

"Thomerion?" Wyver scratches his chin. "That cannot be good." He looks up and about, and orders his tribe, "Stand down." They place their bows on the ground, and begin to huddle in clumps and talk amongst themselves. You feel yourself breathe easier.

"Let us sit." At Wyver's invitation, you all take places upon the large stump. "You gentlemen obviously know my history. But you must also know that I cannot grant your request. This is my life now, connected as it is to the world's creations, not to stone and castles and royalty."

"Why did you leave?" you ask. "There are so many people who would appreciate knowing that you are still alive."

"When I was thirteen, a friend and I had snuck out of the castle, and were roughhousing near the river. We slipped, and both tumbled into the water. I emerged to find he had hit his head on a large stone and was floating, unconscious, along with the current. I was too weak to pull him to safety, and his body was found later by a fisherman. My jealous brother, Patrick, saw the opportunity and threatened to proclaim to all who would listen that I murdered this boy. So, I ran."

You listen, enraptured. Grindle's eyes twinkle with amazement.

"Over time, however," Wyver continues, "I came to accept being a man of the world. The druids took me in, and taught me so very much." He casts a grateful look at Roghet, who smiles. "It is peaceful here. The woodland creatures embrace us, and we them."

You scratch your beard. "You have no feelings of bitterness or resentment toward your brother, of any kind? I find that hard to believe."

Wyver shakes his head.

Bartleby argues, "Would you have the kingdom, which includes these lands, fall to the likes of hordes of undead, should your brother choose to rest on his laurels?"

"Undead?"

Grindle nods with fervor. The three of you look at each other, then back at Wyver.

"I just… don't know. I put my trust in the universe."

Grindle remarks, "Would you put Roghet in harm's way?"

140

"What do you mean?"

"You gave her a valuable artifact. I can even see now that she means the world to you."

Roghet blushes as Wyver glances at her, eyes shining.

Grindle continues, slow and serious, "Sir, the church is targeting dwarves. In revenge for the Battle of Bladepass. I've heard all of this firsthand, and together, we can put a stop to it."

Wyver's smile disappears. He looks about, first at the halfling, then at Roghet, then up at the clouds. He stands. Several moments pass.

"Then, I shall come with you."

The surrounding druids turn towards him and murmur excitedly.

"Upon one condition. I need you to prove that you can get me to the castle safely. Choose one of your own to fight me."

"What?"

"You heard me. Don't worry, we won't use anything lethal. Darby," he says toward a thin, balding druid, "fetch me the padded quarterstaves, will you?" Darby nods, and shuffles off. "This is our arena," Wyver proclaims, gesturing downward. The stump appears barely fifteen feet in width. "Whoever knocks the other off first wins. No striking with anything but the staff, although pushing is allowed. And no outside interference, from either end. Understood?"

A rush bubbles up within you. This might be a bit of fun. Nevertheless, you feel as if you should take the decision seriously. You're the toughest to knock over, while Grindle is easily the nimblest, and Bartleby is probably somewhere in between.

Who will fight Wyver?

To choose Bartleby, turn to the second half of page 97.

To choose Grindle, turn to page 101.

To choose yourself, turn to page 114.

"What are you going to do to me?" he asks.

"This," you answer, "is about what you will do for us."

"There will be no dealing," Bartleby says, "You will remove the Seal of Thomerion from this dwarf,"—he indicates Fedwick—"or face the consequences. Then, you will rot in prison."

The bishop closes his eyes for a moment, and sighs, resigned.

He glances up at you, but seems to look through you at some random thing in the distance. "I will do as you say. But for that, my hands will need to be free."

You nod at Bartleby, who posts himself by the closed bedroom door, his sun talisman palmed and at the ready. Only then do you untie the ropes binding the bishop, your nerves on edge.

He stands as if weighed down by something invisible. He shuffles forward, and scans your dying friend from head to toe, with folded hands. Several moments of silence pass.

The bishop whispers, "My disciple."

You and Bartleby exchange wary glances.

"If our army cannot have you, then no one shall!"

Before you can react, the bishop incants a mystical word. A pulsing, purple blast of energy jolts from his outstretched hand, and hits Fedwick full on. Your friend's body convulses wildly, and the scent of burning flesh pervades the air.

Shouting like mad men, you and Bartleby take revenge, the cleric's divine energy blasts doing most of the damage. Red-faced, your pulse ready to send your heart through your chest, you throw the bishop's body to the ground, draw your axe and hack his head clear off. The undead army's loss serves as little consolation. Your rage gives away to despair, and you kneel by Fedwick's side, your tears evaporating when they hit the still-hot, very dead remains.

Don't let evil win. Read another path!

"We followed the signs," you remind the others, "If the healer we seek isn't here, where would he be?"

Grindle says, quivering, "Just about anywhere else, I'm beginning to think."

"We're turning around," you order, "We can handle it. Trust me."

Bartleby and Grindle exchange incredulous glances.

You push past your cowardly friends and hold your chest out high in realization that you may be getting somewhere. No small wonder, then, that you don't see the lithe, black-skinned body hiding within a nearby alcove until it has already leapt out and knocked you to the ground. The others try to pull him off you, but you are pinned there long enough to gaze into the crazed eyes of a dark elf, as well as hear the insane cackles emanating from somewhere within its gaunt throat.

"I got one," it shouts to no one, "I got one!"

The elf struggles against your companions' grips, wrenches one arm free and spits two more words' worth of arcane gobbledygook in their direction. A deluge of ice shards as wide as the passageway blasts forth from its hands, enveloping Grindle and Bartleby. When the area clears an instant later, they stand before you encased in clear crystalline prisons, able to move their eyeballs but nothing else.

"Wait," you beg as it turns back toward you, "Is there nothing we can do?"

It intones, "You shall come with me, or your friends will die."

It seems you have no choice. The elf beckons you to follow, presses a hidden button, and a door opens near the back of the alcove. Beyond, the elf secures you in a tiny, filthy cell, and tells you something along the lines of being released only if and when the Church of Thomerion pays it a thousand gold pieces for its troubles. It appears you have somehow come between this savage headhunter and his employer, and are now deeply involved in the very conflict that put Fedwick in danger in the first place.

It feeds you mush on a twice-daily basis, and there is little to do but count the nicks in the primitive cell bars, through which others have

143

evidently attempted to escape before you. You duplicate this effort during the first nightfall, but find the cell's integrity far stronger than you would imagine. If Grindle were here, he could pick the lock, but you don't see another friendly soul for an entire day, then two, then three more days. You attempt to negotiate with the dark elf when it passes by, but it ignores every word you say. You realize you have little control over the situation, and far less hope of ever returning to save Fedwick.

I suppose, you reflect with your back to the hall and your head in your hands, *it makes sense that a druid symbol would serve as a warning, as much as anything else.*

Your travels cease here, but don't give up.

Thinking better than to indulge in an unwinnable bidding battle, you ignore further action regarding the chest, taking care not to exclaim or raise your hand again, until finally…

"Sold! To the lady in blue!"

The girl claps her hands, squeals in joy, and bounds up to the stage to pay for and claim her prize. As it is almost as big as her, you wonder how she will get it home, let alone how she will get it open.

Let's see what else they've got…

Anxiety rises within you as the crew presents a few more nice items, including an ancient shield you would be interested in using, outside the immediate context. You hold fast, however, pursing your lips. You wait even longer for gemstone collections, necklaces, anything related to or that might contain pearls. The very last item is a jewelry box of ornate tinted glass, but the auctioneer clarifies that it is being sold as-is, which is to say, empty.

Turn to the second half of page 134.

"Let us head west, if only because we shan't have to stare into the sun," you propose, squinting.

"Fair enough," Zander says.

At first, confidence swells within you, as the tracks appear straight and purposeful. The descending terrain, however, begins to dry out, and the farther along you trek, the more impatience builds within you, until you're convinced that you're stuck in a wild goose chase.

"The trail has faded," Zander grunts, "We may have lost him."

"You waste our precious time dragging us out here," you shout, "and now all you can say is that you've 'lost him'?"

The ranger's eyes widen. He says, "Listen to that."

"To what?" Then it hits you. You hear intermittent pounding and cracking, the sound of rock being struck. You glance in the direction from which it comes, and note a sturdy-looking wooden bridge, hanging over what must be Vagrants' Canyon. It stands about two hundred yards away.

"Do not underestimate me, friend," the ranger preaches. A scowl twists your brow, as Zander calls out, "Hullo! Show yourself!"

The pounding halts.

"What is that on the other side?" Bartleby asks.

As your party approaches the bridge's edge, the mass the cleric had noted becomes clearer. The tracks have led you to a badly mauled, bloody equine corpse. You shudder in horror.

"Who, or what, could have done this?"

"I suggest we leave," you say, "Or we could find out first-…"

Your unfinished sentence proves prophetic, for a ten-foot-tall troll bolts out from underneath the bridge and scoops you and Zander up into the air, one of you in each hand, before either of you can draw a weapon. Bartleby screams and runs, leaving the creature free to smash your skulls together and combine the insides. You're sure to serve as a tasty meal or two, if not also a midnight snack.

Cruel fate has taken your life. Rise again!

You call out, "We seek a healer, for a friend is…"

"The medicine men here are quite occupied at the moment," the guard interrupts, "Now leave this place."

Bartleby presses, "Might you at least tell us their names?"

"You will be given a count of ten." Two lieutenants in the watchtowers nock arrows in their bows.

"Very well," you concede as you hold your hands in the air, "As you say." The two of you retreat partway back up the path, then conceal yourselves within the woods and out of the guards' view. You glance one last time toward Sungaze, and huff to Bartleby, "Do any alternatives come to mind?"

"They may be blocking out visitors," the cleric replies, "but I noted ships approaching their port from a distance. It appears economic activity proceeds per the norm."

You blink. "Your point being?"

"We sneak in by the sea."

This piques your interest, even as, upon further discussion, a dubious plan comes to light. You travel to an Ambrosinian bay, and start sweet-talking some fishermen into lending you a canoe, with which you'll row your way into the Sungaze port, preferably in the wake of a much larger vessel, so as to attract as little local attention as possible.

"Are you not right in the head, or what?" the fourth young angler you approach remarks, scratching himself nervously. "Listen, do you have anything you could give me for the boat? I'd return it to you later. And I like to study weaponry, on the side, it just so happens."

You ponder your options.

What do you offer?

To barter your trusty axe, turn to page 46.

To trade in Bartleby's talisman, turn to the second half of page 244.

"Let's wait until nightfall," you propose.

Bartleby nods. You tail the troop at a great distance, ducking into alleys whenever any being therein turns toward you. At one point, you almost lose them when they turn a corner, but you surmise by the size of the building they enter that they have reached the training grounds. Once all the undead are inside, the necromancer scans the streets one more time with his one gray eye, frowns, and slinks through the door.

You both settle into an alley with an inconspicuous view.

A thought strikes you. "Bartleby," you say, "have you any siblings?"

"One sister, younger," he replies. "Why do you ask?"

"The bond of growing up together perplexes me. While we seek to save the life of the closest thing I have ever had to a brother, I sometimes wonder whether it is quite the same."

Bartleby looks aside, and thinks. "In our case," he says after a moment, "The dozen years that separated us made it feel as if we were in completely separate families. One could argue that a greater bond has developed in adulthood between us than was ever felt when young."

You arch an eyebrow.

The cleric continues, "Even so, just because we are family does not mean that my sister and I have much in common, beyond appearances. While I grew to become a man of the cloth, for instance, she runs a stable in Fort Remnon." He pauses, and looks into your eyes. "With Fedwick, do not forget what you have shared, your ideals, your determination. Your vast array of experiences."

You stretch your sore arms. "How did you know I needed to hear that?"

Bartleby smiles. "Call it intuition."

Over the next several hours, the two of you talk more deeply than ever before, and even come around to laughing at the very obstacles you've had to overcome thus far, after Bartleby picks a clump of seaweed out of his hair. You learn about his sermons, his congregation, the ways in which he spreads peace, while you tell him about military logistics.

A moment of silence passes.

"Bartleby," you say, "Thank you for accompanying me on this quest."

Bartleby nods and says, "It was meant to be. And perhaps," he adds as he glances toward the door to the training grounds, "We shall end up saving each other before it is all over."

A heavy creak interrupts you, as the door swings open once more. The necromancer emerges, but even after several moments, neither undead nor an orcblood follow him.

You and the cleric agree to tail the crony, who by the time you stand has already turned around a bend in the road, nearly diving out of sight. The going proves slow, as the man weaves in and out of several alleys, sometimes emitting a perverse moan as he inspects the very core of night itself.

Finally, he approaches a decrepit wooden home, looks up to the sky, pushes aside the mangled door and shuffles through the entryway.

"A good, old-fashioned kidnapping," you whisper, reaching into your pack and feeling around for your rope.

With knotted coils in hand, the two of you sneak through the door with only the moonlight and the necromancer's mild snoring to guide you. Once, your step upon a loose board elicits a grunt from several rooms in, and you freeze, barely daring to breathe. After an agonizing silence, the snoring resumes.

You pass through a final archway, and see the mottled beam of a hooded oil lamp, which dances upon the face of your target.

You leap upon the necromancer and wrench his arms behind his back. He shouts and protests groggily, but Bartleby holds his mouth shut with one arm and locks his head with the other. You tie him up, and the cleric throws him over his back like a sack of potatoes.

"What is the meaning of this?" the man croaks.

"When we are done with you," you grumble, "You will have shared everything you know about the Seal of Thomerion, about the Black Rose, and especially about your army of undead."

"We shall see about that," he replies, "Dandrel, sic' em!"

148

Out of the shadows bursts the same weasel you'd seen on the man's shoulder earlier, which leaps upon your face faster than you can raise your arms. Murderous fire flaring in its eyes, it scratches at you, digging burning wounds into your skin, even as you scramble to pull the creature off. Bartleby drops the necromancer and approaches to help, but the pet has all fours wrapped around you like a vise.

The cleric wrenches its top half away, and almost has it off, when the weasel flails one last time, and buries a jagged claw into each of your eyeballs. You scream in horror, and feel warm blood spurt out of your face and onto your cheeks and arms.

"Thomerion shall prevail!" you hear.

You can no longer see a thing, but judging by several rapid and loud footfalls, the necromancer has fled. A force pulls hard against your eye sockets, and you hear a squish, but then the weasel finally lets go.

On your knees, you whimper, "Is it dead?"

Bartleby concedes, in a panicked tone, "I lost my grip upon it, and it left with its master. Here, sit. Now."

Your companion guides you toward a bed, and utters some mystical words. You feel warmth rush into your skull, and you feel calmer. Several moments of silence pass.

"I..." you mutter as you feel about, "I still... cannot see. Did you...?"

"At least," Bartleby says, "I was able to stop the bleeding."

"What... what do you mean to say?"

Bartleby sighs. "For me to restore your sight, you would need your eyes."

It takes a moment to sink in, but soon, your soul gives up. Blind and vulnerable, and forced to help yourself more than you could ever help Fedwick, you concede the end of your quest, and would cry, if you could.

Better opportunities await you. Try again!

"Let's get this over with," you suggest, "in broad daylight if we must."

"It sounds like suicide to me," Bartleby counters.

"We don't know where he will go later," you argue, "Strike while the iron is hot."

"We should still wait until he doesn't have quite so much help."

"Speaking of which, what do you suppose he meant by the 'Black Rose'?"

Bartleby shrugs. "This is the first I have heard of it, but judging by context alone, it might grant some expanded level of control over undead."

You scratch your beard. "We shall have to look into it later. For now, they are almost out of sight." You stand.

Continuing to tail the troop at a great distance, you dive into more alleys to avoid detection, and soon you see a sizable arena, built of stone and brick. The orcblood opens a grand door in the side, and enters first. You close the distance and prepare a length of rope as quietly as possible, as the necromancer funnels the undead through in single-file formation. Within moments, the last skeleton has clattered out of sight, and the crony, still outside, pauses to scan the horizon, blinking his one good eye.

As he turns back toward the door, a small wooden item falls from his robes and to the ground, kicking up some dust. The man grumbles, and slowly bends over to pick it up.

"Now," you order.

You both charge out of the shadows and are on top of the crony before he has stood. Bartleby closes and holds shut the door to the training grounds while you knock the crony to the ground, and tie his arms.

He struggles, and shouts, "What do you want with me?"

"Who is responsible for the Seal of Thomerion? For what purpose do you control undead?"

He glares up at you, enraged. "I will become one of our army before I talk!"

Bartleby counters, "Be careful what you wish for."

"Who are you to say so? You assault a stranger in the middle of the streets, without any weapons, with no idea of what is actually happening. You are naïve fools. That is what you are."

How does he know all this? You frown in thought.

The crony shouts, "Carnahinta, Omnivictus, Polaranka, Sergetimpus!"

Something crashes against the door to the training grounds from the other side, throwing Bartleby to the ground and nearly breaking the door in half. As many full sets of boney arms and legs begin to poke through the aperture, you realize the man had not handed over power of the troop to anyone inside the arena.

"Run!" you shout.

You let go of the necromancer just as the door gives way, and the entire troop pours back out into the streets with short swords at the ready. You and Bartleby dash toward the sea, but the skeletons follow. When you reach the pier, out of breath and ready to collapse, you find that anything resembling a boat or other method of water travel has disappeared entirely. Cornered, your mind begins to panic, and you even entertain such irrational thoughts as attempting to drown your enemies, which would certainly fail because they have no lungs.

"Bartleby?"

"Yes?"

"They say in your circles that the afterlife is paradise, do they not?"

"We shall see," he concedes, "We shall see."

Your quest has ended... or has it?

Standing near a large boulder, Zander pulls aside a tangle of moss to reveal an ancient path, which descends into the earth. You carefully light a torch, and proceed with your party into the tunnel. As he could be considered the best scout, Mikhail takes the lead, with Zander right behind. Bartleby brings up the rear, while you march in the middle. The passage turns mustier the deeper you go, and you ponder Argent's living arrangements further.

"For such a legendary figure," you say, "Argent seems to employ little direct protection, at least in the sense I'd be used to."

"I can understand it," Zander comments, "Bodyguards are, after all, quite expensive, and I daresay, old-fashioned."

You frown. "King Patrick employs dozens."

"Which only serves to prove my point."

Bartleby chuckles. Mikhail turns and puts a single finger to his lip, even as you press onward for what seems like many miles.

Finally, you see a light ahead. The passage opens up into a large, well-lit chamber. You quell your flame, and notice wooden doors within each of the chamber's side walls, as well as a large metal double door set into the far wall, which Mikhail approaches. He takes some small tools from his pack.

Zander whispers, "Take caution…"

Mikhail replies, "Why? It couldn't be clearer that the woman we seek is behind this door, of the three."

Zander scratches his head. "Just because it's different from the others?"

The elf says, "Trust me," and crouches over the door's keyhole.

At this, the ranger just stands and gawks.

Meanwhile, you and Bartleby search the area. You find a large hourglass built into a nook in the wall, as well as a strange sheet of glass within the ceiling that protects a copper key. The cleric reports that the two side doors have peepholes, but hide strange mechanisms that seem to keep them shut, as well as a tall ladder.

"Certainly a rather odd get-up," Bartleby says.

"I should think these all have something to do with our overall goal," you note.

"I've got it!"

The shout comes from Mikhail, who with a tremendous heave, pulls open the handles on the metal double door, and opens it wide.

"Then again…" you grumble.

"That was fast," Zander says.

Behind the doors, a tall woman dressed from head to toe in shiny silver sits at a desk, within a small but richly decorated study full of books and scrolls. She turns within her chair, fists clenched.

"What is the meaning of this?" she shouts. "Who are you to barge in here like this, bypassing my…"

Before Argent can finish her sentence, before you can even stop what you are doing long enough to introduce yourself and explain your purpose, Mikhail pulls a dark shiv from underneath his cloak, glides across the study in a few steps and buries the blade in the sorceress's jugular. Blood sprays in streaks upon the walls, and with a lurch and a weak grunt, your best hope for Fedwick's cure falls upon the floor, dead.

Your jaw hangs limp, and shock overwhelms you, to the point where the crimson seal of skull and dagger imprinted into the elf's weapon is almost an afterthought.

Zander sputters, "But… why, Mikhail?"

"I am sorry, friend."

The elf pulls a small vial containing a clear blue liquid from a pouch at his waist. Zander springs into action, and attempts to tackle the elf, but Mikhail twists to one side and trips the ranger, who falls flat on his face. You charge forward as well, but Mikhail pulls the cork on the vial and chugs its contents. He instantly vanishes into the surroundings.

You stop short, and flail your hands around the air where the elf stood. Nothing. You hear quick footsteps trailing toward the compound entrance to your left, but whatever portion of your childhood education that prepared you for the need to intercept invisible assassins seems to escape you at this particular moment. Bartleby and Zander make similarly feeble attempts at finding the traitor, but by the time they recover, the entire compound is quiet once again.

You could go back to Whitetail and start over, you think as you sit heavily. Bartleby checks the body of Argent, but shakes his head, certain that he can do nothing to heal her. Zander hangs his head and lays a hand on your shoulder.

In a way, though, you feel lucky to be alive yourself, let alone Fedwick, or Argent. You were, after all, nothing but leverage. You find yourself wringing your hands, confused and scared.

Acceptance shall come, perhaps, in time.

Don't let evil win. Read another path!

You breathe deeply, suppressing your temper, and remind yourself that this minor financial loss will not break you. Besides, more important issues press upon you.

"Perhaps that wench can use the money more than I," you grumble.

After one last glance toward the treehouse, you stroll toward the wood, where the rest of your party has found the entrance to Argent's compound.

Turn to page 152.

You glance at the floor, but manage a weak smile at the halfling as you say, "I would wish for a way to heal a dying friend."

The little one blinks, pauses, and rubs his neck. "No disrespect intended, good sir," he squeaks, "but… that's just depressing." He sets the book on the librarian's desk, and hustles out the door and into the street. You stare after him, dumbfounded.

"I'd say you'll have to forgive the fellow," remarks the gnome librarian, "Except, it's impossible to say when he'll be back, if ever."

You scratch your beard, and indicate the tome. "May I?"

"Be my guest."

You flip a few pages, and find a short entry:

A native Ambrosinian, Demetria Argent developed superior magical skill as a youth and joined the Council of Royal Magi in the spring of 1472, only to defect eight moons later and become a recluse. Accomplishments during her brief tenure include successful co-negotiation of the Fort Remnon Peace Treatise, as well as supposed innovations in the realm of potion-making, few of which have been tested in the field of battle or anywhere else.

You look up from the book. "Is this all anyone knows about Argent? She doesn't have a family? Someone who would know where she can be found now?"

"Not of which I am aware," says the bookkeeper.

You thank the librarian for her cooperation and follow up on what little you have learned, by asking around about the head of the Council of Royal Magi. The kind old wizard you meet knows even less about Argent than you, and says that the tenure in question must have been before his time. He offers to consult with the entire Council and get back to you, but that option proves unworkable when he notes that the Council won't meet again for another ten days.

By now, your thoughts about the lack of information swirl out of control. As the day winds down, you trek back to the Pig's Foot Inn and

155

Tavern and listen and watch, but the men from which you heard the initial lead are nowhere to be found.

As long as I'm here, you think, *I feel like taking the edge off.*

You order another drink to complement the one from earlier in the day. You begin to feel more relaxed, and so order yet another. With little to do and few people to bother at this hour, you strike up a loud conversation with anyone that passes by. Before you know it, you're intoxicated, and attempt to follow up on Josephine's 'last call,' but she puts a hand out in front of her and waves you off.

"You've had too many, good friend."

"Don't... tell... me," you slur, countering with a rude gesture, "that I've had too many!"

"I would prefer you watch your behavior, sir."

"Oh, now I'm 'sir'!'" you bellow, "What happened to 'good friend,' ya' nasty lil' wench?" You pound the counter a little too hard, and the tankard you hold shatters into a mess of shards, spilling alcohol everywhere.

"That's it," Josephine shouts, "I am sorry for this."

She casts a sober look at two orcbloods near the entrance, and then points at you. The bouncers tromp toward you, grip your arms, lift you up and haul you outside. You want to struggle, but feel a distinct shortage of the energy required. Dizziness sets in as your captors tie your arms with rope and toss you in the back seat of a carriage. The journey to the town jail jostles your stomach, and the bouncers lead you out just in time to serve as targets for your copious vomiting.

Disorderly conduct charges certainly won't help save Fedwick, you think, as your heart sinks and your mind spins. You wonder just how long they'll detain you before a hearing will occur, and manage to pass out onto the cold dirt of your cell, just after the sun sets.

Your travels cease here, but don't give up.

Your stomach feels as if you have swallowed an anvil, as if in anticipation of lifelong spiritual punishment. Yet, something reassures you that the decision you are about to make is for the greater good.

"While few souls can claim my kinship quite as he did," you say, looking at no one, "Fedwick himself would advise me to press forward. We met while at war. And what is war, but a conflict engaged in so as to protect the people? So many more are now involved than he…"

You place a fist over your heart. Bartleby lays a hand on your shoulder.

"Are you certain?"

"Yes," you reply, looking up, "I shall come with you to Koraxon. We need to give ourselves the best chance possible."

You wrangle your horses, and borrow a calm one from the carriage, so that the three of you can each ride. The enemies' rations provide you enough sustenance for the trip; not long passes until you depart from the path at a southward angle. You wonder out loud how to find a good junction at which to meet the main trail without getting lost in prairie, but Vermouth employs a compass with confidence, keeping your path straight and true.

You meet few humanoids during this leg of your journey, save a hunter in green who takes great pains to ignore you. Far more common are squirrels and rabbits, which skitter about randomly and enjoy the luxury of being surrounded by very few predators. Around sunset, the terrain begins challenging you as it changes from prairie to rockier ground, with far sparser vegetation. Brilliant purples and oranges dance along the bottom of a bank of cumulus clouds.

"It seems a good time to rest, gentlemen," Vermouth says, pointing ahead, "And that appears to be the main road. Shall we camp here, while we are still out of sight?"

"That seems… quite reasonable…" Bartleby intones. Something about his tone sounds dreamy, distant. You glance at the cleric, who keeps his gaze locked on Vermouth as he helps her dismount.

You assist in tying the horses to trees and shore up some rocks and tinder for a fire. The three of you soon settle around the flames, feeling comfortable, even as a crisp breeze out of the west whips your faces.

"Once again," Titania says, "I cannot thank you enough. Who knows what could have happened, had you not taken such bold action?"

Bartleby blushes, and replies, "Merely our duty, Miss Vermouth."

You chuckle, and both of the others stare at you for an awkward moment. You clear your throat. "It is nothing," you say. You fiddle with your bootstraps.

"Now then," Vermouth says, "I shall retire a bit early."

"Understandable," the cleric says. "A long distance remains before us."

Vermouth climbs into a bedroll, and soon appears asleep, although her breaths emit not a sound.

"Come," you request of the cleric. He arches an eyebrow, but stands and follows as you stroll many yards away from the fire.

"What is it?"

"You know perfectly well what 'it' is," you reply, nodding toward the woman. Bartleby glances over his shoulder at her.

"So, I find her eyes attractive. And her smile. Oh, and her…"

"My friend, do you know what can happen when you fall into the trap that is the opposite gender? Come to think of it, are you even allowed to have such feelings? Your dogma, and all…"

Bartleby frowns. "I am only human."

"But one 'made in the image of your god.' One whose chastity steers one toward a path of divine devotion. Am I correct?"

Bartleby turns away from you, but you continue, "One moment of distraction could be fatal. I have seen it happen far too often."

"What do you know of this form of love?" The annoyance in the cleric's voice alarms you. "Everything in dwarven society is about clansmanship, camaraderie, brotherhood. I should begin to think you even procreate with reluctance!"

Vermouth stirs and moans, and Bartleby covers his mouth. After you are both sure she has returned to slumber, you take care to speak in hushed whispers.

You puff out your chest. "I shall ignore your petty insults. Just know, however, that your gods, your prayers, they cannot solve everything. When it comes down to it, we must rely on ourselves to survive this quest. And to do that, we must maintain focus."

"Duly noted."

Bartleby turns on his heel, returns to camp, and lies down upon the bare earth, leaving you with watch duty. When the time comes for you to sleep, you rouse the cleric and switch places without a word or even a nod.

Turn to page 169.

If you've ever learned a lesson about elven types, it's to avoid arguing with them. You instruct Mikhail to wake you when the moon is a third of the way to its apex, at which point you will take over.

Sleep, however, does not work its magic quite as you'd anticipated. Multiple rocks poke into your back and hips, no matter how you arrange your bedroll. Huffing, you question Zander's ability to choose a suitable campsite. You breathe slowly, and focus on relaxation. In, out. In, out. You drift through semi-consciousness, when something compels you to open your eyes. As you gaze past the fire's embers and into the darkness, Mikhail appears to be no longer stand at his post.

No matter. This group has gotten you this far. The elf must be nearby, you reflect, merely stretching his legs, perhaps finding a way to stanch the boredom. Your eyelids flutter one last time, and the fog of fatigue finally conquers your bones. You feel reasonably rested when you take watch, which passes without incident.

Turn to page 38.

"This collector could have found just about anything," you assert. "I shall attend the auction."

"Good," Zander says, "I've waited a while for a use for these." The ranger opens a pouch at his waist, pulls out a handful of smooth gray coins, and sets them into your hand.

You notice a difference in the coins' sheen, relative to what you're used to seeing. "These are not silver. Platinum?" you ask. Zander nods. "Impressive," you say. "This could cover just about anything."

"Keep them under wraps," Zander advises. "The last associate that knew I carried that kind of money tried to take it by force."

You arch an eyebrow. "The last associate?"

"Not Mikhail. But a cur of equal deceptive capability."

Heeding his advice, you look over your shoulder, and quickly stash the money in your own coin sack.

"Why is it, Zander," you jest, "That you, an upstanding citizen in your own right, seem to attract such untrustworthy folk?"

The ranger sweeps his hair out of his eyes. "Believe me, friend. That is a question I have asked myself many a time."

Bartleby interjects, "Just in case it is needed, I would like to contribute as well." He hands you a small, multi-looped pouch; a quick count indicates it contains about thirty to forty gold pieces.

"Thank you, both," you say.

"With that, it is time to part, for now," Zander says, "Let us meet again, here, six days after the morrow."

"May divine providence shine upon us," Bartleby says.

You shake hands with both, and a heaviness settles into your chest as you comprehend that, for now, you are on your own. You restock some supplies using a little of Bartleby's gold, and that evening, you trek as far as you can before camping.

The going proves straightforward but hurried for the next full day, and you arrive at the town square exhausted, but just in time to watch the gnome auctioneer set up his podium, while assistants arrange wares into neat piles on a nearby platform. A trio of strong-looking humans flanks the area and keeps the loud throng of potential buyers in line.

You take some space among the crowd, and notice a young girl, who sits on a tweed blanket and fiddles with a thread on her sky blue dress. Intrigued, you approach, and chime, "Good day, madam."

"Good day, sir dwarf." She smiles up at you, her large green eyes twinkling. She sounds and appears no more than ten years of age.

"Have you heard much, perchance, about what these people intend to sell today?" you ask, indicating the auction crew.

"Not much, truly," the girl says, as she glances at the ground.

You kneel next to her. "What kinds of things would you like to buy?"

"I am here on behalf of my mother," the girl replies, "who would like jewelry. Cheaply, if I can manage it, she said."

This is my competition?

"So," you continue, "Your parents are not here to help you?"

"My mother is sick today." The girl continues to avoid your gaze.

Concern rising within, you press, "And your father?"

"He… is with our god. The gods met him on the battlefield, and they took him away from us."

Your heart sinks, and you place a hand over your heart. "I am… sorry for your loss," you console.

She pauses, then looks back up at you. "Are you a warrior, sir?"

You arch an eyebrow. "Why, yes. Why do you ask?"

"The axe at your waist. I could not help but notice."

Your hand brushes against Ol' Rusty, and for a moment you weigh the odds of its blade having ever slaughtered the person in question, or at least someone like him. A twinge of remorse pierces your heart, and you ready yourself to speak further, but she asks first, "And, sir, what do you intend to buy?"

"I attend out of mere curiosity," you bluff, "although, if the desire so strikes me, I am prepared to bid." The organizers appear ready. The auctioneer climbs upon a crate, and holds his hands out to call for order.

161

"Good luck to you, then," the girl says with a half-smile, as she stands and turns to face the gnome.

The auction proceeds with little fanfare, as though its organizers prefer to burn through as many items as possible so as to get home in time for a late dinner. Judging from what's available, you don't blame them in the least; first a plain dresser goes, then a decorative spear, a set of chipped plates and a ream of untouched vellum. The surrounding people bid on some items, although a few properties are so mundane that no one wants them, and the sellers donate them to the merchant's guild.

You tap your foot and grumble to yourself, feeling bored nearly to tears, and have just begun considering other options when you hear the auctioneer's voice swell with vigor, "And, ladies and gentlemen, here we have something quite mysterious, if I do say so myself." Two handlers haul an ornate chest, a couple feet across, of burnished metal with a huge keyhole, to within view of the entire crowd. The auctioneer continues, "Our men couldn't get this puppy open, so whatever is inside goes along with the chest to the buyer. Give it a shake, gentlemen. Quiet, please!"

The men jostle the chest, producing a tinkling rattle mixed in with a few loud thumps.

*The tinkling sounds…*you ponder. *Gems, perhaps?*

"As you can hear, it's far from empty! Do I hear fifty gold, to start?"

"One hundred!"

It takes a moment for you to realize that the bid came from the little girl. She stands on tiptoes to see, her hand extended high in the air.

The chest could be the key to saving Fedwick, or it could contain junk. Furthermore, how much more is the girl willing to pay?

What do you do?

To attempt to outbid everyone else, turn to page 167.

To wait for something better, turn to the second half of page 144.

You take a detour to stock your pack, and meet back up with Paddy and dozens of accompanying followers at the north gate. You depart upon the half-day's journey to the monastery with mixed feelings: a certain lightness and hope comingle with tedium, having already endured this much, with much more to come.

"So," Paddy asks, "what could you be doing with your life that makes so you thrilled about a trip to a monastery?"

"Do you recall Fedwick, of the Canterbury clan?"

"The reckless one, with the dent in his head to match his lack of wits? Clearly. Why?"

You scowl, but remind yourself that in this context, Paddy is just a means to an end. A moment passes as you recover, and tell yourself not to retaliate.

You clear your throat. "He and I became rather like brothers."

"Of this I was aware."

"I was to meet him at his home a mere..."—you stop to count—"three days ago. When I arrived, I found him in a dire state, as someone had inflicted the Seal of Thomerion upon him."

Paddy scratches his chin. "And now?"

"'Tis a long story, but it suffices to say that I need the blood of a monk of the highest rank, to help create a cure for Fedwick."

Your mentor looks away, and sighs. "You've been fed a load of garbage, if you ask me."

You counter, "I know you've long been against the use of magic, and yet, I've met some gentlemen along the way who seem to have such blind faith that I cannot help but..."

"That is not what I mean," Paddy grumbles as he turns back to glare at you. Your eyes widen, and you gesture in encouragement for him to explain. "Sometimes, young man, people fall in the line of duty. This seems to be the nature of things, and there is little we can do to fight it. But what little we can do, we ought to focus in the best direction possible. You talk about saving a dead man, at the same time that the whole lot of us march toward an opportunity to protect dozens of living souls."

You let him pause before you say, "You give the church of Thomerion far too much credit."

"Or, do you give them too little?"

Pursing your lips, you turn your gaze straight ahead, and listen to the conversation of other sub-groups within the convoy. Little seems to quell the irritation rising within you, and yet, a micron of Paddy's message appeals to your brain:

Is this what Fedwick would want? Or would it better serve his memory, our memories together, to move on?

A full minute passes. Above, the clouds drift apart, and the sun's rays blind you.

"We shall have to agree to disagree, then, shan't we?" you say.

Paddy shrugs. The two of you say not a word more to each other, for the entire remainder of the journey.

It is quite late in the day by the time you arrive at the monastery. The abbot welcomes the group, and promises to apprise you of the situation in the morning. As he shows you to an oversized cot within a guest room, you briefly describe your plight.

"You ask of me to give of my life force itself," he replies. "I shall consider it, although I may need as much as I can manage to keep."

You nod your understanding.

At dawn, a breakfast of spiced pork cutlets and sweet mangoes energizes you, and you realize that you hadn't had that good of a night's sleep in ages. The abbot addresses the convoy in a clear voice, "Thank the heavens, and thank you most of all, for your being here today. While we can hold our own when defense is called for, some recent structural work has left weaknesses, literal holes in some cases, within our compound."

You and others look about, noting a door off its hinges in one direction, and a stained-glass window that leans against the opposite wall, waiting to be installed. Piles of raw wood by-product sit visible in the corners of the room.

"We gather that this particular band of miscreants," the abbot continues, "who call themselves the Brotherhood of Dusk, views us as vulnerable at the moment. What they want from us, we do not know. We possess only what we need, and can only guess that they stir up trouble for its own sake."

A murmur of agreement arises from within your convoy. You scratch your beard, and frown.

"That said, the time to fight is nigh. I suggest we begin preparations by designating a strategist."

To this, no one says much; most everyone looks about as if to avoid being nominated. You catch a glance from Paddy, and point at him innocently. He leans into your ear and whispers, "You think you know everything. Now prove it."

You ponder for a moment, then stand, holding your head high.

The audience emits a proud 'aaah,' then breaks out in applause.

The abbot approaches. "If you can win this for us," he says to you, "My blood is yours to do with as you wish. Do we have a bargain?"

You nod, and shake his hand with fervor.

The others finish eating while the abbot pulls you aside, toward an oaken podium, upon which lies a rough map of the compound.

"Our spies have informed us that the bandits' numbers rank about forty, but your volunteers bring us almost even to that. Although a few crossbows are available, we wield primarily staves and our bare fists." He points at a large symbol on the map, which approximates a double-door. "Many aspects to defending the grounds must be balanced, but above all, the Brotherhood must not reach this point."

You listen intently, processing as much information as you can.

"If our temple were defaced, it could very well break morale, not to mention that it serves as a central hub to all other portions of the monastery."

Indeed, the layout shows that the compound sprawls out in multiple branches, which all radiate from one point on the map. Yet, other possible defensive centers include two prominent watchtowers and a system of craggy hills that somewhat protect the eastern and southern sides from the buffeting prairie winds.

"Do we know from which direction the bandits plan to strike?" you ask.

"Unfortunately, we do not."

You grimace.

Upon further examination of the grounds, however, two overarching approaches leap out at you. You feel a rush of nostalgia as you formulate them, a reminder of the intense mental stimulation you experienced in your military heyday, but push it down and away, into your core, so as to remain focused.

At first, you think to place a few people, armed with what ranged weapons you have, at each of the defensive foci you noted, while spreading others around the perimeter at a distance. This gives you the chance to gain the upper hand early, but possibly at the cost of leaving the inner compound more vulnerable, should some enemies break through. On the other hand, if you post large groups of melee fighters near the double-doors and other key locations, you could put the offensive onus on the Brotherhood, while suffering the trade-off of sparser overall spatial coverage. You estimate that there just aren't enough personnel to effectively implement both plans at once.

What do you do?

To propose concentrated fighter units, turn to page 209.

To propose a ranged focus over a wider space, turn to page 207.

You say nothing in response to the surprising bid. Each of Zander's coins is worth about fifty golds; you quickly count them, and estimate you could outdo the girl by six-to-one.

It is now or never.

The auctioneer rattles off more bids, repeating, "Two hundred, two hundred...do I hear two hundred?"

You inhale, raise a fist, and bellow, "Two hundred!"

The girl sticks her tongue out at you and states, "Just like a greedy warrior. Three hundred!"

"I hear three hundred," the auctioneer says, pointing at the girl, "Yes, three hundred. Do I hear more?"

"Three hundred fifty," a stout human near the front calls.

"I hear three hundred fifty."

"This is mine," you tell the girl. "You wouldn't understand why."

"Wouldn't I?" the girl counters. "Five hundred fifty!"

A few attendees gasp, then a momentary silence hangs.

"Well, well," the auctioneer says. "The young lady seems serious! Do we have any other bids? Five hundred fifty gold for this lovely piece..."

If you burn all your money here, and there's no pearl in the chest, this auction will have been a complete waste of time. At the same time, the pile of wares on the platform has dwindled considerably.

What do you do?

To bid all of the six hundred you've got, turn to page 229.

To let the chest go in favor of later items, turn to the second half of page 144.

Saul turns over the jack of hearts, and places it in the last spot. The final grid looks like this:

You have lost.

Turn to page 201.

The next morning, you travel for only a short while. The pebbles underneath your feet sap more of your energy with each step, but signs of civilization eventually appear once more. Several groups of passersby, of many different races and sizes, head in the direction from which you came. Far ahead, however, a bottleneck of some sort seems to grow where cliffs constrict the path to nearly nothing, and a handful of guards scramble to keep up with folk wanting to leave or enter Koraxon.

"We need to keep Miss Vermouth hidden," Bartleby says. "If these orcbloods are authorities of any sort, they might recognize her."

You nod your agreement. Titania guides her horse to a spot behind a large tree, and wrings her hands.

As you look around, two plans present themselves, neither of which thrills your conscience. For one, a band of cloaked troubadours stands several yards off the path; you could try to explain your situation and ask if they could help disguise Titania, or you could even take their hooded cloaks by force, if necessary.

Also, a solitary merchant, whiskered but strong and upright, trudges by you and takes his place in line, hauling a sizable wagon behind him. The wagon's basin appears filled with hay, over which has been draped a tarp of hewn leather. Smuggling Vermouth in by hiding her in the hay strikes you as another distinct possibility.

What do you do?

To engage the troubadours, turn to page 68.

To approach the merchant, turn to page 172.

There's little reason to jump in headlong, you think, as you back away from the altar. Patience is key here.

"This kind of item doesn't get here all by itself," you mutter to Bartleby, "Let's find a hiding place and see if anyone shows up."

"And if no one does?" the cleric asks.

"Then we'd be no worse off than we were before coming here."

Bartleby nods, looks around a bit, and points toward a very large, open crate about ten yards away. It's mostly empty, and holes in the side afford a straight-on view of the Impactium, yet enough of the crate lies within the shadows so as to still be unnoticeable. With a little effort, you're both able to climb inside, grab a nearby lid and close the opening.

Wiling away the time using what little light seeps through the crate's holes, you twist an old awl, then inspect a neglected lathe of some sort. Bartleby's lips move every now and again, as he seems to utter some sort of silent prayer. More time passes, and the importance of this quest begins to settle into your soul. Your mind wanders, replaying Fedwick's jokes about orcbloods, his failed attempt at setting you up with the local armorsmith, and his taking you in while your hut underwent repairs after the Great Raid of 1429. You assert that it's no time to second-guess, but that if this great friend--no, this honorary clan member--is hurt by your dallying here, you would never be able to forgive yourself.

You inch up against the wall of the crate, and glance toward the altar. While the angle of the sunlight has changed, nothing else new has developed. Disappointment drowns your spirit, and you are about to whisper toward Bartleby, when you hear a shuffling.

From nowhere, a fair youth in black and red robes enters your field of vision, stops, glances about, and approaches the altar. He mutters in some arcane language, and holds his hands out over the Impactium. Over the course of several moments, the dwarven holy verses begin to emanate a purple glow, which slowly intensifies.

It occurs to you that this is the time to strike.

You and the cleric exchange glances. You hold up first one, then two fingers while mouthing a count, and on three, you both burst forward out of the crate, sending dust flying. The youth looks up in alarm and backs away, and the book's aura disappears.

Your gaze burns holes into the youth as you charge toward the altar. He steps to the side, flings open his cloak and whips a dagger in your direction, but you deflect it as casually as if a gnat had landed on your shield. The youth blanches, frozen for an instant, then bolts toward the back of the warehouse.

Bartleby says, "I'll cut him off. You take the other side," and takes a wide turn around several crates, toward the east wall. You continue to barrel through the mess, and soon see a trap door, built into the warehouse floor. The robed youth now struggles to open the hatch.

The two of you close the distance. There is nowhere else to go. The youth stands straight and, scowling, raises his hands.

"If you value your life," you posture, "You'll explain what's going on here."

"What business is it of yours?" The youth's voice booms off the walls. His black stubble hides youthful cheekbones and complements narrow eyes that stare blankly into nothing.

"What were you doing to the Impactium just now?"

He glances downward. A bead of sweat hits the floor.

"I will tell you," he says, "if you pledge to let me go unharmed thereafter."

Bartleby replies, "And if we refuse this pledge?"

"The Church of Thomerion will double the price on your head."

The youth has directed these words straight at you.

Unsurprised, you narrow your eyes as if to match his resolve.

What do you do?

To let the youth go in exchange for information, turn to page 30.

To take him prisoner instead, turn to page 33.

The merchant strikes you as more personable. Leaving Bartleby behind with Titania, you approach and ask how his day is proceeding and what he plans to do in Koraxon, to which he replies that he maintains a provisional agreement with the stablemen in the northern forts.

"After all, agriculture ain't never been these orc-people's strong suit," he jests.

You smile at him. "Not to be too forward," you say, "but, could we perhaps enlist you and your cart in a matter of great import?"

"Tell me more," he replies.

"See that woman?" you ask as you indicate Vermouth, even as she remains hidden across the path.

The merchant nods.

"We need to get her into orc country as secretly as possible."

"But, much as you asked me," the merchant replies, "why come here? Surely the mayoress of Sungaze has better things to do."

So, even this random commoner recognizes her?

You glance about you, and then at the ground, hesitant to divulge more than the man needs to know. The man cocks his head to one side, and adopts a curious expression.

"It suffices to say that, together, the orcbloods and the church of Thomerion are up to no good. We intend to do something about it."

The man twists his face into a fierce scowl. "Well, why didn'cha say so in the first place? I have a bone to pick with them skull-and-dagger people, after one of their so-called missionaries harmed my daughter."

You grimace. "Is she okay?"

"Thank the gods, yes."

An idea strikes you. "Would you like to come with us?" you ask.

"Nope," the merchant says, "I am expected back home soon. But whatever I can do to help your cause, I will."

With your help, he pushes aside a large section of hay, and backs the contraption up toward where Titania hides. The old wooden wheels clack upon the rough stones on the way. While the cleric watches around the bend, you and the merchant pile armful after armful of the tan straw over and around Vermouth, until it completely conceals her.

"Can you breathe?" you ask.

"I can," she replies.

"Here goes nothing."

The merchant retakes control of the cart and drags it back into sight of the immigrant line. You let a few small parties fill in the space, and wait until the largest orcblood approaches the man.

"State your business," the guard grunts.

The merchant gulps. He takes a moment to compose himself in the shadow of the hulking semi-monster, but not before he flashes a pleading look in your direction.

"Who are you looking at?" the orcblood shouts.

"Uh… my business is…" the man sputters, "to complete this shipment. I've been through here many times before… I've…"

"Silence!"

The merchant complies. The guard circles round to the back of the cart, and scans its contents, bending over and craning his neck to inspect as much of the payload as possible. He pauses and scratches his chin.

Without warning, the orcblood opens the cart's rear hatch, reaches forward and punches the hay, sinking his arm in to the elbow. Bartleby covers his mouth.

Not a sound emerges, beyond the expected hollow rustling.

The guard backs up, pauses once more, and harrumphs, "Very well. You may pass."

The rest of your party passes through the checkpoint a few moments later, pretending that Bartleby is leading you on a pilgrimage. You help the merchant haul the cart well beyond the guards' range of view, and finally help Titania out from under her concealment.

"That shall leave a bruise," she says, wincing.

"When I need to be the strong-and-silent type," Bartleby comments, "I shall remember you on this day."

"How valiant!" The two smile at each other.

Turn to page 176.

You make sure you are once again out of sight of anyone before speaking further, while resting your tired bodies upon some large stones. Grey clouds shield the sun, as sharp winds buffet the collars of your cloaks. You don't get to keep the cloaks for long, however, as within minutes, the troubadour band catches up with you and reclaims them. They wish you luck and grumble about the weather as they continue past.

"To where in this abominable land were the servants of Thomerion taking you, Miss Vermouth?" Bartleby asks.

"Please, call me Titania," the mayoress replies with a smile.

"Yes, ma'am," The cleric chimes.

"To answer your question, I overheard bits and pieces about what is called the Tower of the Dark Wrath. A prominent orcblood general is to meet with church bishops within its topmost level."

"That could prove our biggest challenge yet," you muse.

"Since we've come this far, I begin to believe we can handle anything," the cleric replies.

You nudge him. "Laying it on a little thick, are we?"

Bartleby shrugs.

"If no one can recognize me," Vermouth says, "We should at least be able to avoid being captured again."

"At the same time," you note, "We can't just march into their meeting place without an explanation. And, where is this tower?"

The mayoress points toward the skyline. An unmistakable structure of dank grey brick, dotted with tiny windows secured with bars of black iron, looms over the entire city from many miles in the distance. The top level must be fifty yards up, you estimate.

"By the gods…"

Bartleby's jaw hangs slack. "I stand corrected," he whispers.

For one of the first times in your life, genuine fear floods your heart, but you force your legs to carry you along as the party rises once more, and prepares to journey toward the tower. As you hike the miles, you recollect many tales of travels to unfamiliar lands from your military years. You have even been in Koraxon a time or two before, but this… you fail to recall ever seeing anything quite so imposing, let alone entering it. Your gaze remains frozen upon it during every step, in anticipation of what lay inside.

When you approach, however, your heart calms. Keeping your distance, you assess that a half-dozen or so orcblood personnel are on hand outside the tower. They talk amongst themselves, and point in various directions as if on the move.

From out of the shadows emerges a wizened human, who wears black and red robes and carries a talisman imprinted with a skull and dagger. He glances down both directions of the mostly deserted street, pulls his cloak tight around a lump, and enters the tower with a slight nod toward an attending orcblood. The door remains slightly ajar.

"Did he look like he might be carrying something valuable to you too?" you whisper to Bartleby.

You watch as five of the guards leave toward the west.

"Not knowing what we're up against," Titania says, "I have two ideas. Deception, or force. As for the latter, these orcbloods may be big and strong, but they're slow, and there's only one left at the moment. We may be able to barrel our way past him, get what we need, and leave."

"And, the other plan?"

"Let's just say the troubadours gave me the idea. As long my disguise holds, we can concoct a story as to why we're here. If it's convincing enough, he might just let us through."

What do you do?

To physically storm the tower, turn to the second half of page 221.

To employ deceptive tactics, turn to page 247.

175

You thank the merchant once again, and let him be on his way.

"To where in Koraxon were you being taken, Miss Vermouth, when we rescued you?" Bartleby asks.

"Several worshippers near my cell in Sungaze let spill that a prominent orcblood general and a key bishop of Thomerion were to meet within the topmost level of the Tower of the Dark Wrath."

Bartleby shudders at the mention of the name. You scratch your head. "Tower of the Dark Wrath?" you ask.

The mayoress points to a distant crag, where a colossus of a building, constructed of dank grey stone and brick, looms large over the countryside. Even upon reflection, you fail to comprehend how you could have missed this the few times your military duties sent you to Koraxon.

Bartleby mutters, "Who knows what awaits us there…"

Vermouth reiterates, "Frightening though it may be, we must stay the course."

You hike to within a hundred yards of the tower's base, and hide behind a cropping of large boulders, out of the line of sight of a corps of about a half-dozen orcblood guards. They discuss something and occasionally point in some random direction. From here, you can see that the door to the tower is unlocked and open by just a few inches.

"So, what is our plan?" you ask.

"I see few options but force," Titania replies, "Although we should still try to avoid battle. Get in, do what we need to do, and get out."

As you discuss, five of the guards march off to the west.

"Now is our best chance," you say.

"One of you, distract the last guard. The other will sneak in with me. If we're lucky, there shan't be much more resistance on the inside."

"I'd like to protect her," Bartleby requests of you.

What do you do?

To distract the guard yourself, turn to the last quarter of page 196.

To order Bartleby to do it, turn to page 184.

Enough of this pussy-footing around, you think.

"We don't know where we're going, other than up," you say to Vermouth, "So, we shall conquer whatever stands in our way!"

Titania smiles at you with warmth equal to her smiles at Bartleby. You don't see yourself partnering with her, but as your soul lifts, the cleric's attraction to her takes on all new meaning.

"Let's do it," she exclaims.

You charge up the stairs and onto the next level to find a single orcblood heading toward you. You engage him in a wrestler's hold, using your weight in an old trip technique that sends the brute to the floor. It shakes its head and blinks, dazed.

Eight more such semi-monsters, however, two of which control barking hounds at the ends of chains, sit on various cots between you and where the stairs continue upward. They turn their gazes toward you in alarm, stand, and draw their weapons.

"Puny dwarf!" the biggest shouts, "You shall pay for this transgression."

You and Titania turn to run, but two more orcbloods intercept you, imposing themselves like statues between you and the door. One grabs the mayoress's arms and binds them with rope, despite her screams. You, however, are not so lucky, as these half-men pound you into dust with their bare fists, imprison you, and decide after a short discussion that your head would make a great decoration upon a spear near the tower's spire.

Cruel fate has taken your life. Rise again!

You pull the mayoress off to one side, and scan a short, oddly-shaped door nearby. It appears unlocked, and safe. Some shuffling sounds come from behind it, but you figure that the worst that can happen is not much worse than how things are now.

You open the door and, crouching under the low entry, sneak into an expansive chamber beyond, within which dozens of implements of torture now surround you. Multiple stretching racks and breaking wheels lay here, as well as a laboratory-like workspace, on which colorful substances in urns bubble and boil despite a lack of any flame underneath.

Nothing living appears to be here, beyond yourselves.

"Hello?" you whisper.

A string of breathy hisses meets your ears, and a dot of darkness appears before you. It expands to wash over the entire room. Vermouth gasps. You withhold from reaching for a torch or walking about for the moment, for fear of knocking into something deadly.

"New experimental subjects!" exclaims an impish voice from somewhere within the void. You whirl about in place and hold your hands out, but still hear light footsteps approaching, as well as the wooden thump of a wand or club-like object hitting a palm.

"Hold!" Titania pleads, her voice trembling, "Is there any way by which we can…"

You have already thought that there is no way to talk yourselves out of this, and retreat toward the triangular door--potential obstacles be damned--when a sizzling jolt of electricity bursts from the direction of the voice and hits you square in the back. Perhaps your unseen enemy, at the very least, will have some trouble with you, given that you're a bit short to fit properly within an iron maiden.

Your quest has ended... or has it?

"We may not get another chance," you say, "so let's delve deeper."

Bartleby nods his agreement. You pull upon a metal handle built into the hatch, to find that the passage opens easily. Underneath, a short ladder, with steps far apart as if built for humans, is implanted into the near wall, and the ground slopes into a dark tunnel heading to the east.

You retrieve flint and a torch from your pack, and light the torch. You lead the way in, climbing down with caution to avoid slipping on the round, slick rungs, while Bartleby trails behind.

The tunnel seems featureless, beyond the fact that the dirt floor stretches for miles. No offshoots provide a choice or challenge of any kind. Finally, your light illuminates a plain stone wall ahead of you, which blocks your way.

"How boring," the cleric complains.

"Why in the world would Crolliver want to come down here?"

"There must have been some reason."

Several moments of silence pass. You look about you, and scratch your head.

"And yet, here we stand," Bartleby says. "And stand some more."

You search for anything interesting, under rocks and within crags, on the floor and within the ceiling, and find nothing. The cleric even knocks on the wall, but the resulting tone sounds somewhere between hollow and muffled, and fails to shed any real light on the situation.

"We could end up spending all day down here," you observe.

"That lackey must have known something we could never guess."

You sigh, "And it certainly is too late to extract it from him now."

Turn to page 35.

It seems unlikely, you reflect, *that that is an actual oasis.* You turn up your nose and wonder what kind of monster might hide behind the very sand dune you considered traversing.

You march further, forcing your legs to lift and move one after the other, even as the remaining clouds clear and the sun's rays intensify. Minutes later, you check your waterskin, to find it empty, and turn, only to discover that either the supposed oasis has disappeared, or you've walked clear out of sight of it. The winds sharpen, and pelt your eyes and face with sand. You can now barely breathe, and no standard path is in sight.

Stories replay in your head, of desert wanderers that never find their way out because of a strange tendency of one leg to walk in longer strides than the other, causing one's path to become circular rather than straight. Without personal assistance, a camel, or so much as a compass, the foolhardiness of undertaking this leg of your quest alone sets in now. And yet, what did you know? Somehow, in all your years, your adventures never sent you this way, even though the Ambrosinian military headquarters is in Fort Remnon.

Were they keeping secrets from me in some way? Here I am, believing that I was stationed further east for no real reason...

Over the next hour, your head becomes so clouded that you cannot form coherent thoughts. Utterly spent, you collapse in a heap, alone in the middle of nowhere. You smack your tongue against the roof of your mouth and observe that buzzards circle overhead. You hope in a perversely wicked way that your parched body, even if already dead, will provide them little sustenance.

Your travels cease here, but don't give up.

You reluctantly conclude that continuing might not be wise, and steer yourself toward the oasis. The closer you get, the realer it seems, until you stand within the refuge's crystal clear pond, surrounded by about twenty weary travelers of all races and sizes. The breeze blowing through this valley cools your cheeks and scalp.

You ask around, and discover many souls willing to help, from a boy who refills your waterskin to a muscled saleswoman, from whom you purchase an old compass at a deep discount. You share stories of your travels with a congenial newlywed couple, who in turn bestow a blessing upon you. By the time you're ready to depart, hope once again courses through your veins, like invigorating manna from heaven.

The remainder of the journey to Fort Remnon seems almost effortless. There, the gate guards guide you to the military headquarters, and in turn toward a specific hall therein.

Around the corner approaches a black-haired, wiry human, dressed in long white pants and a white cloak, who smiles at you and extends his left hand for a shake. "Welcome!" he bellows. You wonder why he's not using the customary right hand, until you notice that he has no right arm. His shirt sleeve hangs limp over a short stump.

"Are you Saul?" you ask.

"Indeed I am. What brings you to these parts?"

You explain what you've been through, from your desire to save Fedwick to rescuing Titania, as well as the church's plans and its alliance with Koraxon.

"And, you left my sister with only a servant of the sun god to protect her? A peace-monger?"

"You underestimate him," you reply, "In fact, you have never met him. You cannot judge."

"I admire your dedication to your clansman," Saul continues, "yet, the idea that my sister expects me to help you automatically is now thrown into question." He frowns, and scratches his chin.

You blink, and cross your arms.

"An expedition to Managhast happens to depart within the morrow. But, let's make it interesting. We like to play a game around

181

here to pass the time, called nine-card poker. You play me, one on one. You win, and I'll come all the way with you to Managhast. You lose, and I'll still let you aboard my ship, but I will then choose to stay here, for as you see, responsibilities abound." You look about you, as footmen in chainmail shuffle from room to room within the compound, issuing orders and carrying weapons, food, and other supplies.

Saul guides you into a private chamber, where he pulls two squat stools up to a table, and offers you one. You sit, while he retrieves a deck of cards from a nearby cupboard. He spreads the cards out on the table and mixes them with his one hand.

"I shall deal out a total of nine cards," Saul says, "one at a time. By the time the game ends, the cards need to form a three-by-three grid, but before then, we shall take turns choosing where a card goes within that grid, one card at a time. And each card beyond the first must border another by at least a corner.

"Your job, as the player, is to attempt to arrange the cards so as to form three-card poker hands in any of the rows, columns, or diagonals. For example, if two cards of the same rank are in the same row, you earn a point for the pair. A straight, three cards of consecutive rank, or a flush, three cards of the same suit, earns you two points, while three of a kind or a straight flush, the rarest possible hands, earn you three points. Your goal is to accumulate a mere four points by the end. If you do so, you win."

"That's it?"

Saul nods.

You huff into your beard, unimpressed.

"I'm ready, then," you say.

"Dealer goes first," Saul says, as he turns over the queen of hearts, which he places on the table without comment. "Your turn."

The next card is the ace of diamonds.

"No help just yet. Where would you like it, relative to the queen?"

You think for a moment. It doesn't much matter where this card goes, other than that you shouldn't block places conducive to scoring hands. You place the ace one spot below and to the left of the queen.

Saul deals another card. This time it's the seven of spades.

182

"Still not much help," he says, placing it to the immediate right of the queen.

So, this is how the grid has shaped up so far…

Your heart leaps upon seeing the seven of clubs next. Along with the seven of spades, it can make a pair.

"Lucky dog," Saul grumbles, "In which of the two spots do you want to place it?"

What do you do?

To place the seven of clubs above the seven of spades, turn to page 76.

To place it below the seven of spades, turn to page 36.

"If brute force becomes called for," you explain, "I'd best be inside with Titania. You distract the guard."

Bartleby frowns, but shrugs. "May the gods smile upon us on this fool's mission," he mumbles, before he steps out of the shadows.

"Excuse me, good sir," Bartleby chimes to the orcblood, "But I wonder if you could help me. Do you know the way to Saint Martin?"

"Wha?"

"Saint Martin. 'The last time I was there, there was this old man who wouldn't stop talking to us about the island of Managhast, something about how it had the most beautiful flowers in the world, and..."

Bartleby prattles on and on, until the guard begins sputtering and blinking, and holds his hands outward in a placative pose. "Wait, wait," he grumbles. "I have never heard of a Saint Martin in these lands."

"You are joshing me!" The shock in Bartleby's voice is only halfway convincing, but you lead Vermouth down the lane on tiptoes, through the door and into the tower. You hear, "Do you not have a map of some sort?" from outside as you peruse the dark interior, boosting your confidence that you won't be interfered with, for now.

Ahead of you lay a flight of dimly-lit wooden stairs, which coil upward in a helix. The bizarre architecture here offers no rhyme, reason, or pattern to the arrangement of alcoves. Foreboding arches throughout form L-shapes, diamonds, and half-stars; you wonder whether the shapes hold any meaning. Some are spaced only a few yards apart, while the southern wall contains no entryways at all.

You hear low voices and the tromping of boots on the ceiling. The sound progresses toward where the stairs rise upward.

What do you do?

To go through a triangular door to your right, turn to page 178.

To go under the undulating arch to your left, turn to page 88.

To take on whoever walks above, turn to page 177.

After you place the ten of hearts, Saul deals the three of spades, arches and eyebrow and slowly places the card to the left of the queen. The grid now looks like this:

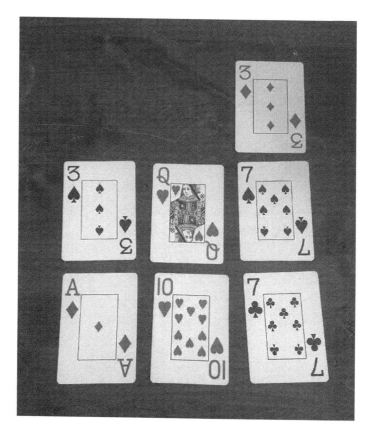

He then deals the eight of diamonds, and there are only two spots left to place a card.

Where do you place the eight of diamonds?

To place it above the three of spades, turn to page 242.

To place it above the queen, turn to page 193.

You reflect upon whether you would ever be back to these mountains during your lifetime. Concerning this egg, it is now or never.

Your muscles twitch with trepidation as you slowly approach the nest. You keep the egg in your peripheral vision while focusing on whether the mother seems nearby, but soon realize there isn't all that broad an entryway by flight. A few more steps, and the smooth texture of the mottled shell meets your fingertips. You reach around the egg, and need the whole width of your grasp just to lift it from its perch...

"Squawwwwwwk."

At that moment, a pair of golden claws land between you and the passage with a tremendous thud. The perturbed gryphon connected to them calls again and spreads it wings, blocking out your view of the sun.

Panic causes you to forget about the feather. You first feint to the right, but the bird is too quick, and cuts you off. To the left lay the precarious cliffside, with its shattered rocks. An idea strikes you.

You dash straight forward, and duck between the gryphon's legs. The bird whirls about in confusion, and you are just about home free when your foot catches on a branch sticking out the far edge of the nest. You stumble forward, one, two, three full steps, and crash face-first into the stone; the egg smashes into hundreds of pieces in your arms.

Yolkish muck now smothers your face, chest, and hands, and in the moments you have left, you can barely breathe, let alone get your wits about you. As you recover, the gryphon bull-rushes you, burying its massive head into your chest and shoving until you no longer find ground underneath your feet. Mercifully, you're knocked out by the first blow, and don't feel the next several times your limp body smashes against the hard mountainside as gravity does its work. Calling your corpse a mess, at this point, would be quite the understatement.

Cruel fate has taken your life. Rise again!

"Looks like you need a bit of a miracle," Saul says.

He turns over the jack of hearts, laughs heartily, and places it in the last spot. The final grid looks like this:

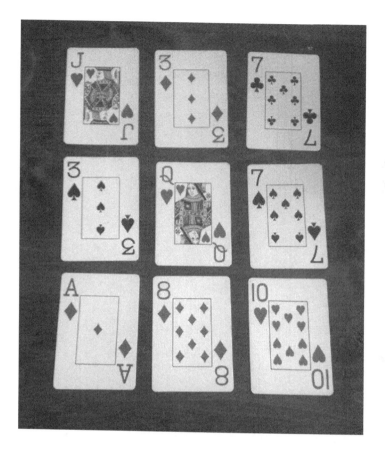

A straight-flush and a pair, for four points! You win!

Turn to page 191.

You circle around a large boulder and approach the tower from many yards to the east. It appears to offer no visible back entrance, or you would be tempted to return to your party and redirect them.

You peer around the edge of the stone wall, and see the backside of the orcblood guard. He's armored in leather, cinched together with thick cords all the way up his spine, and a short sword hangs in a weather-beaten scabbard at his waist. The creature sways from side to side every now and again.

"Hey, wart-face!"

The words shock you as they escape your mouth. You duck back into the shadows and brace yourself as you hear the brute turn and stomp once in your direction.

"Excuse me?" it grunts. "Who's there?"

You dash further around the tower, hoping to incite a game of follow-the-noise. "You heard me! Your mother wears army boots, and your father smells of cheap wine!" You make a mental note that you're going to have to work on your skill regarding witty insults.

"That may be true," the orcblood shouts, "But what business is it of yours? Show yourself!" The guard now heads straight in your direction, having abandoned his post.

Now three-quarters of the way around the tower, you see Bartleby and Vermouth rush toward the front door out of the corner of your eye. They make it in, just before you note that the rest of the orcblood band is on their way back from down the avenue.

Loathing the idea of leaving your companions behind, you nevertheless dash away from the tower and into the core of the capital city, as fast as your legs can take you. In the name of self-preservation against overwhelming numbers, you can now do little but watch from a distance, and hope.

For several minutes, nothing seems to happen. Then, you hear a blood-curdling female scream pierce the afternoon air. An indistinguishable body runs by one of the tower's barred windows, then another in the opposite direction. The latter appeared to carry somebody else upon its shoulder. The guards outside the door look upward and murmur amongst themselves briefly, but soon rush into the tower, and it appears more clearly than ever that this was a fool's mission.

"Care to apologize yet?"

The deep voice startles you; you whirl about to find that the original guard looms over you, and he swiftly punches you in the jaw. Your last instant thought before falling unconscious involves something about how persistence can sometimes make up for a lack of smarts.

Better opportunities await you. Try again!

You cross your arms and grumble to yourself, but admit that it's too early and too dangerous to trust just anybody you run across. Further, you realize you may need what gold you have elsewhere in your quest.

You glance up at the old woman and tell her, "It seems I am outvoted. No offense intended."

The elf smiles warmly, her eyes crinkling at the corners. "None taken. Good day to you all, and good luck."

She turns, shuffles toward the door of his treehouse, gazes at the horizon for a moment, and retires.

Undeterred, your group hurries further into the wood. After a brief search, Zander declares that he has found the entrance, and you rush to join him.

Turn to page 152.

Saul wordlessly turns over the jack of hearts, and places it in the last spot. The final grid looks like this:

You have lost.

Turn to page 201.

"Nicely played," Saul says, "even if you did get a little lucky." He winks at you.

As I said, I shall accompany you to Managhast. I'll leave some lieutenants in charge here, although the way they play cards, perhaps I should think twice."

You chuckle. Saul and three strong-looking men stock a generous supply of food and water, and lead you through the desert and back into the temperate lands beyond, then to a small port village. There, a handsome, medium-sized ship lay in wait, docked and rocking on the waves. On its side is a wooden placard that reads 'The Grand Titania.'

"You do not normally captain your expeditions at sea?" you ask Saul, as the evening winds down into night.

"I merely own the vessel," Saul explains, "and occasionally oversee its maintenance. But do not interpret that as meaning it holds little value. A ship is, after all, much like a woman."

"In that, if you give it some attention, it will love you back?"

Saul laughs out loud. "In that you can't live with them, and you can't live without them."

You board, and suddenly notice how tired you are. As you retire to a small chamber under decks, a skeleton crew prepares to shove off, pressing through the night to arrive at Managhast by mid-morning.

You awaken refreshed, if a little sea-tossed, and meet a fellow sailor near mid-mast. Curious, you ask, "What does Fort Remnon hope to accomplish on this expedition?"

"This is an exploratory commercial venture," he replies, "to gather fruits and other flora native to the area."

"From any specific tree, one that might, say, earn a specific title?"

"Not of which I am aware."

You scratch your beard.

So, even they don't know about the Tree of Purity...

The weather holds fair as the sun climbs higher into the sky, and soon, you see a broad isle poke its way over the horizon. Shaped like a crescent, its dense jungle wraps around an inviting bay, but the shore contains no man-made piers of any kind. Upon a brief scan, it becomes clear that the sailors weren't the only ones with only partial information. A throng of wiry, fur-covered dog-men—you think you've heard them referred to as gnolls—chokes the land. They jump and point at you, and wield sharp-looking, smoothly-hewn spears. You also think you seem them readying a catapult of some sort, pulling it out from among the island's deepest foliage. Yet, the ship sails on.

"What do you plan to do about them?" you ask Saul.

"What does it look like we'd do?" he asks with a touch of disbelief. "We defend ourselves." To the crew he shouts, "Load the cannons!"

You arch an eyebrow. *But, they haven't done anything to harm us yet...*

As you get close, the gnolls howl and holler, scowling all the while. Your corps lets loose a deadly volley, but many of the dog-men dodge the projectiles, while a few jump behind trees, so few attacks hit their mark. The sailors drop anchor, then press into the throng, drawing daggers and swords. With a mighty swing, one pierces the heart of a dog-man, who collapses. The other targets, however, prove themselves capable adapters. They disarm, trip, and compensate for their shortcomings in weaponry. Soon, two or three of them have surrounded each of your men, and some of the latter have already fallen.

The tide turns, you think, as your short legs cause you to straggle behind, *and I'm not here to fight, ultimately.*

You dash across the shoreline and around the battle, and look over your shoulder as you penetrate the foliage beyond. The natives seem to not have noticed you, but one small problem still plagues you.

Where in this land can I find the Tree of Purity?

Two options present themselves.

What do you do?

To push through the core of the jungle, turn to page 196.

To traipse catty-corner along the shoreline, turn to page 194.

Saul wordlessly turns over the jack of hearts, and places it in the last spot. The final grid looks like this:

You have lost.

Turn to page 201.

Your boots sink into the soft sand as you traverse the shoreline perpendicular to the landing site, and the sounds of battle fade as you put miles between you and the sailors. You find your target arcing high above the landscape, but nestled such that you never could have seen it had you immersed yourself within the jungle. From a distance, it appears much the same as the adjacent trees, but soon, you notice that a bluish sheen envelops it. Small pulses of magic shoot across it in a distinct and predictable rhythm, like oxygenated blood to a beating heart.

Glancing around one last time, you begin pulling berries off the outstretched branches, filling your pockets to the point of bursting. As you do so, you ponder aloud, "These could fetch a pretty penny in the wrong hands. I find it hard to believe Vermouth never uttered a word about it to her brother."

You return to the shoreline to find that most of the remaining gnolls have been subdued or captured, although a surprising number of humans lay unconscious or hurt. While some sailors treat their peers' wounds, most go about what they came here for, and completely ignore you. Even Saul turns his back when the two of you make eye contact. So, you board the ship, lower a lifeboat and start to row back to the mainland.

Over the days that this requires, you begin to wonder whether Fedwick still clings to life. The sea, desert and prairie all blow by in a flash, as your rush to salvage his spirit drives you forward despite exhaustion and exasperation.

Carrying the berries as carefully as possible, you hustle through the streets of Whitetail and burst through the door of your hut, to find the attending cleric still on duty, even if asleep.

You press a hand to Fedwick's chest, and feel it rise. You are in time!

You use a mortar and small bowl to crush the berries, and mix them with water from your basin. As you pour the solution down Fedwick's gullet, the color begins to come back to his cheeks. Suddenly, he sits up and launches into a wild coughing fit. Your smile couldn't be wider. You embrace him.

"Brother," he grunts, "What happened?"

"'Tis a long story," you reply.

Your overwhelming joy leaves you oblivious to all else, as meanwhile, mere kilometers away, near the northern gates, a convoy of undead skeletons approaches, armed with swords and commanded by a handful of wizened necromancers. At their head is an orcblood general, the hatred in his heart soon to set the entire Ambrosinian capital aflame.

You have revived Fedwick!

But is there more to the story?

Read through The Seal of Thomerion again to find out.

We're in enough trouble as it is down here, you think, *with no need to risk more.*

You take a last glance at the rubies, tempting as they are. You descend, with little fanfare or difficulty.

Bartleby asks, his arms crossed, "So, nothing of interest is up there?"

"Oh, nothing that doesn't probably have another trap rigged within it."

You ponder your other options.

To take the squat passage, turn to page 50.

To take the wide passage to the right, turn to page 71.

You search among acres upon acres of wilderness, pushing aside huge branches and sloshing through damp undergrowth as you go. An eternity seems to pass, but no one plant stands out among all the rest. You take a moment to think things over, and estimate you haven't even covered a fifth of the island's land mass, when it hits you that the surroundings have become eerily quiet. Either all battle at the landing site has ceased, or you have long since traveled out of earshot.

Then, the trees start to move. They seem to rise at a slow but steady pace, and you begin to think your eyes play tricks on you, until you look downward.

You're sinking into quicksand.

"Help!" you shout, flailing your arms. You sink even more rapidly, then remember that panic will make things worse, and breathe deeply. You look about, and see little recourse. Almost a half-circle behind you, a thick vine snakes outward, which you grab and start to pull upon, but by now, you're up to your waist in the sand, and the vine snaps off near its base, unable to take the strain.

You holler for assistance once again, but no one comes. The brown menace consumes your chest, then your arms and neck. Although you take one last breath knowing just how close you to came to success, the earth consumes you whole, knowing in turn just how far away you are from home.

Your quest has ended... or has it?

Your heart softens a bit from your earlier stance, as this might give your companion a chance to get on the mayoress's good side.

"Wait to act until I can lure him away from the door," you instruct.

"That's the way," Bartleby says. "Good luck."

Turn to page 188.

You think for a while, during which time the youth makes it out of the temple entirely.

"It's just as well," you conclude.

"He left something behind," Bartleby says, while heading toward the prayer box. He leaves you musing near an altar, your arms crossed.

The parchment the cleric retrieves is barely larger than your hand, yet he pores over every word for several long minutes.

"What is it?"

"See for yourself."

You rejoin Bartleby, and inspect the script over his shoulder:

May the victims of Thomerion find solace in this gesture, a symbol of peace and harmony in a world of discord, and may the gods forgive my transgressions, as I seek to repent.

"A prayer," you remark, "and little more."

"Not so," the cleric counters, as he turns the parchment over. The obverse contains row after row of hieroglyphs and ciphers. A strange curlicue in the lower-right corner punctuates the message.

You scratch your head. Bartleby clarifies, "Magical scroll paper. In fact, while I know only some of this language, I can say with reasonable certainty that the spell contained herein can be used to inflict the seal of Thomerion itself."

You smack your forehead in amazement. "Does it," you ask, "have the power to reverse such an effect already in place?"

"I'm afraid this kind of magic doesn't work that way. But, this definitely counts as something that the church would want back."

You now know how to set the trap; the question left is where.

What do you do?

To return to the warehouse, continue to page 198.

To recommend somewhere more public, turn to page 199.

"We know that something odd is going on underneath the warehouse," you note, "and might get their attention by employing the place in the same way they did us."

Bartleby arches an eyebrow, but accepts your idea. You hike to the warehouse once again, enter, place the parchment on the altar, and hide in the same large crate as before. Time passes, yet nobody comes.

"Out of curiosity," you whisper to Bartleby after about an hour of waiting, "you said that the church of Thomerion finds ways to cover up what they've done. Can you give examples?"

The cleric thinks for a moment. "Mostly, they use up something as quickly as possible, then move on before those who could prosecute them catch on. I only know that much from a few isolated incidents involving defectors, such as what that youth had appeared to me to become."

You grimace. "Was it rather hasty of me, then, to let him go?"

Bartleby blinks, then says, "I am not one to judge."

Suddenly, seven men, all dressed in black and red robes and carrying lit torches, enter your vision from various directions and converge behind the altar. The shortest barks an order, and four others disperse. They spread some kind of liquid over the floors and many crates, including your own. The smell of alcohol wafts into your nostrils.

You glance at Bartleby, whose face betrays his panic.

By the gods...we're trapped, and outnumbered...

"As this temple has been desecrated, it is of no more use to us," you hear, "May this sacrifice please Thomerion!"

"Hear, hear!" the others shout, before each touches his torch to the nearest wooden surface. Within seconds, all you can see is fire, and smoke begins to seep through the holes in your crate. Hacking and coughing, you burst open the lid to find that the worshippers have fled, but there is no open escape route. Charred beams fall from the ceiling, and you hear the building's infrastructure creak as its support weakens.

"What do we do?" you shout.

"It's a temple, after all," Bartleby sighs. "We pray."

Don't let evil win. Read another path!

"So, to a commoner, this paper is just a bunch of nonsense."

Bartleby nods. "More or less."

"If we put it someplace highly visible, then, anyone who tries to take it must already know the purpose for which it is used."

"I think I follow you, but, what did you have in mind?"

"The Pig's Foot."

You exit the temple, and cross several streets to get to Whitetail's most popular watering hole. There, you sweet-talk a local carpentress into lending you her hammer and a nail, post the parchment on the public kiosk and order brews for both you and Bartleby, with no intention of drinking them. You snag a table that puts the kiosk to your direct left, but well within your peripheral vision. Work notices and wanted posters around the parchment help it look like just another normal document.

Everything is going according to plan...

Noon strikes, and you've exhausted all casual topics of conversation with both Bartleby and random passersby, when a plain-clothed man in his fifties, with stringy white hair and deep black eyes, approaches the kiosk. The man reads for a moment, looks about him, and snatches the scroll, before turning toward the tavern entrance.

You stand, and the man increases his pace. You follow. He attempts to walk toward the west, but frowns at you over his shoulder.

"What do you want with me?" he shouts.

You grab him by an arm, and Bartleby seizes the other arm. He struggles, but you hold tight.

"You are of the church of Thomerion, yes?" you grunt.

"So what if I am? You can't prove anything."

Bartleby forces his way into the man's pockets, and pulls out a medallion emblazoned with a skull and dagger of deep red hue.

"Certainly more than a lackey," the cleric theorizes, "In all likelihood, a bishop. You shall come with us."

You retrieve rope from your pack and tie the man's hands behind his back. You lead him toward your hut, and enter.

Turn to page 142.

After you place the ten of hearts, Saul deals the three of spades, and places it in the lower-right corner. The grid now looks like this:

He then deals the eight of diamonds, and there are only two spots left to place a card.

Where do you place the eight of diamonds?

To place it to the left of the queen, turn to page 225.

To place it below the queen, turn to page 29.

You inspect the cards' arrangement one more time, just to be sure, but no matter how you look at them, your score falls short of the necessary four points.

"Well," you grunt, "A bargain is a bargain, is it not?"

"Worry not," Saul consoles, "for my ship employs some of the finest men this side of the mountains. They will get you to where you want to go."

With some guidance, your journey from Fort Remnon to an unmapped coastal village proves quick and uneventful. There, you find the vessel; of moderate size, sturdy-looking and well-kept, it displays a placard on its side that reads 'The Grand Titania.' You board, and the crew shoves off. For the next few hours, the by-proxy captain says little to you, other than to occasionally bark an order to help with the sails during patches of rough weather. As dusk approaches, the crew pushes the ship to its limits in rotating shifts, as you drift into sleep under-deck.

The next morning, you stretch your weary bones, yawn widely, and ask one of the men, a red-haired lass of about twenty, "Have you, perchance, journeyed to Managhast before?"

"We have not," she replies as she hoists rope above her head, "The mission is supposed to be exploratory, but others have failed to fill me in on the details."

"Maybe," you offer, "that is because the natives, I have been told, are not so friendly. Deadly, perhaps."

"Is that right?" The sailor adopts a quizzical look, saying this with a touch of bitterness. A moment passes as she glances at the sea.

"So," she continues, "this is a suicide mission?"

You concede, "I do find it surprising that you were expected to participate without full knowledge of what you were getting into, but…"

"No, no," she counters, "I've known him for quite some time. This is just like Saul, to throw everybody around as if we were mere pawns, while he sits on his rear, comfortable and safe."

You blink, and say, "Paranoia will not help."

"Perhaps not. But, I know what will."

The sailor hastily finishes her work, then retreats to under-deck. You stare after her, pondering.

More time passes, as the Grand Titania cuts through miles more of surf. The sun has risen considerably when the proxy-captain shouts, "Land, ho!"

You scan the horizon, and see a crescent-shaped island that hugs a pristine bay, straight ahead. Expansive jungles paint your destination a glorious mixture of brown and green.

"I can already taste those exotic fruits," the captain says.

You reflect upon the chances of getting at the Tree of Purity within such an expanse. You reflect so deeply that you fail to see a half-dozen crew members until they have already snuck up behind the captain. Two of them grab his arms and hold him fast, while another binds his hands and wraps his torso with immense lengths of rope.

"This is a mutiny!" the red-haired sailor shouts.

"Now, just… just, wait a minute," you grumble, "I need to get to that island!"

"Stand in our way, dwarf," another sailor says, "and get thrown overboard."

You can't swim all that well, so that isn't an option, and when you approach the lifeboats, the mutineers cut them loose. Thereby, you can do little but watch as the crew locks the proxy-captain into a holding cell and steers the ship far away from Managhast. Where you are headed now, these mangy miscreants don't, or can't, tell you, and anger and frustration rise to the boiling point within you. Your last bits of hope that you'll head toward the Ambrosinian mainland within the next few days dissolve when one of them makes clear that they've wanted to sail the seas randomly for years, and just needed a reason.

So much, you lament, *for trust.*

Your travels cease here, but don't give up.

"So, good sir," Wyver says to you as you trek, "tell me more about your friend, and about what ails him."

"He is Fedwick, of the Canterbury clan. I fear many more souls share his plight, for he has been marked with the seal of Thomerion. A disease of pure evil accompanies the seal."

Wyver scratches his chin. "I know of magic that may be able to help. But be warned, the spell is taxing upon both the caster and the recipient, and takes quite some time to cast in its entirety."

"Taxing?"

"In the same sense that our bodies fight illness naturally, this spell exploits and encourages automatic defenses by restricting the target's exposure to only a controlled dose of what is bothering it. Many ways exist in which it could go wrong, including sudden overdose."

"Therefore, we cannot afford to rush."

"Or be tired, or distracted," Wyver agrees, "while casting it. The earliest I shall be able to heal your friend is tomorrow morning."

You acquiesce to this, since dark has indeed enveloped the landscape by the time you emerge from the wood. Many miles still remain between you and the capital.

"Shall we rest here?" Grindle suggests.

"There is still time," Wyver says, "to see what we can do about the throne. I'd venture a guess that we are less likely to run into resistance after most of the royal staff has retired for the night."

You press on, despite grumblings from much of your party, and a distinct sense that your personal goal has been lost, or at least minimized, within the greater context.

Suddenly, a horse bolts past you from behind, in full gallop and carrying a stout rider in a hooded green cloak. You couldn't see who it was, and the pair ignored your party. As its path ran many yards to the south of yours, and Bartleby and Grindle were locked in conversation, it seems nobody else noticed the rider but you.

You scratch your beard, but continue your trek, nonplussed.

More time passes, as owls begin to emerge and fill the night prairie with ominous hooting. Your legs ache and your head swims, but finally, you see the torchlight of the Whitetail border guard ahead. You enter the city without trouble, but as you approach the castle itself, two helmeted footmen confront you near the edge of the moat.

"The drawbridge is up for the night, sires," the younger one explains, "Whatever your business with King Patrick, it will have to…."

"Wait," the older orders. He approaches the druid, places a hand upon his neck, and traces the birthmark with a finger.

"Prince Wyver…" he says, amazement tinging his voice, "You're alive! How is this possible?"

"Indeed, it is I."

"Who?" the other guard asks.

"I shall spread the word."

"You are not worried that I am a killer?" Wyver says.

"Of course not. Such grudges ceased being important long ago. Ambrosinia needs a new leader, one spurred to action."

The support behind placing Wyver back at his deserved post quickly spreads, from the guard to a group of tired passersby, to the rest of the castle staff. The footmen issue an order to lower the drawbridge, and the internal guards comply. Your party enters, and finds Patrick's royal chambers, on the second floor of the southwest tower.

"Let's see him try to fight us, now," the prince says. He knocks loudly upon the door.

From within comes a cough and a splutter, and the sounds of sheets being ruffled. "Wha? Who dares to wake me? What could be so important that you…"

The door opens, and within the archway stands King Patrick himself, stooped and blinking, his disheveled head bare of the crown, which sits upon a wooden bust on an armoire, mere inches away. Patrick grows silent, and the two men glare at each other.

"Brother," the king says.

"Patrick."

The king wrings his hands, and mumbles, "I know that what I did was unconscionable. Years, and trials of many a kind, have taught me that hard lesson."

Wyver stares at him, listening.

"But, my friends," Patrick asserts as he scans the four of you, "I do not give up the throne that easily."

"Even in the face of the will of your people?" Wyver retorts.

"What do you mean?"

The prince offers an arm to the king, who takes it and accompanies your group to an open window, from which can be heard chanting. A servant offers Patrick a robe, which he pulls around himself to combat a stiff breeze as you step out onto the balcony. Below stands a throng of over a hundred citizens, many of whom pump their fists, pitchforks, or torches in the air, and all of whom call Wyver's name.

Patrick stares at the populace for a while, then hangs his head, and sighs. "Perhaps the time has come. After all, royalty becomes weary of criticism, of hatred. I had become the 'do-nothing' king... when all I had ever done was what I felt was best."

Wyver puts a hand on his brother's shoulder.

"All you need do now is to say the word. Then, rest easy."

With the tiniest bit of a smile, Patrick nods. You accompany him back to the bedroom, where he takes the crown and places it gingerly upon Wyver's head. Once again, you return to the balcony, where Patrick leads Wyver to the very edge of the stone railing.

"May I present to you," he shouts, "His Royal Highness, King Wyver of Ambrosinia!"

The throng cheers their new ruler, and you detect an air of bittersweet irony, as you watch Patrick wordlessly retreat beyond the bedroom and into a deeper recess of the castle, his brow furrowed.

"As we discussed," Wyver tells you, "go on ahead. I shall meet you at your home, with bodyguards in tow."

Your other teammates accompany you through the city as far as their homes, but then bid you a good night, and retire. While you traverse the rest of the distance alone, your heart both leaps and aches for Fedwick, feeling closer to a peaceful end. You check in on your clansman when you reach your hut, and dismiss the attending cleric. The moon rests high in the sky when you lay down in your bed.

You awake to hear the clash of metal and grunts of pain and exertion from just outside your door. It is dawn. You rush outside to find that Wyver, Grindle, and Bartleby, along with a small group of armed soldiers, fight for their lives with a cordon of animated skeletons, commanded by men in black and red robes.

We've been found...

You draw your axe and shield, and jump into the fray with a yell. You hack the skull of one skeleton clear off its body, then duck a sword swing before disarming a second undead. You find Wyver among the commotion, who crouches and casts a spell of some kind. Some nearby vines grow and wrap themselves into, through, and around two skeletons' bones, entrapping them for the time being.

"What is going on?" you shout.

"We don't know," Wyver shouts back, "We had moments ago approached to within yards of your home, when we were ambushed."

"How did they know you would be here?"

You notice a familiar face among the attacking corps. Her jealous scowl telling all, Roghet stands within a pocket of relative calm, mud still streaked down her cheeks, staring at you and the new king.

"May my spear drink of your traitorous blood," she taunts. With that, she charges her former love, whose back is turned.

There's too much din going around you to shout to get his attention. You don't have much choice but to intercept her, since the safety of the king is at risk. But a tiny part of you feels responsible, even guilty, for her rage.

What do you do?

To attempt to kill Roghet outright, turn to page 230.

To merely subdue her instead, turn to page 239.

After considerable deliberation, you outline to the abbot a plan to post a trio of crossbowmen at each major tower, plus monks with slings behind most of the hillocks. He nods and follows your orders, issuing movement commands down through the ranks, until everyone is armed and in place. You take a post high atop one of the towers, so that all are within earshot.

Now, you wait. And wait some more. You wonder for several minutes what Bartleby and Zander are doing in order to fulfill their portions of your mission. All is silent.

Then, the pounding of paws against ground meets your ears. You look up, and see in the east a few dozen halfling riders wearing black bandannas and riding burly dogs, who barrel toward the monastery at a full sprint. Each bandit also sports a wicked-looking scimitar at his waist.

"It's the Brotherhood, all right," the abbot says.

"Now!" you shout. "Open fire!"

A smattering of bolts and pellets pelts the countryside, although a delay in a few shots indicates that some fighters hadn't loaded yet. Even the shots that go off early sail yards over the heads of the bandits, whose sheer speed has already put them nearly upon you.

"Regroup! Everyone descend to ground level!"

Your men punch and trip and pull several bandits off their dogs, cutting off much of the onslaught. Within, the abbot himself grabs a quarterstaff and, breathing heavily, composes himself to fight. The strongest three halflings yelp and shriek like banshees, press forward, and bash through the temple doors as easily as if they were made of matchsticks.

As a scrappy-looking male wearing a set of spiked armor across his shoulders shouts orders, the others stash fruits, meats, weapons and assorted miscellany into their packs. The monastery's defenses scramble to keep up.

"Cease this!" the abbot shouts.

The leader merely laughs, and slashes at the abbot with his scimitar. The abbot backs away several steps, but regains his footing. He swings his weapon wildly, catching the halfling in the arm. You would help, but two unmounted bandits have trapped you in a corner. They hesitate as you swing your axe around your head, but hold their ground.

More bandits pour through the doors, and some begin to chop at the compound's infrastructure. A supporting beam cracks and gives way, and an entire section of wall collapses onto three of your men. Meanwhile, the abbot climbs onto and then over a table, using it as cover as the bandit leader attempts to close the distance.

"Come here, monk-ey-man! I ain't gonna hurt ya!"

An enemy lunges at you, but you dodge the strike, grab the halfling by the wrist and twist hard, then bash its arm at the elbow with your shield. The bandit screams in pain, just as you hear a similar yell from somewhere within the temple. His friend's eyes widen, and both quake for a moment, and then run clear out of the monastery and into the horizon.

"That will teach you punks a thing or two," you grumble.

You turn toward the center of the room, where the abbot lay on his back in the dirt, with a gaping blade puncture in the middle of his chest. You approach and lean over him with a heavy heart.

"I am sorry," you say.

"It matters not now," he professes, his tone peaceful. "My time has come, but I will be born again. Take what you need of me, and go."

You scan the area. Looting continues, and more men fall by the moment, but no one notices you. You hastily pull your vial from your belt pouch, allow several ounces of the abbot's freely flowing blood to fill it, and secure the opening with a cork.

As you run toward the wilderness, you pass by Paddy Coberfitch one last time, who, even while fighting, flashes you a look that says again, 'you think you know everything, don't you?'

Turn to page 235.

"It sounds as if your compound's strengths lie in melee," you theorize. "We shall have to take a slight risk in letting them get close, but a concentrated defense should keep them at bay."

The abbot nods with enthusiasm, and issues orders through the ranks until fighters with staves and shields cover all sides of the compound two-deep. You post only one man in each tower, each with a crossbow. You join the men by the temple doors, conscious of the expense of being unable to issue orders from above.

Now, you wait. And wait some more. Your mind wanders, and you wonder for several minutes whether Argent reset her magical traps, or whether she changes them each time someone conquers them. An image of Fedwick flashes in your mind's eye once again. All is silent.

Then, the rhythmic thump of galloping mounts meets your ears from somewhere in the distance. You look up, and see in the east about twenty-five halfling riders atop burly dogs, wearing black bandannas and barreling toward the monastery at a full sprint. All are armed with unsheathed scimitars.

"The Brotherhood have arrived!" the abbot says.

From above sail three crossbow bolts, two of which hit targets square in the chest, who fall with a grunt. Their dogs whine in confusion for a moment, then dash off in random directions. The remaining bandits are already almost upon you, such is their speed.

"Hold!" you shout, "Do not meet them in the middle!"

The bandit leader, a scraggly youth wearing spiked armor, shouts a charge to bowl you over, just as ten more of your volunteers wrap around the compound from the other sides and close in. As he bolts in your direction, you switch from a defensive position to an open one. Two monks flanking you hold a staff between them and counter-charge; the halfling's momentum carries him headlong into the weapon, which clotheslines him off his mount and onto his back.

"That works, too," you admit.

The battle escalates, even as you now have the clear advantage in numbers. Quick as they are, the bandits prove only a small challenge, and those that you manage to disarm flee. The final five stubbornly fight on, but your men slay them without mercy, and by the end, you have also taken another three prisoner. A quick inspection reveals that your militia has suffered only a few injuries, without a single casualty.

The abbot approaches you. "Brilliant work, my friend," he says. You notice a large gash in his arm, and order a volunteer to fetch a dressing for the wound.

"I am surprised," you comment, "that you joined the fray."

"A true leader does not put himself above his men, for we are all made of the same *ki*. An energy that pulses through us, that has driven us toward a communal victory this day."

You smile, proud.

The volunteer returns with a large spool of gauze, but the abbot asks him to hold off for a moment. Without a word, the abbot extends his open palm toward you. It takes a moment for you to understand, but you retrieve your vial from your pouch, and give it to the abbot, who holds it under the trickle of blood on his arm for several moments. When it's nearly full, he gives it back to you and allows the volunteer to do his work, while grimacing a bit.

Since they are busy, you cork the vial and prepare to depart. Just as you turn away, the abbot calls one last time, "Sir dwarf,"

You turn back.

"Thank you," he says. "And good luck to you."

All in a day's work...

Write down the keyword BLOOD.

Turn to page 235.

You inhale until your lungs might burst, then let loose a long, warbling yodel that echoes against the snowy mountainsides. In answer comes an ear-piercing squawk, and within seconds, a gigantic gryphon swoops into the nook and lands on the opposite side of the nest with barely a sound. It steps toward you, flaps its wings and tosses its head about. You notice something different about it than you expected: a long crest of white feathers that stretch from its forehead to the base of its neck.

The male, you realize in panic, *I've attracted the father!*

You glance behind you.

Then, despite your fear, you brace yourself as you jump forward. You almost touch the nest, then hop back again, hoping to lure the beast to within your natural reach. Confused, it squawks again, and mimics your actions. As you hold a hand outstretched, you establish eye contact with it, and for a long moment, it seems to want to hold on to that connection for dear life.

"I won't hurt you," you say.

It squawks a third time, this time a long, plaintive wail, and holds very still. You step toward it, and reach for the very tip of its right wing.

You grab hold of a feather, and yank.

The gryphon lurches backward with shock in its eyes, pounds the ground with its claws, and roars a challenge.

Clutching the feather, you duck a tremendous swipe from the creature, and run back toward the cavern. You hear it bite at you from behind, once, twice, and on the third time feel its beak nip the seat of your pants, but are able to dive to safety, putting many yards between you and the creature before looking back again. The gryphon pokes its head into the tunnel, calling out, but cannot fit inside. With a whine, it slinks back to near the nest, hunched over, but does not sit upon the eggs.

It seems to take forever to wind your way back down through the mountainous passages. Assuming Bartleby's estimate of two weeks holds, Fedwick currently has less than five days to live. You reassure yourself that you have enough of a buffer, that nothing will stand in your way, and that you trust your companions will fulfill their portions of the mission.

Or will they?

211

These thoughts and others fill your otherwise uneventful journey back to the City of Storms. Security at the city limit is laxer than ever, and everything appears normal, until you reach Argent's compound. The moss covering the boulder appears to have been pulled aside recently, and there is no one here but you.

You scratch your head, and look about.

I expected to be the last one here, not the first...

Curiosity gets the better of you. You light a torch and enter the tunnel with caution. The walls and floor somehow seem damper than usual, creating an oppressive atmosphere.

When you reach the puzzle room, you wish with all your soul that you had been faster. Argent and Zander lay on the floor. The sorceress is clearly dead, eyes closed, her skin already turning white, and her silver robes stained with immense amounts of blood. Zander lay on his side, motionless, but is also wounded, and groans in obvious pain.

You close the distance and kneel over her. "Zander! Thank the gods you're alive. What happened here?"

"I was able..." he wheezes, each breath difficult, "to get the blood... and return..."

"Who attacked you?"

"I tried... to fight... undead assassins... too many..."

"We need to get you to a healer," you say as you lift the ranger up. Bartleby would do, but is nowhere in sight.

Argent was a fool, you conclude, to stay here. As one of the only people in the nation with the knowledge to destroy the Black Rose, she could have employed the entire royal guard and still been a vulnerable target. And yet, you could not have afforded to stay behind.

The only question that remains is: *What now?*

Better opportunities await you. Try again!

The hour grows late, and your legs and back ache.

"Shall we attempt to find shelter along the way?" you ask.

Bartleby asks, "Will these orcbloods even rent us a room?"

"You forget," Crolliver chides, "that as far as most here know, I still work for the church. I can say that you are with me, if our robes aren't enough to protect our true identities in the first place."

Another hour passes before you encounter a small village just off the main path, the name of which you have never heard. A decrepit wooden building sits in the center of the main avenue, with a sign hanging by one of two hooks that reads 'The Ugly Pigeon.' From it rings the sounds of simultaneous, deep-voiced conversations. The three of you exchange glances, but trek onward, as it appears to be the only inn around.

You enter by the faint light of two oil lamps flanking the door. Every being in the room is an orcblood, and they all stop what they are doing. Most are armed and armored. Their stares bore holes into you, and several tense moments pass.

Bartleby breaks the silence, "So... have you heard this one?' he says, "A priest, a lackey, and a dwarf walk into a bar..."

Crolliver rolls his eyes. A slender female tromps out from behind the counter toward your party, and scans every inch of you.

"I keep this inn," she declares through a cheekful of tobacco, "What do you chumps need?"

"Have you any vacancies?" you ask.

The woman considers for a moment longer.

"Have you the silver? Five per night."

With that, the surrounding patrons return to their business. You pay your fee, and each settle onto a cot within a sparsely-furnished room. The walls stand bare, and cobwebs pervade the upper corners.

"Lovely accommodations," Bartleby remarks.

"At least they chose not to keep us in some sort of communal bunk," you note. "This way, we can discuss our plans in relative privacy."

"For now, let us retire," Crolliver requests, adding as he brushes a spider off his tunic, "...to the best of our ability." You weigh the likelihood of learning anything new from this point forward.

213

You wake with a start, to the bash of a body against wood. Someone repeatedly rams the door from the other side, straining the multiple locks and chains to the point where they hold by a splinter. Bartleby and Crolliver sit up, and draw weapons.

The door gives way, and through the entryway bursts a tall, square-jawed human in black and red robes. He sees Crolliver, shouts a battle cry and points a black talisman in the lackey's direction.

Thinking quickly, you tackle Crolliver, and your momentum carries you both to the floor in a heap as a beam of crackling energy shoots from the talisman, over both of your heads. Bartleby dashes behind the man, closes the door, grabs the man's arm and twists it behind his head in a bar-style lock. You stand, retrieve rope from your pack, close the distance and help press the man against the wall. You tie his hands, rendering him harmless within seconds.

"What do you want with us?" you ask him.

"Isn't it obvious?" Crolliver remarks from the floor. "The church thinks I'm a threat!"

The attacker says nothing.

You shove the man into a corner, where he falls onto his face, then rolls onto his side. "What is the meaning of this?" you demand. "This must have to do with more than just one lackey."

The worshipper looks up at you with a silent, sadistic grin.

You pace back and forth, nervous irritation rising. "Do you understand what we've been through? The sheer nerve of it. For a church that has too few numbers to prove a threat, you sure seem to pop up wherever and whenever it is most inconvenient!"

Two hard knocks ring on the side wall, and you realize you're disturbing other tenants. You hesitate, but speak to the worshipper further, this time in a hoarse grumble: "Do you know just how destructive you fools are? Could you undo what you have done, if you wanted to?"

An idea strikes you. "Would you spare Fedwick, if you received something else, something more valuable, in return?"

The man's smile disappears. He still says nothing.

"No bargaining, eh..." you mumble, as despair mixes with anger, "After all, I can't... make you talk."

Bartleby and Crolliver exchange glances.

Just as you turn your back upon the man, he intones, "What a fool..."

You stop in shock, and wheel around. "Excuse me?"

"Your friend," he hisses, "Of the Canterbury clan, was he not?"

"How do you know that?"

The worshipper emits a slow, evil chuckle. "You truly are even more oblivious than you appear."

You wait, as the knuckles of your clenched fists turn white.

"You want to know the truth?" the worshipper hisses. "The truth awaits you. Go to the place known as the Farbringer's Pool. It is well known, on the easterly side of the capital city. Gaze into its waters, and it will tell you all."

Your breath returns to you, albeit shrouded in confusion. You glance toward your companions, in a silent request for input.

Crolliver nods. "I've heard of it. It might be worth the time, and we were headed that way anyway."

On the other hand, you reflect, *what if what we need is already right here in front of us?*

What do you do?

To visit the Farbringer's Pool, turn to page 258.

To try to force more information out of the worshipper, turn to page 218.

After you place the ten of hearts, Saul deals the three of spades, say, "Hmph… no sense in giving you another pair," and thinks for a moment, and places it directly to the left of the queen. The grid now looks like this:

He then deals the eight of diamonds, and there are only two spots left to place a card.

Where do you place the eight of diamonds?

To place it in the bottom-middle, turn to page 187.

To place it in the upper left corner, turn to page 190.

You swing your staff hand over hand, over and over, aiming high and putting all your muscle behind each blow. Wyver crouches as you whirl, and deflects most strikes. His expression betrays a red-faced ferocity you've rarely seen in real combat, let alone this type of arbitrary exercise.

Just as you've turned to your right side to rear a finishing push, the druid flails outward from the left; his staff connects at lightning speed, just above your ankles. Both feet fly out from under you, and you crash into the stump head-first.

Everything goes black.

When your eyes next flutter open, you look about, and find that you lie on a mattress of straw, still within the wilds. Within seconds, a terrific ache pulses from where your head meets your neck, so strongly that your vision blurs and your stomach turns.

A human clad in furs notices that you're awake, and alerts others, who crowd around you, all jabbering at once. You vaguely recognize a kind-looking human standing among them, as well as a small, brown-haired being with a shiv strapped to his waist. Another gentleman blurts something about "an accident" and that he "didn't mean any harm."

Although Bartleby's magic closed your gaping skull fracture before too much of your brains spilled out onto the arena floor, it seems the impact left you a bit of a vegetable, in ways no one can heal. You try to speak, but what comes out is a mess of garbled tongue-tripping. Others try to explain that you've been in a coma for several weeks, but none of it sinks in; the information floats away among your damaged neuroses like a rotting log down a river. Something, however, tells your heart that you will be taken care of well. Perhaps Fedwick's spirit will look over you.

Your quest has ended ... or has it?

You frown, and approach the worshipper once more.

"Not good enough," you grumble. "Why can't you just cooperate, here and now? Why do you have to…"

The thud of heavy footsteps from outside interrupts you.

"What's going on in there?" comes the voice of the innkeeper. You open the door to find her with a bodyguard in tow, and they force their way into your room. She glances at you at first, but then zeroes in on the worshipper, who still lay tied in the corner.

"What kind of pureblood trash do you think you are, barging through here and disturbing my customers?" she shouts, her hands on her hips. Then, her eyes widen and her jaw drops. She covers her mouth, before looking back at you. "Do you realize who this is?"

"He had not given us his name," you reply.

"What do you mean by that? You should know better than anyone that he no longer has a real name," she comments.

You pinch your robe between two fingers. *I forgot.*

"But," she continues, "I recognize him."

You arch an eyebrow.

"This chump crossed paths with another bishop, a friend of mine, no less, who didn't take kindly to it. A warrant's been out for his capture for many moons."

The bodyguard remarks, "Unfortunately, it does mean we're going to have to take you all in for questioning."

The air whooshes out of you as defeat sinks into your bones. You cooperate with officials, revealing in the process that you're not really with the church. You end up negotiating a deal: stay out of Koraxon's business, and they will allow you to leave peacefully. The alternative, unfortunately, seems to be imprisonment in hostile territory. As orcbloods record your general description for future reference and escort you back to the border, you wonder whether there wasn't some way to get what you truly wanted in the long run.

Better opportunities await you. Try again!

Your instinct, fueled by battle adrenaline and bubbling up within you like a steaming cauldron, screams at you to follow it, just this once. You assault the druid's lower half with sweeping strikes, some of which he jumps over. But then, one catches his knee at an awkward angle. Wyver drops his weapon, clutches his leg, and shouts in agony.

"Stop the fight!" Bartleby yells.

His words fall on deaf ears. You take advantage of the opening, and use your staff to shove upon the druid with all your might. He falls off the edge of the arena limply, as if a rag doll.

Nary a semblance of pride rises within you as you begin to calm. Rather, a twinge of shame grows as you step down and help the druid up.

"I owe you an apology," you mumble, "That was…"

"Genius," Wyver interrupts.

You reel at the enthusiasm in the druid's words. He claps you on the shoulder, and a collective sigh of relief, smattered with mild cheering, arises from the crowd.

"Those kinds of tactics," the druid reassures you, "may turn out to be quite necessary in the days to come. Your experience has shone through this day."

You manage a half-smile.

"As pledged," Wyver finishes, still wincing a bit, "I shall return to claim the throne."

Turn to page 109.

You tell the others you'll follow through on Bartleby's idea. Zander frowns, looks through his coin purse for a short while, and says, "I suppose I shall have to find some other use for these."

"You were going to lend me money?"

"In these parts," the ranger comments, "auctions are not cheap."

He dismisses the idea quickly, however, and turns toward the east. Bartleby wishes you good luck, and departs as well.

No time to waste.

You ask around some public locations, and learn from a retired sailor that the best reef in Ambrosinia for oyster fishing lies almost due north, in the frigid waters of Ethias Gulf.

"I'd be surprised," she cautions, "if you find what you need. It isn't the greatest season for this kind of thing. But if you're insistent, talk to whoever you can up there, and tell 'em Sharona sent you." You thank her, and give her a silver piece for her trouble.

You decide that time runs too short to take the trip on foot, and so use your last few silvers to rent a horse. Little trouble stands in your way, save heavy winds and early sundown, and you arrive at the bay just a day and a half later. A small cluster of fishermen guide you to the reef.

"This is our last go-round 'til spring," a youth explains. "Help us, and you can keep half the value of whatever you find. Deal?"

Ouch… not sure I can keep up my end of that…

"Deal," you say.

With some guidance as to how to use the fishermen's rakes and nets, you cull the shores with relative ease. During the first several passes, however, you find only a few small specimens, just one of which has even produced a pearl. Several large dents and scratches mar the gem, making it virtually unusable.

Tedium begins to set in, and your joints creak from the moisture. Soon, you become sick of breathing brine and cracking shells, and just when you turn away from the others and admit to yourself the fruitlessness of this venture, a gigantic ship rounds a corner of the bay and approaches the reef at full clip. At its main mast flies a black flag imprinted with crossbones and the face of a tiger.

"Not the pirates again," the youth says, "Run!"

Before you can speak to them, the fishermen clear out, taking as much as they can with them, although several crates of oysters lay left behind on the shores, as the surf laps their sides. You take cover behind a large tree further inland, just as the ship drops anchor. A handful of armed men lower the gangplank and run onshore, whooping and hollering about 'easy pickins.'

If anyone has a stash of valuable gems, you think, *it'd be a pirate band.*

You don't feel that you need to run, and yet, there are too many of them to fight. Still, you think of two other ways to proceed.

What do you do?

To attempt to bargain with them, turn to page 243.

To sneak aboard the ship, turn to page 240.

"Let's just get in there and do this," you propose. "These brutes may be dumb, but I doubt they're dumb enough to fall for whatever we could come up with."

"A reasonable conclusion," Vermouth admits, "But, it might help if you try to distract the last guard. Bartleby here will sneak in with me, and together, we pray to the gods that there isn't much resistance inside."

The cleric nods soberly.

Turn to page 188.

That evening, you wait until dark, when the catacomb seems at its quietest and the slightest whisper echoes down the dank corridors. As you thought you remembered, a goblin sits on general watch duty, with his back to you against the bars of your cell. He listlessly slices at a section of wood with his dagger, while humming a guttural tune.

"What are you making?" you ask him from your cot, in your friendliest tone.

"Nothing," it hisses, staring forward.

You pause before continuing, "Surely some sort of artistic intent lies behind it. It almost looks like a flute."

The guard turns his head, but does not stand. Contrary to how you would guess he'd been trained, his eyes belie fatigue and heartache.

"Oh," he remarks, "sometimes I create these little nothings as a reminder of my aunt. She and I would spend entire days carving and whittling, when I was younger. It was our shared passion."

You arch an eyebrow. Bartleby chimes, "I never knew that goblins value family so highly."

"There is a lot you humanoids do not, and will never, know." The goblin turns forward again, and stares at the wall. Several moments of silence pass. From your side view of the creature, you think you see a tear in its eye reflect the light of the hall's sole torch.

"You would like to see your family..." you note, "to be home?"

It stands and turns toward you. "I cannot," it counters, "for the church forbids it."

"And your service, nay, your loyalty, to them is voluntary?"

To this, the goblin says nothing, but hangs his head.

"If you help us," Bartleby says, "we can in turn help you."

"You tempt me. But trust is short around here. You are now servants of chaos, just as are the men that brought me here."

No one says anything for a long time. The goblin continues whittling. *Snick, snick,* goes the repeated sound of the skimming blade. A stalactite somewhere in the tunnel drips moisture into a growing puddle.

"What is it you want, humanoids?"

The voice rouses you out of a half-sleep, and you meet the goblin at the bars. "Your master possesses a wand he used to influence our actions. We need that wand, to turn the tables and force him to cure a friend who is dying."

"And, for this, you would take me home?"

You and Bartleby exchange glances.

"We will do our best," you vow.

"That is good enough for me!" the goblin shouts, a moment before you hear a loud clank and the shifting of wood against dirt from down the hall. The guard covers his mouth and returns to his post, but nobody else shows. Within moments, all is quiet again.

"Wait here," he instructs, barely containing his excitement.

Where else would we go?

You crane your neck to follow the goblin as it skitters down the hallway to near where a large dog lay. He reaches over the dog and retrieves a golden key from a hook on the wall, then returns and carefully unlocks your cell. You file out, keeping your eyes and ears open for potential trouble, and tromp down the hall ahead of the goblin. Your heart beats a mile a minute, and you exhale with force.

"Wait..." the goblin calls, "I need to tell you something first..."

The goblin scampers behind as you and Bartleby charge down the hall and around several twists and turns, arriving at a metal door, different than the first one you encountered. This one is draped with a black and red banner, and has an obvious peephole. You attempt to turn the knob, but the door is locked.

Panting hard, the goblin catches up.

"Master's door...is sealed... by a divine rune."

"This one, here?" Bartleby asks, pointing to an angular symbol just below the doorknob, painted in off-white.

"I don't know how to read it."

"I do," the cleric whispers. "Articulus Romunus..."

You hear the faint click of a lock releasing.

"I knew you would come in handy, although some patience would benefit you," hisses the goblin.

223

The door creaks open by a small margin, and you tiptoe into the room beyond. Thick rugs, personal service items and a four-poster bed in the far corner decorate this bedchamber. On the mattress snores the bishop, dressed in a grey nightcape. The wand lay in plain sight on a nearby nightstand.

You glance at Bartleby, who palms the item.

"Do you know how to use such implements?" you whisper.

"Only a basic sense," the cleric whispers back, "Divine magic such as mine doesn't typically employ wands."

First, he merely concentrates, as if willing it to do what he wants, but that seems to accomplish little. Raising the wand above his head, he then waves it back and forth twice, over the body of the bishop. Nothing.

He tries more complicated patterns, including curlicues, exes, figure-eights and even the kinds of maneuvers reserved for fencing or jousting. By all accounts so far, it seems to behave no more magically than a regular stick of wood.

Confound it, you think. *There must be some kind of keyphrase.*

The wand gives no clues, as it boasts no etchings or markings of any kind. You take a moment to evaluate what to do.

What do you instruct Bartleby to do?

To have him wave the wand and say 'Abracadabra,' turn to page 118.

To have him wave the wand and say 'Thomerion shall prevail,' turn to page 133.

Saul smiles smugly, turns over the jack of hearts, and places it in the last spot. The final grid looks like this:

You have lost.

Turn to page 201.

You think better than to offer the guard something, as if gold or other valuables could so easily sway a Thomerion devotee. You examine the floor late that night, however, and note that a particular chunk of stone displays a pattern of regular cracks. The formations snake out along the floor at unnatural angles, and then wind back toward the wall again.

"Bartleby," you whisper, as the goblin guard snoozes just outside your cell, "Take a look at this."

The cleric crosses the length of the cell toward you, and crouches over the stone. "Curious," he says, "Do you think it could be removed?"

"Only one way to find out."

You find some chunks of brick and an old nail within your cell, with which you begin to dig among the cracks and pry the layer of stone away. When you give it a strong shove, the stone makes a horrendous screeching sound, and the goblin guard stirs. You hold fast and still as a statue; your muscles ache from holding the slab in place.

After an eternity, the guard begins babbling in his sleep once again. You turn back to the stone and discover that you have unearthed a narrow passage that leads deeper into the ground.

You say to Bartleby, "Let's do this."

The cleric nods as you set your feet into the gap. You shove forward and land several feet below. Bartleby follows. No light exists down here whatsoever, beyond the faint glow from the torches in the hallway above, and since you were stripped of your packs when the bishop 'recruited' you, you have no way to light your own torch.

Bartleby incants a mystical word, and touches the corner of his tunic. The garment begins to emit a soft, white glow.

"This spell will not last long," he cautions. "Let's move."

In exploring this catacomb, you find only that more tunnels branch off from the first, each of which results in either complete dead-ends or more tunnels. After hours of this process, you almost wish you would encounter something hostile down here, just for the sake of variety.

You and the cleric backtrack through the maze, mentally tracking where you turned in the first place, until you are sure you are within just a few yards of the prison cell. Then, Bartleby's light fizzles out with a poof.

Groaning, you feel against the walls, and almost trip on a patch of pebbles, and turn away from the cleric as his footsteps trail just behind you.

You see nothing above. No hallway torchlight shines upon you.

It should be here, you think, exasperated. *Are we lost?*

You flail about, and suddenly realize that you can no longer hear your companion.

"Bartleby?"

"I'm here…"

"Where?"

Silence. Then,

"I don't know."

"Bartleby!" Your shout echoes throughout the catacomb.

Defeated, blind and unarmed, you slump against a wall, and remind yourself that there are probably worse ways for this to have ended.

But, not many.

Your travels cease here, but don't give up.

You reassure your companions, "I ask no money of you, and will be as quick as possible." The woman giggles.

You reach into your belt pouch, count off five gold pieces, and hand them to the fortune-teller.

"I thank thee, good sir," she says, pocketing the money, "And now, your palm, please."

You look her in the eye, and hold out your hand, your fingers thick and leathery in comparison to her dainty digits. The latter now traverse the lines in your palm; over several moments, the woman occasionally cocks her head to the side, or squints, the signs speaking to her in ways mysterious and unspoken.

She releases your hand, and looks at you. Her lips twist into a smirk. The three of you glance at each other with apprehension.

The fortune-teller flips her hair aside, removes her pack, and retrieves a ripe, shiny apple. She steps back a short distance, takes a bite, and scans you up and down. You summon patience.

"Your soul," she says through chewed food, "is pure, a product of a solid upbringing. Family is everything. But your journey is a contradiction. You respect life, just as you also kill to protect it."

You arch an eyebrow, and wring your hands.

She swallows, and adds, "And that is where the desire for revenge comes in. Just as a worm in an apple works from the inside out, it may not be noticeable at first. But it is insidious. You have been tested once in this respect, and will be tested once more. When that happens, look elsewhere, beyond your immediate impulses, for fulfillment."

This news sinks into you like bricks in water.

"I had hoped…" you say, "For something a tad more positive."

"Continue to hope," she advises, "And act. Your goal is near."

You nod, pensive. "Is there anything else I should know?"

The woman shakes her head, and releases your hand. "Go. And, when all else fails, look within."

"Thank you," you say sincerely, "And… what is your name?"

"Katalina," she replies.

"Madam Katalina, what might you be doing here? Surely better opportunities for a prognosticative career exist in Ambrosinia."

Her smile fades. "I was exiled. An influential duke did not appreciate the honesty in my services."

You nod. "Some people cannot handle the truth, as much as they may also need to hear it."

"You are kind to say so."

Katalina waves, turns, and attempts to earn the attention of other passersby. You rejoin your group, reflections swimming in your head.

Write down the keyword APPLE.

Turn to page 213.

You raise your hand and shout, "Six hundred!"

"Six hundred," the auctioneer replies, "Do I hear six hundred fifty? Six hundred fifty... six hundred to the gentledwarf in the armor..."

The girl shoves her fists into her hips and glares at you. "I hope you're happy!" She stomps upon your foot, turns and harrumphs her way down the lane.

"Going once, going twice... sold!"

Your heart heavy, you approach the podium. "Just a moment," you tell the auctioneer. You chase down the girl and splutter, "Listen..."

Pouting, she wrenches free of your grasp. "Leave me alone!"

"All I want from that chest is a large pearl, if it has one. I should have just told you outright. Let us share whatever else is in it."

Her countenance softens. "You would do that... for me?"

You nod, and smile. "And... for your mother."

A moment passes. She smiles back.

"Maybe I was wrong about warriors, after all."

The two of you approach the podium. You pay for your purchase, and together you haul the chest off the platform.

"Let me go find my uncle," the girl says. "He's a locksmith."

The remainder of the auction proceeds behind you, without much fanfare. Within minutes, the girl returns with a freckled man of average build, who greets you and promptly begins his work on the lock. You watch as he manipulates the cylinders with a slender brown pick. He and the girl consult, but you can't make out what they say.

"One... more..." the man says.

You hear a distinct click.

"Voila!" He opens the lid just an inch, and asks, "Are we ready?"

After you have all gathered round, he flings the lid wide open.

Inside are animal bones. Some are as large as a femur, while most are tiny, but none offer any use to you. Canine teeth rattle loose about the chest. You dig through it all, swiping away large swaths of dust, but find nothing resembling a pearl.

Turn to the second half of page 134.

The life of the king must be saved at all costs!

You run as fast as your legs can take you, rearing your axe as you go. Roghet draws back her spear, and is nearly upon Wyver, when you step between them at the last possible moment. Her strike clanks off your shield, and she reels back in shock, just as Wyver turns around.

"How dare you, foolish peasant!" shouts the druid.

"Roghet," Wyver says sadly. "Must it come to this?"

"No one will stand in my way!"

The king nods. "Then, I daresay, I question who, between the two of you, is the fool."

Roghet's jaw drops, and tears well in her eyes.

"Have at her," the king orders. He turns away to continue the fight.

The druid screams and lunges at you, over and over. You block one blow, and dodge another, but the third catches you in the shoulder, and you reel in pain as she rips the spear's serrated point out of your flesh. You counter with several swings of your axe, but she is too quick. She steps backward and starts to recite a mystical spell.

You brace yourself, and charge the druid in the middle of her chant. You crouch as you run, and bash her knee with your shield, which twists at an impossible angle. Roghet collapses and writhes in agony, and as you stand over her, you note a broken bone sticking out of her leg.

"I don't want to have to do this," you note calmly.

"Then... don't," the druid replies, tears streaming down her face.

You bend over, to within inches of her face. "It is too late."

With that, you finish her with a blow to the heart.

Turn to page 245.

You growl at the goblin, "We don't trust you," and turn to begin sneaking past the hound, further into the tunnel.

The goblin stamps its feet and flails its fists. "Then," it shouts, "You leave me no choice!"

It grips the cell bars with both hands, throws back its head and screams at such volume that you both cringe and cover your eardrums. The hound wakes and leaps to its feet, its eyes swimming in evil. You back up a step, but by the time you reach to wield a weapon, it has knocked you to the ground and clamped its jaws around your jugular.

You push and twist your body with all your might, but remain pinned, while Bartleby fumbles to ready his magical talisman. You feel your heartbeat send blood spurting out by the pint, onto the dirt floor, onto the prison bars and the dog, onto everything. All the while, the goblin claps his hands and cackles with delight.

Finally, the cleric aims the talisman and focuses for a moment. A beam of bright energy erupts from it, and strikes the dog full in the chest. It keels over with a loud whine, and the smell of seared flesh pervades the air. Your companion approaches, and kneels over you.

"This is bad..." he moans.

"We've..." you groan, "got to get out of here." You try to sit up.

"No, don't. Stay still."

The cleric holds his hands out over your wounds and concentrates. The spell envelops your neck with a white, opaque fog, some of which you breathe in, but it doesn't tickle or irritate your lungs. If anything, it feels relieving. This continues for several moments, then the cleric relaxes and allows the fog to disperse.

Bartleby hangs his head, and wrings his hands.

"The wound won't close," he says, his voice wavering with panic, "It's just too serious." A pool of blood soaks your tunic, and is now altogether larger than you. You feel your eyes begin to roll backwards.

"Stay here," the cleric says, "I'll get help."

Bartleby takes off, first further down the tunnel, and after a few moments, comes back and heads in the direction from where you first came. More time passes.

"Filthy humans," the goblin mumbles. It retreats to a corner of its cell, sits on a cot and curls into a ball, knees held to chin.

Minutes stretch into hours, and you conclude that Bartleby either was downed or has had unusual trouble looking for an exit. Your head becomes faint as the life force drains out of you. While someone may eventually find you, you admit that at this point, it will be too late. Your final thoughts are ones of pride and gratitude, that while you know you have tried your best to save Fedwick, it's good to know that others would attempt the same for you.

Cruel fate has taken your life. Rise again!

"Perhaps we do not need them, after all," you theorize.

"No need for a fight, on the chance it would turn out two against two," Bartleby concedes.

The two of you gather your supplies, return to the path, and quietly trek several miles further northeastward, before establishing a new camp many yards into the wood. You breathe a sigh of relief, and glance back in the direction from where you came.

All of this occurs before you realize that only Zander knew precisely where Demetria Argent is to be found.

Turn to page 124.

That wand sounds too good to be true, you think. The thought of forcing those Thomerion villains to heal your friend makes your mouth water.

It might even be worth a temporary association with this kind of scum.

You stare the goblin right in the eye.

"Fine," you whisper.

You hand your torch to Bartleby, who stands by as you tiptoe around to the dog's far side, where the key dangles temptingly. Taking great care not to skim the dog's fur or skin, you reach over the hulking mass. A pebble at your foot skims over the floor, making scratching sounds, and the beast stirs.

You wait, frozen, until its muscles calm and it returns to a normal pattern of snoring. You reach further and slip the key off its hook. As you hold it in your palm for a moment, you realize that you hadn't been breathing, and inhale with great relief.

You return to the cell door, and unlock it. The goblin barely contains his excitement; its tongue wags and it hugs you around the waist as it bounds through the opening. Whether you were more repulsed by the dog or by this creature could be a matter of debate.

"Come," the goblin whispers. He assumes the lead, and beckons you toward an area beyond the hound.

Several hundred yards further down the tunnel, a tall, natural chamber sprawls for many yards, and contains few features, except one: A strange block of stone juts out from the rest of the surface of the far wall. You approach, and see that a short series of runes has been painted onto the wall just below the block.

"It's in one of the divine languages," the goblin croaks, "But master always says it too quietly for me to hear..."

Bartleby nudges his way between the two of you and toward the runes, where he scratches his chin. "Varlancia Departicos?"

You grab his arm. "Wait just a..."

233

The block glows for a moment, retreats into the wall, and shifts to the side, revealing a nook, within which a wand rests. The goblin snatches the wand, admires it for a moment, and takes several large strides toward the exit.

"Stop," you blurt in shock, "We made a bargain."

"Oh, we did, did we?" the goblin snips. It squints in concentration and waves the wand at you. Your mind fogs over, and suddenly you feel a strong craving for birdseed, or perhaps a spot of corn. The goblin repeats the process at Bartleby.

As your head bobs and your arms flap in random circles, you wonder for several moments to where all your fellow chickens went. You see some sort of creature acting like one, mind you, across the chamber, but something about the situation doesn't seem right. A memory of interacting with a green-skinned monster flashes by, but you can't process it, and besides, any such monster left the area long ago. Its chuckles, though, reverberate down the tunnel from where you came.

Was the mind control spell the wand cast permanent? It's hard to say, at least for the first few days.

Your quest has ended... or has it?

With the vial of abbot's blood stashed in your belt pouch, you borrow a horse from the monastery stable, and cover the distance back to the City of Storms within a day and a half. The hour runs quite late when you find Argent's compound, but this time, she meets you at the mouth of the tunnel.

"Am I the first one back?" you ask, glancing about.

"It appears so," the sorceress concedes. "And, I see you were successful."

You nod, humble.

"May the gods' providence shine equally upon your companions. For now, would you care to retire for the night?"

"'Twould be a blessing."

Argent guides you to her study once more, then opens a door you hadn't noticed before, within a back wall. Inside is a nondescript but respectable living space, including a bed with crisped sheets and, as one could expect, a generous supply of reading material. She bids you good night as you sit, and closes the door behind you.

You stare into space for several moments, and the sheer proximity of your goal hits you, deep within your soul. *Yet,* you think, *how can I trust that things are as they appear? Every time I think we are close to healing Fedwick, another obstacle presents itself.*

You breathe deeply, and meditate.

Can you hear me, friend? you pray. *I will not give up.*

The next morning, during tea, you ask Argent about her defenses, to which she replies that she has established some frightening illusions relating to dragons, set to trigger if intruders enter the compound without her knowledge.

"If only I could recruit the real creatures," she laments.

"You seem calm, even as you know you are a target."

"One cannot afford to live in fear," she philosophizes, "for paralysis of the soul is worse than death."

At that moment, intense shuffling breaks out from somewhere in the compound. You and Argent exchange glances, put down your cups, stand and proceed to a viewing room, where Argent quickly casts a spell.

An ethereal image arises on the otherwise blank wall in front of you, of two men running down the tunnel, jostling each other. You can't tell their identities from the image's murky detail.

You hear laughter.

"Stay here," you advise, drawing your axe as you rush out of the room. You reach the compound just as two bodies burst out of the tunnel, but sigh in relief when you see that they are Bartleby and Zander.

"Forgive us," the cleric says, out of breath, "for we thought we could see who would make it here first."

"A spot of fun, as it were," says the ranger.

"I am just happy you made it back," you rejoice, shaking hands with each. "Did you find what we need?"

"Indeed," Bartleby says, "The richest ladies in the kingdom couldn't stand a chance at rummy."

You blink. "Wait. You... won a pearl of that size at cards?"

He reaches within his pack, and takes out of it a specimen of perfect sheen and roundness. "You would think they would not be so loose with their assets," he chuckles.

You smile, and turn toward Zander. "And you?"

"After much digging around, I learned that the giants in the Noblehorn steppe own some domesticated gryphons. They are friendlier than you would guess, and were willing to bargain." Similarly, he produces his ingredient with a flourish.

You shake your head in amazement. "I wish I thought more like you two."

Bartleby chuckles again, and pats you on the back. "Thinking is overrated. You are a man of action."

"And, along those lines," Argent interjects, "action is what we must take, with haste."

She leads the group to a workstation, where a small black vat sits over a controlled flame. Within it bubbles and boils a clear liquid, from which emanates a tart odor. An ancient book sits open on a nearby stool, a reed marking a specific page, to which Argent now refers.

"This is the base solution," she explains, "to which we first add the pearl."

Bartleby hands it over, and Argent holds it between two fingers for a moment. "It must be allowed to dissolve for exactly twenty-three seconds, at which time we add the abbot's blood. Have it at the ready, if you please."

You nod, and uncork the vial. Argent turns back to the vat, bumping it. A small amount of liquid splashes out of it and onto the floor.

"Must remember to take care," the sorceress mumbles, ignoring the steam rising from the stone underfoot. She drops the pearl into the vat, and together, you count off the requisite time. At fifteen seconds, Argent nods to you, and you hand the vial off. At the correct interval, she pours the blood in without incident. The bodily fluid swirls alongside the murky white grains of the dissolved pearl, tainting the solution a dank maroon.

"Now, watch, if you will," she instructs. She takes the gryphon feather, and begins stirring the potion with it. "This infuses the Bard's Brew with the natural energies of the creature from whence the item came." After a while, the potion starts to change color. It now shines a fluorescent green. Another moment later, it changes to a sky blue, then again to a bright apple red, and back to green again.

"It seems to be stuck in some sort of cycle," Zander observes.

Without stopping her stirring, Argent scratches her head. "I cannot recall at the moment what to do next. Would you be so kind," she asks you, "as to check?"

You nod, cross toward the spellbook, and read:

When thrice the potion's shown its hues,
Raise the flame and cook it through,
Then stop upon a moment's news,
As the color turns to...

You stop in horror as you realize the next words have been smudged, as that small portion of the page sits soaked by splashed liquid. As a result, you can't read the rest of the instruction.

237

"Oh," Argent says. "Oh, my."

Nobody says anything for several moments.

"It appears intuition will have to fill in the rest," Bartleby says.

"If intuition is incorrect, we have lost the Bard's Brew," Argent warns, "There is no trying again."

On top of it all, you think you hear the clattering of large numbers of skeletal bones, along with the clank of armor and weapons, approaching from down the tunnel. Time is once again of the essence, as the army of Thomerion has come to stop you.

Consider carefully the keywords you've gathered throughout your adventures in this book when deciding what to do next.

What do you do?

To have Argent stop stirring when the potion is blue, turn to the second half of page 241.

To stop when the potion is red, turn to page 260.

To stop when the potion is green, turn to the second half of page 246.

This is the king's former love, you remind yourself. *There has to be some semblance of good left in her.*

You barrel toward your best guess at a cutoff point as Roghet rears back her spear, and close the distance in a few grand strides. She downswings upon Wyver's exposed back, but you tackle her just in time. The impact wrenches your shoulder hard, and pain lances through your torso. The king, wide-eyed, finishes off a skeleton, then turns toward the source of the commotion.

"Roghet," he says sadly, "This is my new destiny. Surely you can understand."

She struggles as you lay upon her back, and her cheeks acquire more grass and mud from ground contact. As you put your entire weight upon her in a submission hold, she goes limp, and you tie her hands with rope. You help her up while tightly holding her arms.

"Wyver," she says through tears, "I love you. And, I hate you. For this. I just... don't know how I want to feel."

The king approaches to within inches of the druid, stepping quietly among the chaos, and strokes her face, wiping the tracts of moisture. They lock gazes, and he kisses her, long and deep. Her eyes flutter like sprites in the wind, and for a moment, the pair look beautiful together, highlighted by the blazing morning sun.

"You will see me again," the king tells her. "Of course, for now, you know what I have to do..."

Roghet smiles. "I understand," she replies. At Wyver's command, you haul her away from the battle, to be taken into the local prison and arraigned on charges of assault upon royalty.

Write down the keyword LOVE.

Turn to page 245.

You let the pirates go about their business onshore, and pretty soon, it appears that no one monitors what's going on within the actual ship. You dip further behind the trees and circle toward the shoreline, and see that a gigantic treasure chest sits just behind the near railing, onboard.

You glance about one last time, and make a beeline for the boarding ramp. Your footsteps are silent against the sand, but it hits you that you could attract attention by clomping upon the ramp, so you hold fast, and hide behind it.

You overhear the pirate band discussing something about raiding further inland, which is what they do next, leaving you alone.

Unbelievable luck!

You board the ship with little trouble, open the chest and look inside. Gems of all sorts, along with platinum and gold pieces and a few small weapons, fill the container to the absolute edges. You marvel at it all for several moments, digging through and tempted to take far more than what you need.

There it is.

The biggest pearl you have ever seen sits in the lowest recesses of the chest. You palm it, as excitement rushes through your veins.

"Can I help you with something?"

You jump out of your skin, stand and whirl about to find that a wiry human, armed with a broadsword and wearing a large feathered hat, confronts you. A nearby door to what you can only assume is the captain's quarters, closed when you boarded, now stands wide open.

"I helm this vessel," the man says calmly, "And whoever you are, you are trespassing."

The two of you draw weapons, but the captain kicks you in the face, sending you onto your back. You roll twice toward portside, shifting a couple large barrels by several feet. The ship jostles, causing you to fall again just as you gain your footing. With better sea legs, the captain closes the distance and swings his sword once, twice, three times, each blow missing by mere inches.

Breathing heavily, you look aside just long enough to note that you have circled around to the boarding ramp once again. You rumble down it and toward the forest once again, but are only a few yards from the ship when you hear,

"Never turn your back on a pirate."

Something whizzes through the air from behind and strikes you between the shoulder blades. You fall to your knees. As unbearable pain shoots through you and blood begins to seep through your clothing, you look down to see the very point of a dagger protruding from your sternum. The last things you hear are the footfalls and murmurs of the rest of the pirate band, returning to investigate the commotion. Soon, all fades to black.

Cruel fate has taken your life. Rise again!

The rhyming structure speaks to you, and by now, three cycles have completed, so you direct Argent to stop when the potion next becomes blue. The tromping of skeletal warriors grows louder.

When she stops, the potion just sits there, boiling mundanely for a few moments. Then, its color fades, leaving a perfectly transparent and unremarkable liquid.

Argent hangs her head. "We have failed," she mutters.

Bartleby shouts from the open door, "We have company!"

Dozens of undead, all armed with swords, burst into the laboratory and zero in on Argent. The other three of you defend her to the best of your ability, and she unleashes a volley of destructive spells, but the enemy outnumbers you by at least six to one. Whenever you down one, another takes its place, overwhelming your small corps, until you find yourself exhausted and badly wounded.

With no regard left for the contents of Argent's compound, you try to force your way back through the tunnel, but the skeletons' sheer force bowls you over and onto the dirt ground, where they trample upon you, shrieking in glee.

Don't let evil win. Read another path!

Saul remarks, "Looks like you need a bit of a miracle." He then turns over the jack of hearts, and nearly falls out of his chair in shock. He laughs heartily, and places it in the last spot. The final grid looks like this:

You have made a straight flush and a pair, for four points! You win!

Turn to page 191.

You consider what you can offer. You don't have much money, and can't afford to part with your axe or shield, for your own safety.

The way to get a pirate's attention off something valuable, you theorize, *is with something more valuable.*

You clear your throat, and several pirates look in your direction. You step out from behind cover, but keep your distance. "Excuse me, gentlemen," you bellow, "but you seek pearls, am I correct?"

The men glance at each other, snicker and jab elbows, as if they haven't seen a dwarf in their lives. "What of it?" one grunts.

"I seek pearls also. But if you can give me the largest one you have on board, I promise to lead you to the most powerful concoction on earth. It can cure anything, it can destroy anything. It can do whatever you want it to!"

They stand, stunned, scratching their heads.

You continue, in dramatic tone, "It is called the Bard's Brew."

At this, the pirate crew bursts out in hearty laughter, bending over themselves and slapping their knees. You feel your face flush.

"What is so funny?"

"You speak of useless legends," one shouts, "The Bard's Brew hasn't been made in centuries!"

You cross your arms. "That may be true, but I seek the ingredients to make it again."

A stout pirate composes himself and shouts, "He's serious, fellas." They begin to calm. "You'd best be warned, landlubber," he continues, "the last man to imbibe his attempt at such a potion got his insides eaten out by magic gone haywire."

Another says, "That's why we don't believe in them mystical stuff, ain't that right, boys?" The crew growls and shouts its agreement.

So, this has been a wild goose chase? you think as you scratch your chin. *Although, these people are likely just misinformed.*

"But," the stout one resumes, "If it's pearls yer lookin' fer, I might be able to talk the captain into letting you join us. You seem harmless enough. Hell, it had been forever since our last good laugh."

An inside track strikes you as nearly ideal, for now.

The men guide you on board. The taste of victory becomes more tangible right away. Over the next few days, however, while you sail, you search among their stash several times over, but each time, the goods end up getting sold or traded for pure cash. To get off the boat and back home, besides, would require stealing a lifeboat, and by now, you're too far away from the mainland to get back to Fedwick in time, even if you did.

You eventually resign yourself to the life of a pirate, and in many ways, it excites you. You get to use many of your military tactics in new and refreshing environments, and the smell of sea salt, along with stiff maritime breezes, invigorate you every time you step above decks. Even your attitude regarding theft begins to change. But you never do get rid of the nagging feeling, sitting there in the back of your mind, that your friend would not approve of such behavior.

Forgive me, you ask of the universe, as you raise the mainsail, before heading to the mess hall for a bite.

Better opportunities await you. Try again!

After some consultation with Bartleby, you present his talisman to the fisherman. You show off the intricate carvings in the face and the painstaking efforts that went into the finish.

The youth laughs. "You can talk all day long, but it's still just a hunk of wood," he complains, posing with his fists on his hips, "Show me something I could use if I had to."

Your heart sinks and you mutter to yourself, as it appears you'll say goodbye to Ol' Rusty for a while after all.

Turn to page 46.

The battle is nearly won. Skeletons lay still, in twisted piles over a large swath of land abutting your home. Facing certain destruction, a bishop issues the remaining enemies an order, and they retreat back up the hillside and out of sight.

"Is everyone all right?" you shout.

Grindle and Bartleby check in with you and the king, having suffered only minor scratches. Wyver dismisses some of his men, but keeps the ones that profess to have energy left over, before proceeding to the door of your hut. Bartleby winces at the sight of your shoulder, but recites a minor incantation, which relieves most of the pain.

You meet the king within your bedroom. He kneels over Fedwick, feels for his pulse, and wipes his brow. When he sees you, he stands.

"I was correct. The spell I had in mind should still work, but I need to start immediately. He may only have hours left."

Wyver pulls a stool up to the bedside, and closes his eyes as you and the others stand watch. From a sitting position, he enters a meditative state, his features composed, no frown or other tension anywhere on his person. He extends both hands, holding one over Fedwick's chest and the other over his forehead, and Wyver's palms begin to glow white.

Finally, you think. The joy of being able to speak to your friend again, to know he will make it, washes over your whole being. You are tempted to tell Wyver to hurry things along, but remind yourself that, as he said, patience is required.

You scan the scene, as gratitude swells up within you. *These people,* you ponder, *they devoted themselves to a revolution.* You smile, even as you stare into nothing.

There is not much left to do but wait. Since things appear to be under control, you step outside, sit against the outer wall of your hut, and bask in the sun.

A young boy dashes up over the hillside and stoops over you, out of breath. You stand, put a hand on his shoulder and ask, "Are you all right?"

"I bring a message," he pants. "King Wyver is needed. Scores of undead attack the capital, and the castle!"

245

You feel the news suck the air out of your chest. "What?"

"The royal army seeks orders, and as they are without a leader, their ranks are a mess. We're losing!"

You look back toward your hut, as the circumstances sink into you like bricks. The spell shouldn't take that much longer, and the idea of coming this far only to give Fedwick up now floods you with sadness. The difference in time, however, could mean doom for Ambrosinia itself.

What do you do?

To stall until Fedwick is healed, turn to page 27.

To relay the message immediately, turn to page 75.

You decide to take a stab in the dark. By now, three cycles have completed, so you direct Argent to stop when the potion next becomes green. The tromping of skeletal warriors grows louder.

When she stops, the potion just sits there, boiling mundanely for a few moments. Then, its color disappears, leaving a perfectly transparent and unremarkable liquid. Argent hangs her head.

Bartleby shouts from the open door, "We have company!"

Dozens of undead, all armed with swords, burst into the laboratory and zero in on Argent. The other three of you defend her to the best of your ability, and she unleashes a volley of destructive spells, but the enemy outnumbers you by at least six to one. Whenever you down one, another takes its place, overwhelming your small corps, until you find yourself exhausted and badly wounded.

With no regard left for the contents of Argent's compound, you try to force your way back through the tunnel, but the skeletons' sheer force bowls you over and onto the dirt ground, where they trample upon you, shrieking in glee.

Don't let evil win. Read another path!

"We wore their cloaks," you note, as a sly look crosses your face, "But, what if we 'were' troubadours?"

Vermouth grins. "My thoughts exactly," she chimes.

"Only one problem exists with this idea," Bartleby says.

"What is that?"

"We have no instruments to play."

Vermouth giggles. "That's what you think."

You discuss until you come to a consensus, and glance one last time at the orcblood guard outside the tower. You strip yourselves of weapons and anything that might appear threatening. Upon a silent count of three, your group bursts into his full view and sings at the top of your lungs. Bartleby belts an effeminate tenor, while you struggle with the bass notes. Vermouth's voice, a silky soprano, holds you together just well enough to make you think that this crazy plan could work.

"Old MacGregor, he was a fine lad..."

"He was a fine lad..."

"Oh, was he?"

"Old MacGregor, he was a fine lad!"

"He was a fine lad, so sue me!"

You dive into another verse as you close the distance, the shock on the guard's face notwithstanding. Soon, you stand before him, as he scratches his head in confusion, but you do not let up for a single beat. On the final note, the three of you shout an almost-simultaneous 'Huzzah!'

The guard claps slowly and grunts, "That was... interesting."

Vermouth says, "We wish you a jolly day, sir, and request that you make our presence known within the tower, for we have been sent for, to help celebrate the recent achievements of the church of Thomerion. We are... the Three Blind Mice!"

You glare at her, incredulous. She winks at you, and curtsies for the guard. You follow suit with an awkward bow.

The guard arches an eyebrow and grumbles, "Let me see what my boss says. Stay here." He turns and enters the tower.

You ask, "Three blind mice? Really?"

Vermouth thrusts her fists into her hips. "You think of something better!" Bartleby snickers, but looks aside and whistles when you glare at him in turn.

Quite some time later, the guard returns. "He's never heard of you," he says.

Your group exchanges innocent glances.

"However..." the orcblood continues, "he's in a pretty good mood, and will give you a try. I'll guide you. Just don't take forever."

You follow the guard into the tower, and enlist its help in ascending the stairs, as they are built with orcblood proportions in mind. You see the contents of some open rooms you pass out of the corner of your eye: first an armory, then a recreation area of some sort, and even a mystical laboratory, out of which fly sparks of magic, like bits of molten metal from a blacksmith's anvil. At numerous points, other orcbloods frown at you or pound their fists, but relax when your escort explains that you were allowed in.

Finally, the guard stops in front of a plain wooden door, and uses the knocker to rap upon it.

"Thomas," he shouts.

"Let them in," comes a voice.

You enter a small study, where the human you thought you saw hiding something earlier sits at a table. He consults a deck of cards depicting what you guess is a demonic version of tarot. He does not look up, but dismisses the orcblood with a wave of his hand.

"So, you are singers, eh?"

Vermouth curtsies and smiles.

"It so happens," the man continues, head still down, "that your services could be used at an upcoming event in this area. For, you see, I am soon to mark my fifty-fifth year upon this earth."

Vermouth gasps and says with thick drama, "Oh my! Is that true?" At the same time, she jabs her head in the direction of a shelf on the far wall. When you look there, you notice that upon it, just behind a bank of ancient books, sits a goblet of deep hue, marked with mottled swirls and a rough texture.

The Black Rose…

At that moment, the man looks up and sweeps his cards aside. You avert your gaze.

Vermouth continues, "In that case, good sir, a solo is called for. Would you care for a sample, just to cement that contract in your mind before we even draw it up?"

The man stares straight at the mayoress. He scans her entire body as she moves closer, seductively throwing her hips from side to side.

How cocky must he be? you marvel.

Vermouth slinks into Thomas's lap, and throws her arms around his neck, her gaze locking his. He chuckles, having the time of his life. She swivels the both of them around in the chair, so that the goblet is now at the man's back. She coos, while stroking his hair and cheek,

"Happy birthday… to you,"

"Haaaappy birthday. To you."

Bartleby tries to nudge you, but you have already snuck your way toward the shelf. You reach for the goblet on tiptoes…

"Happy birthday, dear Thomas,"

You grip the item you came for, carefully lower it to your level and slip it into your pack. The rustle makes just enough noise…

"Hey!" shouts Thomas, "What are you doing over there?"

Vermouth's tone becomes angry. "Happy birthday to you!" She stands, digs a heel into the man's chest, and shoves, sending him head over heels. The three of you run as fast as you can. You hear grumblings and curses from the study. "Stop them! Don't let them out of the tower!"

By the time the orcblood personnel catch on, you have already hustled past most of them, and now hear, and feel, the rumbling thud of their pursuit behind you. At one tricky stair, you stumble, but catch yourself against the rocky wall, scraping your hands and wrists.

You make it out onto the street, to find that the half-dozen footmen return from the east. You cut a sharp right turn through the surrounding terrain, but find yourself against the walls of two adjacent buildings, facing a steep drop-off where the third would be. For all practical purposes, you are at a dead end.

"Now! You have no choice!" you command, while digging into your pack. "Activate the Black Rose now!" Shaking with adrenaline, you hand the goblet over to the mayoress, who nods in trepidation.

She raises the item over her head, and declares, "Gods, hear me. May the tempest of Thomerion be quenched! Sunbringer!"

The goblet glows red in her hands, and her eyes grow wide.

"Are you all right?" you ask.

Vermouth nods. "It's like… it's telling me how to use it. I can just… feel it." And with that, she closes her eyes, and focuses on broadcasting her orders.

In every corner of every land on earth, skeletons and zombies, wraiths and other horrors raise their heads in cognition, and turn toward one point within a tiny country, ruled by orcbloods, called Koraxon. Most have never been there, nor would they ever be. But upon hearing their new master from afar, they retreat, climb back into graves, settle into coffins or fall upon the ground, inanimate. They do so gladly, feeling a renewed connection to the afterlife, as if one step closer to reclaiming their lost souls.

Then, she throws the Black Rose over the precipice.

You show the orcbloods that you have nothing of theirs in your possession, and they begrudgingly let you be on your way. By the time Thomas himself catches up, you are well on your way back home. Your chest swells, and your eyes well with tears of both relief and regret.

Fedwick would be proud.

You helped save Ambrosinia!

But is there more to the story?

Read through The Seal of Thomerion again to find out.

"This best be taken care of while it still can," you postulate. Bartleby nods. Resolute, you wake Zander, and whisper in his ear what you have learned. Zander stares first at you in surprise, then at Mikhail, who still dozes.

The three of you gather around the elf and perform a silent count: "one, two, three…"

You kick Mikhail in the midsection, not to injure so much as to alarm. He wakes with a start and shouts, "What the…?"

Zander grumbles, "You have some explaining to do."

The elf stands, and whirls about to each of you in turn, although none of you have a hand on him as of yet.

"What are you talking about?"

"The church of Thomerion," you say, "sent someone to meet an elf at this location."

Mikhail's already pale skin turns whiter.

Zander shouts, "What business could you possibly…"

The elf punches Zander in the gut, and the ranger doubles over. Seeing his opening, Mikhail begins to run back toward town, but only takes a few strides before Bartleby raises his sun god talisman; from it projects a focused blast of white light, which strikes the elf in the shoulder. The traitor screams and collapses, and the priest's divine energy continues consuming the elf's flesh, searing it to the bone.

You and Bartleby converge over him.

"I'll take that," you boast, "as an admission of guilt."

Bartleby says to him, "Is there anything else you'd like to tell us, lest we send your soul to the flames of hell?"

"Thomerion… shall… prevail!"

With an exchanged glance, you and the cleric agree that you've gotten as much out of him as you will. It doesn't seem appropriate to let him go, nor does killing him outright—your spirit won't let you stoop to his level— so Bartleby mutters some rhythmic words while passing his hand over Mikhail's eyes. The elf falls unconscious. The two of you grab some rope from your packs and are about to tie him to a tree, when a pang of curiosity rises within you.

"Wait," you implore.

A quick search of Mikhail's cloak pockets reveals, of course, the Black Rose, as well as the expected implements for a stealthy chap of his caliber, but also two articles that alarm you: a shiv with the Seal of Thomerion imprinted upon it, and a beaten parchment. You carefully open the latter.

It reads:

> *You are to pass the goblet on to our messenger when the moon is at its highest point. Upon confirmation that all proceeds according to plan, infiltrate the cavern and assassinate the sorceress, then return her head and this note to me.*
>
> *Commander Grekk Del Arken*

The name doesn't ring a bell for you, but it sounds a lot like that of an orcblood. For elves and orcbloods to associate for any reason is unusual, but the additional connection between orcbloods and the Church of Thomerion strikes you as downright bizarre.

By the gods, you think, *what is going on?*

"Someone should be alerted," Bartleby notes. He crouches and mutters a few words in an archaic tongue, toward a nearby squirrel. It glows for a moment, chirps briefly, then skitters off toward town.

You arch an eyebrow.

The cleric says, "It will carry our message to the authorities, and Mikhail should be taken into custody before dawn."

"Have you ever encountered a situation for which you don't have a spell of some sort at the ready?" you ask, amazed.

Bartleby snickers, just before you remember Fedwick's predicament. You clear your throat and feel your cheeks flush. It is time to move on. The two of you relieve Mikhail of the goblet, work together to secure him, and walk back to where Zander sits recovering.

The ranger looks up at you, saddened. "Is he…?"

You shake your head.

Bartleby says as he lays a hand on the ranger's shoulder, "We've merely subdued him."

Zander closes his eyes, full of unspoken sentiment.

The pain of a lost comrade… of being deceived…

You let several moments pass.

"So… What now?" you mutter.

"My resolve may be eroded," Zander says, "but if the gods be kind, we continue in the morning. After all, perhaps I should count our blessings, in that we are all still alive. Who knows in what ways the bastard could have used us?" Bitterness pervades Zander's voice.

You and the cleric exchange glances.

"I shall resume watch," Zander says, "You've certainly done your part."

The two of you retire as the ranger turns to stare at the moon.

Come dawn, you rise with a crick in your back, but overall, you feel rested and relieved. Zander reports there were no further disturbances overnight. You prepare your horses and resume your ride in relative peace, while keeping an eye on a patch of storm clouds gathering strength in the northern sky.

Turn to page 54.

"We should attempt your plan," you say to Zander, who nods, removes his pack and retrieves from it a thick rope of tanned, well-aged fiber. In a flash, he ties a solid knot, and then adjusts the loop until it spans about ten inches wide. You take your place at the door's peephole, to facilitate verbal instruction.

"You keep an eye on the time," you request of the cleric. He turns and jumps in alarm. The hourglass's top half now contains about half the sand it did when you got here.

Zander gets the knot through the U-portion of the funnel, but the straight section that runs to the back of the chamber proves trickier.

"You'd think that…" he says through occasional grunts while reaching into the funnel further and further, "the constriction of this space would actually make it possible to push a rope."

"It's doubling back on itself. Use your staff to stuff it in harder."

"This reminds me of a joke," Bartleby quips, "There once was a man, scheduled for hanging, and he…"

"Just a little bit more," you interrupt, only to watch the rope stick near where the tube turns downward and back itself up into a wad.

"Stop. Try pulling it back out."

He yanks hard, but the rope doesn't budge.

"By the gods…" you mumble.

"I suppose we try the other plan now," Bartleby groans, with a twinge of bitterness. All three of you retrieve your waterskins and begin pouring, but the blockage redirects the vast majority of water, such that it sloshes back out and onto the stone floor.

You throw your hands up and grumble a dwarven curse.

Zander takes a good long look at the hourglass.

"I hate to bear even more bad news," he says, "but…"

At that moment, the last grain of sand drops to the bottom.

Everything turns white.

Turn to page 65.

"The rope idea just seems like too much effort," you huff, "Let's fill the tank with water." Zander frowns, but acquiesces.

You grant Bartleby the honor of pouring first, while observing through the peephole. The clear liquid sloshes and settles around the bottom third of the tank; Zander steps into the cleric's place in front of the funnel and repeats the process. The rate of filling appears well ahead of the required pace; you may even have enough water left over for a celebratory swig, once the key is retrieved.

While you pour, Bartleby watches the tank, and soon, he declares, "The lever's rising!" A thud rings out, followed by a short pop, and the door creaks open, releasing a small burst of steam into your faces.

"Huzzah!" you all shout. The end of the braided wire now lay in front of you; its glint entices your senses. You vaguely recall seeing an experimental implement of this nature long ago; memories of sparks and the smell of burnt metal ripple through you. Bartleby scratches his head as he scans the rest of the chamber, while Zander checks the hourglass.

"Time runs short," he warns.

"Hand me the nearest torch," you command. The ranger retrieves one from the wall, and hands it to you. You hold the torch to the end of the braided wire. Zander reels, and catches his breath.

"What are you doing?"

"Just watch." Confidence bubbles inside your chest.

The thick strands catch aflame, burn quickly, and start to travel down the length of the wire, into the ground. Now, you can no longer see the flame, but hear the strange fizzing and hissing so vividly that you can tell it has already almost reached the opposite end. As you look through the second door's peephole, the dancing orange bursts forth and snakes its way into the metal box...

Kablam!

The force of the explosion knocks you off your feet. At your frown, your companions help you up as you rub your bruised hip. The door to the ladder now stands wide open.

Zander and Bartleby enter the chamber, take opposite ends of the ladder, and feed it out into the open space as you take one final look at the key, as it hovers above you within the stone. Taking care to set up the steps below your target, your breathing accelerates and you feel a bead of sweat accumulate above your brow. The final layer of flowing hourglass sand taunts you from just within your peripheral vision.

You climb.

You undo a metal latch securing the glass tile, and let the toothed hunk of iron slide into your palm. You scurry down, and all three of you hustle toward the central door. Upon your turning the key, at the same instant the cylinders click, the hourglass tips, coming to rest on its side.

The double doors glide open. A moment passes.

Behind the doors, you find a small, rectangular antechamber. Banners of cream and sky blue hues line the far wall. A desk of ancient walnut sits underneath a blazing lantern. At the desk sits a smooth-skinned woman in spectacles, whose pointed hat, robes and slippers all boast the shiniest silver tone you have ever witnessed. She finishes scribbling something on a parchment, and looks up at you.

"Good day, gentlemen," she says, calm, and stands.

You all stare at each other for a few moments.

"Need I any introduction?"

"Erm..." Bartleby sputters, "Madam Argent, we..."

"You may call me Demetria," Argent interrupts.

"Demetria," you implore, "We are in need of your help. Since it appears we passed your test..."

The sorceress stands and takes your hand in both of hers. "Of course," she acknowledges, at which point everyone begins talking at once:

"A close friend is dying..."

"We need to find a way to destroy..."

"It's hard to know where to begin, but..."

Argent silences the room with a forceful gesture of outstretched hands. "Peace be in your hearts. One at a time, now." She looks at you.

You explain Fedwick's plight, then concede the floor to Zander as graciously as possible. He tells what he knows about the Black Rose.

Argent scratches her chin. "Please, come," she beckons. "Let us sit as we talk further." She leads you to a side room, and indicates a table with three sturdy chairs. She pulls up a fourth, this one shorter than the rest, which strikes you as remarkably accommodative. She then places a delicate cup in front of each seat. Although the urgency of the situation strikes you as at odds with taking time for tea, you figure politeness is warranted, and settle into a chair. You realize how much tension you carry; your calves beg to be stretched and your shoulders ache.

Argent shares, "I had my suspicions about this artifact, ever since I first handled it years ago. If you will leave the Black Rose with me, I would like to perform some magical tests upon it." She pours a deep brown liquid in your cup, and proceeds to do the same for others. You shuffle in your seat a bit to accommodate her squeezing past, and you hear the crinkle of paper within your pack.

"Oh, yes," you say, "There is one more rather... important thing we should mention. We discovered this upon the body of a spy." You retrieve Mikhail's note, and hand it to Argent, who squints at it, then begins to move her lips as she reads to herself. Several moments pass.

Argent looks up at you. "I am not surprised. Part of the purpose of this compound and the magical traps weaved within it is for personal protection, as I have long been perceived as a threat to the status quo. But this text..." she points at the general's name, "Del Arken has great power. I can only guess that he would seek to abuse it via the goblet. What can it do that is worth harnessing, that is worth this much trouble?"

You sip the earthy tea, and listen intently.

"So," Zander says, "The question becomes: what is our plan?"

Turn to page 90.

You scowl at the worshipper.

"Let's see what we'll see, then shall we?" you muse. "Meanwhile, the authorities will deal with you in due time."

You gather your companions and hastily exit the room, locking the door behind you as you go, incurring a raised eyebrow or two.

"Are we sure we want to travel immediately?" Crolliver asks. "We didn't even get a full night's rest."

You turn and shoot him a glare that says it all. Your determination is not about to be deterred or minimized in this context.

He puts his hands up. "All right. Sheesh."

With the lackey's help, you cover the rest of the territory between the inn and the capital of Vartzog--mostly made of the same craggy plains and rock formations you have seen before now--by the time the moon is high in the sky. The buildings here, many of primitive adobe, are exclusively single-story, so it strikes you that it should be relatively easy to see landmarks from a distance. You comb the sparsely-lit streets with an uncertain wariness, but your spirit lifts when, while turning past a ghostly stable, you hear the flow of falling water.

The Farbringer's Pool, you note, is more of a fountain than anything. A thin stream, pure to the point of seeming out of place, arches from the outstretched hand of an angel to a plain cement depository below. Architecturally, it would seem completely mundane, if not for the faint blue glow emanating from the water itself. Ivy crawls up the sides, and crackled leaves peacefully float within, as if inviting anyone who passes to dangle a digit or two.

We know better, you reflect. Nevertheless, a spark of energy draws you toward the landmark. You think you hear a ting of metal from somewhere in the surrounding air.

Crolliver and Bartleby exchange glances. The cleric whispers, "It's like it knows you've come."

As you inch toward the pool, a burst of white air begins circling above the water's surface, slowly gathering strength; it coalesces into a recognizable face.

Fedwick!

You reach out, but feel nothing there.

The face turns away from you, and another image appears next to it, both now floating just above eye level. The second personage wears clerical robes, and stands near an ethereal entrance to a temple of some sort.

You wait, and watch. The murky beings make no noise, even as the cleric extends a holy symbol toward your friend, who nods apprehensively, and points. A few more gestures occur, a few more moments pass, and all becomes clear. Fedwick takes the talisman into his hands, and looks down at it as if with an anxious heart.

The symbol is a skull, pierced by an evil dagger.

"No..."

This is... the past?

You grip your face in amazement.

It can't... be the future... Fedwick looks too young.

Then, your dear friend's ghostly image enters the temple, and the vision disperses.

You sit on the bare walkway stone, in a daze.

"Fedwick... joined the church of Thomerion?"

Bartleby places a hand on your shoulder, and speaks comfortingly, "He had to have changed his mind soon after. Why else would they know to target him with the seal?"

Revenge cannot be yours now. Who knows where the worshipper that pointed you in this direction has been taken? But even if you were to go backwards in your story, you would do so now with the knowledge that nothing is as it seems. Your clansman, your brother, he betrayed everything you thought he stood for, for reasons yet unknown. You can taste the bitterness within the insides of your parched cheeks.

Is he even worth saving?

Your travels cease here, but don't give up.

Something intangible speaks to you from within, in the sense of what it took to get to this point. After some thought, you instruct Argent to stop stirring when the potion turns bright red.

For several moments after she does so, the Bard's Brew simply sits there and boils. Then, the pace of the bubbling increases, and the mixture crackles as the clanking of the undead militia grows louder and closer.

"Yes!" Argent shouts. "We've done it!"

"Quickly," you order, "We need to save enough for Fedwick and the Black Rose, but I have an idea for the rest."

The others take pots off the shelves, and scoop large quantities of Bard's Brew from the vat. You remove your tunic and wrap your hands in it, then grip the vat's hot handles. You haul it into the main chamber, its girth forcing you to waddle as you go, just as skeletons burst out of the tunnel and barrel toward you with swords drawn.

You tip the vat, spilling its contents onto the stone floor. As the oblivious undead run straight into the mess, their feet dissolve under them, then their legs, and within moments the compound is saturated with liquid bone. Not one enemy makes it anywhere near you, Argent, or the goblet.

The stuff merely dampens your boots as you confidently stroll back to the laboratory, where Argent has already retrieved the Black Rose.

"Would you care to do the honors?" she asks.

You hold the goblet in your hands for a little while, and reflect. The pain it has caused, the evil it carried, all comes to an end now. You drop it into the liquid, and watch. The potion envelops the item, like it has a mind of its own. Suddenly, the goblet cracks and breaks into dozens of pieces, which sink to the bottom like stones in a riverbed.

All present erupt in cheers. You hug your friends, as the significance of their help buoys your spirit toward the heavens. You stash a corked vial of Bard's Brew in the pocket of your tunic, and thank Argent profusely, who professes in turn how she learns something from every adventure:

"As in, slow down when mixing potions," she jokes. You laugh.

Zander and Bartleby follow as you exit the compound. The ranger teases you about how he'll collect his due, and how that was what made the whole thing worthwhile. He turns and heads toward the prairie.

It's just the two of you now.

"As long as everyone has something to say about it, Bartleby," you say on the journey back to the capital, "What was your real motivation for helping me?"

The cleric keeps walking. "Would I lie to you?"

"I don't know. Would you?"

"Curiosity," he answers. "Service to my ideals. But one reason stands above all others."

You pause. "What is that?"

"Because... Fedwick is my godfather."

You halt in place, stunned. Bartleby continues for a few steps, then turns toward you.

"He never told you he converted to the sun god? Even the youngest of budding clerics needs a role model." At this, your quest partner's eyes shine with pride.

You make it back to your hut without further incident, and proceed without pause to the bedroom, where an attendant lay beside Fedwick. You approach, open Fedwick's mouth, and slowly pour the potion down his throat. Before the vial is even half-empty, your brother and lifelong friend jolts upward and launches into a violent coughing fit. The two of you embrace.

"What happened?" he grumbles.

Your grin stretches from ear to ear. "It's a long story."

You have saved both Ambrosinia and Fedwick, the ultimate victory!

Keep reading The Seal of Thomerion for more alternate endings.

Something about the name Vagrants' Canyon puts you off, and although you also wonder what you'll find in the other direction, you recommend the eastern trail to the others, who vehemently agree.

An eerie grayness casts over the sky as you travel. You realize at one point that you run low on rations, but ripe apples from an untended orchard help compensate for this. Now and again, Zander comments upon how the tracking has become easier, given how Mikhail leaves behind scraps of miscellany. No concrete indication that the elf might be nearby, however, presents itself, even as your muscles ache and the sun retreats underneath the hills.

"I'd prefer not to admit it," you say, "but the best way to find Mikhail may be to push through the night."

"And what then?" Bartleby gripes, "We have no guarantee of finding him. He surely knows of many ways in which to hide."

"Better to give ourselves a small chance than none," Zander counters, although his voice carries as much fatigue as the cleric's.

The party lights torches and continues riding, moderating its pace so as to not lose the trail. The moon has climbed a considerable distance when the thick underbrush gives way to rocks, dirt and pebbles. Cricket chirps echo in the cool air. The terrain begins to hurt your horses' hooves, so you leave them to rest at a nearby spring and continue on foot.

The ranger halts, and scans the emptiness.

"You should know better than to have come here, Zander," intones a familiar voice.

Out of the shadows of the cliffs slinks Mikhail. An uncharacteristic scowl dominates his countenance. Zander approaches him, but the elf extends a hand in a halting gesture. They stand inches apart, leagues of shared experiences separating them.

"All I ask," the ranger says, "Is that you explain what's going on. We had a partnership, a goal, and then it all just..."

"All you need to know," the elf interrupts, "Is that now, you have seen too much." He shouts over his shoulder, "We have company!"

There soon appear two additional men, the first a stout, gray-haired human carrying a talisman and wearing black and red robes. The other, a scarred, shirtless orcblood, towers over all of you. He flares his nostrils and pounds a fist into his palm.

The robed man rubs his eyes and asks Mikhail, "What business have you with these ruffians?"

"We were on our way to the sorceress, but they turned out to be more disruptive than helpful," Mikhail answers with a dismissive wave.

"The Black Rose," grumbles the orcblood, "represents something far greater than your pathetic minds could comprehend."

"To interfere is blasphemy," adds the robed man.

The three of them advance. You draw your axe, and step back.

Zander asks, "Must it come to this?"

"Thomerion shall be pleased," Mikhail responds.

The elf performs a backflip to one side, throwing off Zander's balance, then slashes the ranger's Achilles with a hidden shiv. Your companion collapses in a heap, holding his foot and screaming in pain.

You react quickly, and swing your axe at the traitor's head, but the blow clangs off a gigantic shield. The orcblood carrying it has stepped between the two of you.

Bartleby shouts a primal cry, charges the brute and attempts to wrench its arm behind its back, but the orcblood hip-tosses the cleric against a dead tree. The robed man raises his talisman at the stunned cleric and cackles as black energy begins to gather around the item, but with a thunk an arrow lands in his shoulder. He shouts and tumbles backward.

You glance toward the prone ranger, who holds his longbow in front of him, his arm cocked to nock another missile.

"I'm not dead yet!" he exclaims through gritted teeth.

Mikhail strips his companion of the shield, dashes toward the ranger and bashes him across the skull with the shield's metal edge, knocking him out. The orcblood draws a sword and calmly approaches Bartleby. You see an opening, and attack the monster full on, but he turns just in time to parry your blow, tangle the shaft in his arm, and wrench your weapon free of your grasp.

A second later, Bartleby seems to come to his senses, just in time to watch the orcblood's sword pierce his heart.

The moment stretches on for what seems an eternity.

"Nooo!" you scream, as rage and sadness explode from within you like a supernova.

The monster roars, "Who else dares challenge the alliance?"

Fear replaces all else within you. You turn, and run. You run for mile after mile, through the countryside in random directions, your instinct propelling you toward whatever tiny chance of survival remains, until you can run no more. Heaving and wheezing, you let yourself fall into a patch of clover, and stare up at the merciless stars.

What have I done? How is it right that two should die to save one?

You command yourself not to return to town, not to involve any more innocent lives. But you also know you cannot survive for long in the wild. Whatever larger plans these evil men referred to, you are now just one dwarf, alone and powerless to stand against them.

Better opportunities await you. Try again!

"If this is where this symbol-searching leads us," you grumble, "I'd just as soon change my mind."

You lead the group back to where you stood when you first told the halfling to put away his whistle.

Turn to page 119.

You concede that Zander and Mikhail's concerns seem larger on the surface; upon your encouragement, the two men enter the compound. You look toward Bartleby, who has already sat on a nearby rock, and stares toward the horizon. Starting up a conversation seems somewhat moot, at least, that is, for the first hour. As more and more time passes, however, it slowly dawns on you that your companions may have encountered trouble.

"At this point," you grumble, "I'm not sure breaking the rules is of much concern..."

"Agreed," the cleric says.

The two of you push and stumble your way into the passage and through a system of damp tunnels, proceeding deeper and deeper into the ground. Utter silence meets your ears from ahead; you were sure that by now you should have received some proof that progress was being made.

Instead, what you witness when you reach a large circular chamber makes your stomach turn. Zander and a lithe woman lay sprawled in gigantic pools of blood, the latter dressed in what would be shiny silver robes, if not for the horrendous staining. This being is clearly dead.

Your pulse racing, you approach the ranger, who by some miracle opens his eyes. He winces, and groans, "The elf...."

You scan the premises. A door stands built into each stone wall, and the backmost one is widely ajar. Not through it, however, nor anywhere else in this setting can you see whether Mikhail is still here, nor whether he ever was.

"What about him?" you ask. "What happened here?"

"The elf... is a traitor..."

While doing your best to tend to Zander's wounds, and thereafter get him back to town, you wonder aloud, multiple times over several days' time, just where everything went so awry. Having unwittingly led an enemy to an ally weighs upon your soul, and you pray to the dwarven gods, if only to avoid living in fear and distrust, as the future of the Black Rose itself wallows in uncertainty.

Better opportunities lie ahead... try again!

Daniel J. Heck

Daniel is a 2004 graduate of Iowa State University with Bachelor's of Science degrees in Technical Communications and Computer Science, and has been writing fiction for approximately five years as of publication of this volume. He thanks the universe for all blessings, including and especially his home, family, and loving wife Michelle. Daniel's hobbies include competitive Scrabble, Lego design, and acting in central Iowa community theatre productions.